THE INVENTOR

A Penny Green Mystery Book 4

EMILY ORGAN

THE INVENTOR

Emily Organ

Books in the Penny Green Series:

Limelight

The Rookery

The Maid's Secret

The Inventor

Curse of the Poppy

The Bermondsey Poisoner

ALSO BY EMILY ORGAN

Penny Green Series:
Limelight
The Rookery
The Maid's Secret
The Inventor
Curse of the Poppy
The Bermondsey Poisoner

Runaway Girl Series:
Runaway Girl
Forgotten Child
Sins of the Father

First published in 2018 by Emily Organ

emilyorgan.co.uk

Edited by Joy Tibbs

ISBN 978-1-9809840-9-2

CHAPTER 1

LONDON, 1884

The Crystal Palace shimmered in the fiery rays of the setting sun. The sound of bells and drums assaulted my ears and the smell of frying sausages hung in the air as we pushed our way through the crowd at the Midsummer Fair.

"Mother, there's the fortune-telling pony!" exclaimed my niece, Fenella, tugging at Eliza's arm. "Please can we give him a penny?"

"The fortune-telling pony is mere trickery," replied my sister. "We should save our pennies for the sweet stall."

"But we have enough pennies for the pony as well," protested Fenella. "Please can we go and see him? Please, Mother, please?"

At the age of nine, Fenella already bore a strong resemblance to Eliza. Both had fair hair and brown eyes. Fenella wore a large yellow bow in her hair to match her summer dress, which had puff sleeves and a wide lace collar. Eliza wore a large straw hat and a loose-fitting cream cotton dress, deliberately ignoring the fashion for a tightly-laced waist.

A crack of gunshots rang out from the red and gold rifle gallery. The stall next to it housed Mademoiselle Chloe's Marvellous Clever Cats, who I hoped would be able to withstand the noise.

"I don't think I have ever seen so many people in one place," Eliza remarked. "Once we've stopped at the sweet stall I think we should take a walk by the lake and visit the dinosaurs."

"But we've seen the dinosaurs before!" complained Fenella. "What about the pony?"

"I've heard enough about the pony."

"Please may I have some lemonade instead?" Fenella pulled Eliza toward a stand selling carbonated drinks.

I pushed my spectacles up onto the bridge of my nose and gazed over the stalls and flying horses to the Crystal Palace. Its fiery orange panes were slowly darkening to red. Built for the Great Exhibition more than thirty years previously, the glass building remained an impressive sight.

"I read recently that the arch over the central transept is more than one hundred and sixty feet high," I said to Eliza.

"What transept?"

"The transept in the Crystal Palace."

"Oh, that."

"And you do realise that it was Isambard Kingdom Brunel who built those two enormous water towers either side of it? They feed the fountains, and it's said that each can hold more than a thousand tonnes of water."

"I can't imagine what a thousand tonnes of water looks like," replied Eliza. "A lake, I suppose. Was it ginger beer you asked for?"

"Thank you."

"I just asked someone where the sweet stall is," she continued. "And they told me it's next to the Man with the Iron Head."

"The illuminations will begin shortly," I said. "We shall need to be up on the upper terrace."

"But what about the dinosaurs?" asked Eliza.

"I think they will also be illuminated. We can walk down there a little later."

"Did you hear that, Fenella?" said Eliza. "The dinosaurs are to be illuminated!"

I followed Eliza and my niece to the sweet stall, trying to prevent my ginger beer from being spilled as I was knocked about by the crowd.

I hadn't come for the fair. I was hoping to speak to the inventor, Simon Borthwick, who was about to put on the greatest display of illumination ever seen. More than sixty thousand fairy lights were to light up the grounds of the Crystal Palace, and I had been eagerly anticipating the spectacle.

Simon Borthwick was well known for his work on the incandescent electric lamp. Three years earlier he had installed lamps in the Savoy Theatre, making it the first public building in the world to be lit by electricity. I hoped he would have time for me to interview him at some point in the evening for the *Morning Express* newspaper.

"Your Aunt Penelope is going to meet the inventor who created all the magical fairy lights you'll see this evening," I said to Fenella, but she was too distracted by a woman dressed as an Arab princess to listen.

"Did I tell you that I've interviewed Mr Borthwick before?" I said to Eliza.

"I don't recall you telling me that," she replied with an expression of complete disinterest. "Oh, look! There's the

Man with the Iron Head! That means the sweets must be here somewhere. There they are. Look!"

We pushed our way over to the sweet stall.

"Oh, Fenella! What will you have, do you think?" asked Eliza. "How about some lemon fruit slices? Or there's sticky toffee or butterscotch. And honeycombs! I shall have some of those."

"They have alphabet liquorice, Mother!"

"So they have. And caramel rolls and gum raspberries. What's that? Oh, it must be peanut candy. What will you have, Penelope?"

"Are there any fruit jellies?"

"Yes, there are. Which flavour would you like?"

"I don't mind."

"Are you all right, Penelope? You seem rather distracted."

"I'm fine, thank you Ellie. I'm hoping that Mr Borthwick will have enough time to speak to me this evening. If I can make my way to the upper terrace shortly I shall ask someone where he is to be found."

"Oh, you're distracted by your work. I should have known."

"It's the reason I'm here, Ellie! I asked you and Fenella to accompany me because I thought you would enjoy the spectacle."

"And I'm sure we will," she replied curtly. "That's enough honeycomb to be getting on with, Fenella. You don't want to make yourself sick."

"Mother, can we go and see the Man with the Iron Head, please?"

"I'm afraid not. Your Aunt Penelope needs to carry out some work on the terrace, I believe."

"You don't need to come with me," I said. "Take Fenella to see the iron man."

"The Man with the Iron Head," Eliza corrected as she handed me a paper bag filled with fruit jellies.

"I'll meet you later by the dinosaurs," I said.

"Very well. In forty minutes' time? Will that allow you long enough to complete your work?"

"I hope so. I shall see you then, Ellie."

CHAPTER 2

The noise of the fair receded as I followed the path up to the Italian-styled terraces in front of the Crystal Palace. A light breeze played with the brim of my hat and the evening air was pleasantly warm, so there had been no need for me to wear a jacket over my blouse and skirt. A brass band played the jaunty William Tell Overture as I made my way past splashing fountains and climbed the wide stone staircase to the lower terrace.

Chatter and laughter drifted over from the refreshment bar, which sat between two flights of steps leading to the upper terrace. I wondered where I might find Mr Borthwick. I conjectured that at this moment he would likely be making final preparations for his switching on of the illuminations.

I had first met with the inventor two years previously when he had worked with Richard D'Oyly Carte on the production of Gilbert and Sullivan's *Iolanthe*. Borthwick had created miniature lights for the lead fairies to wear.

I had visited him at his laboratory in Southwark and could still recall the strong chemical smell which had stuck at the back of my throat. The walls had been lined with shelves and glass jars containing powders and liquids of all hues. We'd stood at a well-polished table in the centre of the room, upon which stood a variety of apparatus, glass bulbs and lamps.

About forty years old, Mr Borthwick had been clean-shaven with an aquiline nose. His eyes were large and dark, and his brown hair was long around his ears and collar. I had thought him surprisingly well dressed for a man who spent much of his time in a laboratory. His jacket was fashionably cut, and he had worn a carnation in his buttonhole.

"*Iolanthe* must be the first occasion upon which performers have appeared on a stage with electric lights in their clothing and hair," I said. "It's quite astonishing!"

"It was a pleasing effect, wasn't it?" he replied. "I had to provide quite a bit of reassurance that the lights wouldn't catch fire. People are still rather fearful about the dangers of electricity."

"But the dancers weren't in danger, were they?"

"No, not at all! Small battery packs were sewn into their costumes and they were quite safe at all times. Here you are, you see, it's quite simple. This is the battery pack." He pointed to a small box encased in rubber.

"It looks like one of those electrical medical devices I've seen advertised for curing neuralgia and rheumatism," I said.

"It's not dissimilar. Think of it as a miniature electrical generator."

I saw that a wire was attached to the battery pack and branching off from this were thinner wires, each ending in a miniature lamp.

"The fairy lights are pinned into the dancers' hair and onto their costumes," Borthwick had continued. "The wires are too thin to be noticed by the audience, so they find the effect quite magical. I'll turn the lights off in here and pull the blinds down over the windows. Then you'll be able to see the full effect."

The room was almost completely dark once he had closed the blinds.

"Oh dear. It's rather dingy, isn't it?" Borthwick had said from his position by the window. "Just make a noise, Miss Green, and I'll be able to find you again."

"Over here, Mr Borthwick."

I had stifled a snigger as I heard him bump into a table, then eventually I saw his figure emerging from the gloom.

"Thank you for that, Miss Green, I was lost for a moment! Now, where's the battery pack?" He fumbled about on the table. "Here it is. Now watch."

I heard a slight flick of a switch and the little lights had instantly glowed yellow.

"They're beautiful!" I exclaimed.

"They are, aren't they?" he replied with a smile. "It's quite a pleasing event when the dancers are lined up on stage."

"The effect has been much talked about."

"I'm rather pleased with the result, and what matters the most is that the audience appreciates it. I very much hope that Mr D'Oyly Carte asks me to provide lighting effects for his future productions."

Stone sphinxes guarded the steps to the Crystal Palace's upper terrace, and when I reached the top I found myself standing before the central and highest point of the grand glass palace. My neck ached as I looked up to where a few windows were catching the final rays of the sun. Peering in through the palace windows I could see a tree filling the central atrium, while palm fronds framed statues and fountains.

A distant voice sounded through a speaking trumpet. I couldn't quite discern the words, but I felt sure this had to be the moment at which the illuminations would be switched on. I turned to look around at the vast grounds sloping away from me, and then a collective gasp rose from the terrace as thousands upon thousands of tiny electric lights burst into colour.

Cheers and applause rippled through the evening air.

Every statue and stone urn was lit, and the lights spread from left to right and ahead of me as far as my eyes could see. I walked up to the balustrade, along which ran a trail of vari-coloured lights: bright reds, blues, yellows and greens. Below me were clipped hedges and topiary shapes twinkling with light, and the fountains were a sight to behold; splashing with incandescent colour.

Bells rang out from the fair and I wished there was someone by my side with whom I could share this magical sight.

James.

As soon as his name entered my thoughts, I shook my head in a vain attempt to drive it out.

James would have loved this evening, I thought sadly.

A young couple stood a few yards to my left, excitedly pointing out the sights to one another. As I watched, I felt a heaviness in my heart. Perhaps it was envy.

CHAPTER 3

"Isn't electricity a marvel?" a voice boomed into my right ear.

I turned to see a wide man in a tweed suit with thick, grey whiskers and a glass of champagne in one hand.

"Such a dangerous and unpredictable element, and yet see how man has tamed it!" He gestured at the coloured lights with a broad sweep of his hand. "That Borthwick fellow is a genius. We'll soon have this in our homes, you know. You and I are looking at the future." He paused and glanced around the spot where I was standing. "Are you here on your own?"

"I'm here with my sister and niece," I replied. "They're wandering around the fair. I came here to report on this spectacle for the *Morning Express* newspaper."

"You are a news reporter?" He raised his eyebrows. "By Jove! I have never set eyes on a lady news reporter before now. This evening will receive a favourable write-up, I trust?"

"Of course," I replied, wondering why this should be any concern of his. "My name is Miss Penny Green, by the way."

"Goodness, how rude of me. I blame this stuff," he said, raising his glass. "Mr Roderick Barrett."

I recognised his name. "You're the organiser of this evening's entertainment, are you not?"

"Yes, and if I must blow my own trumpet I'd say it's gone off rather well, hasn't it?"

"It's gone off extremely well, Mr Barrett. Extremely well indeed. Would it trouble you if I asked where I might find Mr Borthwick? I've met him before and am keen to interview him this evening for the newspaper."

"What a capital idea! The last I saw of him he was by the generator with Mr Repton. Let's not allow the genius of Repton to go unremarked. If it weren't for his generators, Borthwick's lamps wouldn't do a thing."

"Indeed. Where might I find the generator?"

"At the engine house, close to the maze."

"Thank you, Mr Barrett."

The hiss of steam and the pounding thud of the steam engine grew louder as I approached the engine house in the evening gloom. There were few people in this area and I hoped to be the only news reporter so that I wouldn't have to compete for Mr Borthwick's attention.

Suddenly, I heard someone shouting and I noticed a shadowy figure striding towards me, a lamp in one hand.

"Mind the wires!" he cried out.

I looked down at the path and saw a thick black cable snaking past me.

"Don't worry," I called back. "I see it!"

"Go away!" came the reply. "You shouldn't be here!"

"I'm a news reporter," I replied.

The figure marched towards me. As he drew nearer I could see that he was a square-faced, clean-shaven man of about thirty. He wore a top hat and a light grey frock coat.

"Madam, may I kindly request that you leave this area? It is unsafe."

"I'm Miss Penny Green, a reporter for the *Morning Express* newspaper. I should like to interview Mr Borthwick. I don't believe anyone has ever lit up a place with sixty thousand electric lights before. As Mr Barrett has remarked to me just now, we are looking at the future."

"You have spoken with Mr Barrett?"

"Of course."

I noticed his stance soften a little.

"Well, I suppose you could speak to Mr Borthwick if I knew where he was."

He held up the lamp and looked around him, as if the scientist might suddenly appear from behind a shrub.

"Who is it, Jeffrey?" called out a woman's voice.

I hadn't noticed the silhouette of a small, slender woman walking towards us.

"Just a news reporter looking for Simon," he replied. "I'm Mr Maynell," he explained. "And this is my wife. I'm a colleague of Simon's and... Oh no, you're in for it now. Here comes Repton."

I was aware that Mr Repton was Simon Borthwick's business partner.

"Hullo?" called out another shadowy figure with a lamp. "Who are you speaking to, Jeffrey?"

"A news reporter," replied Mr Maynell.

"A news reporter, eh?" exclaimed Mr Repton. "We like those chaps! Oh, hello. It's not a chap after all."

I introduced myself to the lean, stooped man, whose shock of white hair protruded in tufts from beneath his top hat. His bright eyes twinkled in the lamplight and he smiled broadly.

"What a spectacle Mr Borthwick has created this

evening," I said. "You must feel extremely proud of Repton, Borthwick and Company."

"I am indeed," Mr Repton replied. "Come and have a look at how it all works."

He began to walk back toward the engine house and I followed in his footsteps.

"Please mind the wires, Miss Green," warned Mr Maynell. "You mustn't trip on any."

"Of course she'll mind the wires," said Mr Repton.

"Is Mr Borthwick available for an interview?" I asked.

"He would be," replied Mr Repton, "if he hadn't disappeared off somewhere. He's in rather a bad temper this evening."

"That doesn't sound like him," I replied. I explained to Mr Repton that I had visited Simon Borthwick at his laboratory in the past.

"The chap reminds me of a pendulum," replied Mr Repton as we entered the engine house. "His temper swings from one extreme to the other." He had to raise his voice so that I could continue to hear him above the pistons. "Some days one encounters cheerful Borthwick and other days he's glum Borthwick. This chap here, however, is perpetually glum."

He laughed and gestured at a thin-cheeked man with bulging eyes and dark, drooping whiskers, who was examining a dial on the steam engine. "Meet Jack Copeland, Miss Green. He's one of our engineers at Repton, Borthwick and Company."

Mr Copeland acknowledged me with a nod and I smiled weakly. Towards the back of the engine house a man in overalls was shovelling coal into a furnace.

Where was Simon Borthwick?

In the gas light I could see that Mr and Mrs Maynell made a handsome couple. They were both fair-haired and

Mrs Maynell was a young woman of slight build with pretty features and a retroussé nose. She said little but seemed friendly, listening patiently to Mr Repton as he embarked upon a shouted explanation of the machinery before us.

The generator was a machine about the size of a divan and consisted of two large barrels encased in wire coils. It hummed and rocked unnervingly, powered by the rapid belt of the steam engine. The pounding of the engine's pistons made my heart race and the spokes of the large fly wheel were nothing more than a blur. I couldn't hear much of what Mr Repton was saying, but I jotted odd words down in my notebook regardless.

Once Mr Repton's explanation was complete we left the engine house. It was dark by this time and the thousands of coloured lights looked even more beautiful.

"It's quite remarkable, Mr Repton," I said, "to think that this spectacle is powered entirely by coal and water."

"Incandescence is quite something, isn't it, Miss Green? It's almost four years since Borthwick obtained the patent for his light bulb. He paved the way by parchmentising cotton with sulphuric acid. And that was all there was to it."

"Indeed. Although I'm sure it's not as simple as it sounds."

"You're right, it's not. But thank goodness the weather's been kind to us this evening," said Mr Repton. "Rain would have completely ruined the event. You must come and visit us again in Southwark, Miss Green. Perhaps you can meet the elusive Borthwick then."

"I should like that. Thank you, Mr Repton."

"Very good. When are you planning to eat your sweets?"

He glanced at the paper bag clutched in my left hand.

"Oh, I forgot about those. Would you like one?"

"What are they?"

"Fruit jellies."

He considered this for a moment. "I'm more of a toffee man myself. Maynell might be interested, though. Are you a fruit jelly man, Jeffrey?"

"I can't say that I am," he replied. "But thank you for the offer, Miss Green."

Mr Repton shrugged. "Never mind. I'll have a raspberry jelly then, if I must. Unless you've eaten all the raspberry ones."

"I haven't eaten any of them yet," I answered, proffering the bag.

CHAPTER 4

"I'm sorry I'm late!" I was breathless by the time I arrived at the dinosaurs, having run all the way to the lower lake from the engine house. My corset barely allowed for such exertion.

"There you are! We were about to leave without you, weren't we, Fenella?" said Eliza.

They were overlooking the lake where the illuminated concrete statues of the dinosaurs stood on small islands and lay about in a lagoon.

"That's a Megalosaurus," said Fenella, pointing at a fearsome, dragon-like beast with four sturdy legs.

"Can you remember the name of the one in the water?" Eliza asked her, pointing at a creature which appeared to be half-dolphin and half-crocodile.

"An itchy thing."

"Ichthyosaurus," corrected Eliza.

"There is some suggestion that these dinosaurs may not be completely anatomically correct," I said.

"Well, they're about thirty years old now," said Eliza. "It

wouldn't be too surprising if they had some details incorrect back then. Come on, we must leave for home. It's late."

We walked back across the illuminated gardens toward the Crystal Palace. Beyond it was the high-level station from which I planned to take the train to Victoria Station.

I felt disappointed that I had been unable to interview Simon Borthwick about his illuminations; however, I found solace in the thought that I would have the chance to meet him when I visited the Southwark works again.

"When will our next excursion with the delightful Mr Edwards be?" asked Eliza.

Mr Edwards was a clerk from the British Library reading room whom I had met socially a few times with my sister acting as chaperone.

"I don't know."

"Show some enthusiasm, Penelope! The chap is extremely keen on you."

"I'm not sure it's reciprocated, Ellie." I offered her and Fenella a fruit jelly and took one for myself. It was strawberry flavoured.

"Why not? He's an intelligent man from a good family, and he has sensible and stable employment. He's a good influence on you, Penelope."

"How so?"

"I like to picture the pair of you on a set of scales. Your impetuosity and flightiness are perfectly balanced by his pragmatism and sagaciousness."

"In other words, he is rather boring."

"Oh, Penny, don't say that! He's the best suitor you have come across for more than ten years. And you can't be too particular now. You're almost thirty-five!"

"I am thirty-five now, Ellie."

"Oh, that's right! We celebrated your birthday a fortnight

ago, didn't we? Silly me. Though that merely emphasises my point. Most thirty-five-year-old spinsters have no chance at all to rectify their status. At least you have someone to show an interest in you."

I laughed. "Should I marry Mr Edwards simply because he's interested in me?"

"I know the notion seems ridiculous, but the older you are the less you can afford to be particular. If you're still a spinster at forty you will have no opportunity to be particular at all."

"The alternative is that I remain a spinster for the rest of my life."

"Oh, Penelope. What a bleak thing to say!"

"Aunt Margaret did it."

"That's because she had those rather odd earlobes. Sadly, she never had a suitor as a result, though she tried her best to cover them with her hair."

"It wasn't just the earlobes, Ellie. She had no wish to be married."

"If she'd had normal earlobes she might have wanted to. I think her appearance made her wary and shy. I suspect your true reason for dismissing Mr Edwards is the affection you harbour for Inspector James Blakely."

"That's nonsense! He's engaged to be married. How could I possibly harbour any affection for him?"

"Indeed. It would be most improper."

We reached Crystal Palace Parade, a tree-lined avenue which separated the Crystal Palace from the train station. The gas lamps flickered, and the road thronged with hansom cabs.

"Fenella and I shall travel home by cab," said my sister. "Will you join us, Penelope?"

"I'm quite happy to travel by train," I replied.

"You must be careful travelling on your own."

"I shall be quite all right. There are many people around this evening."

I bid my sister and niece a fond farewell. They climbed into a cab and I continued along the parade toward the entrance to the station.

The air was still warm, and a tuneful blackbird sang in one of the trees. I finished the last of my fruit jellies, enjoying the sweet flavour of blackberry. Then I paused to cross the road.

As I did so, the unmistakable sound of a gunshot rang out.

Horses shied and birds scattered from their roosting places. My heart pounded as I pushed myself up against a tree, fearfully looking around me to see where it might have come from. Some people ran in different directions, while others remained rooted to the spot.

An eerie hush descended and then came a clamour of voices.

"What in the devil's name?" said a man beside me.

Our attention was drawn to a nearby hansom cab, which stood stationary in the middle of the road. The driver had jumped down from his seat at the back of his cab and was attempting to calm his horse.

"Get a doctor!" he called out.

"Doctor!" I cried. "Is there a doctor about?"

People began to gather around the cab, and I hoped that one of them was a medical gentleman. I looked around frantically for the cab into which Eliza and Fenella had climbed.

Were they all right?

The sickening thought occurred to me that it was their cabman who had called for a doctor. I ran over to join the small crowd.

"Get 'im out!" ordered the cabman.

A thick-necked young man tried to lift the catch of the door at the front of the cab. "It's locked!" he shouted.

The cabman asked someone to hold his horse while he jumped up onto his seat and pulled the lever to open the door.

I stepped back as four or five men pulled the passenger out of the cab. As they did so something clattered noisily onto the cobbles.

I felt relieved to see that it wasn't the cab my niece and sister had been travelling in. But something terrible had happened and my stomach turned anxiously.

The men laid the passenger out on the ground, but I couldn't get a good look for all the people crowding around.

"Does he have a pulse?" someone asked. "Is he breathing?"

"I think he's dead," said another.

"A shot to the head," added someone else.

I winced and averted my eyes from them. Something on the cobbles glinted in the dim flame of the cab's gas lamp. I stepped closer to examine it and realised that it must have been the object which had fallen out of the cab.

"A gun!" I exclaimed. "He had a gun in there with him!"

"I'm a doctor!" called a man as he ran toward the cab, top hat in hand.

"Don't fink there's nuffink yer can do for 'im, sir," said the cabman, climbing down from his cab. "'E's gone an' shot 'imself."

"Here's the gun," I said, pointing it out to whoever chose to listen. I didn't wish to touch it or pick it up.

"He had this case with him," said the thick-necked man, opening it up and standing close to the cab's lamp to get a better look inside. He pulled out some papers and examined them.

The doctor took off his jacket and placed it over the passenger's face and chest.

My throat grew tight as I realised that he was dead.

"Simon Borthwick!" the man with the case called out. "These papers suggest he's our man. Does anyone know anything about him?"

"Yes." My voice sounded weak. "Yes, I do."

CHAPTER 5

"So the chap spends a week setting up the largest display of illuminations in the world and then shoots himself in the head as he takes a cab home?" queried my colleague, Edgar Fish. "But why?"

We sat at our desks in the hot, cluttered newsroom at the *Morning Express*. Edgar Fish was a young man with small, glinting eyes and a thin, mousey-brown moustache.

"Irrational," added the corpulent, curly-haired news reporter, Frederick Potter.

"I attended the inquest this morning and the coroner ruled his death as a suicide," I said.

"Clever fellow, that coroner!" laughed Edgar. "I think a chap far less qualified than him might have deduced the same thing!"

"Simon Borthwick left a letter explaining his actions," I said. "It was found in the case he was carrying and read out at the inquest. I managed to transcribe it in shorthand, and I think it's rather intriguing."

"What were his reasons?" asked Edgar.

"He said that he had a persecutor," I replied.

"Don't we all?" Frederick chipped in.

"Who might your persecutor be, Potter?" asked Edgar.

"The wife."

Edgar snorted in reply.

"Simon Borthwick said that someone had turned his friends against him and besmirched his name," I said.

"It sounds like sour grapes to me," said Edgar.

"Have some sympathy for the poor man," I replied.

"I do. I meant sour grapes on someone else's part. And that's why they persecuted him. This is why I don't ever want to be too successful at anything. It breeds resentment among friends and acquaintances."

"That's your excuse is it, Fish?" laughed Frederick. "You deliberately try not to be successful."

"I'm being serious, Potter. It's the old head above the parapet, isn't it? If you raise it too high, boom! You're decapitated, or you fetch an arrow to the eye or similar. Nobody wants that, do they?"

"It's why I try not to be successful too," said Frederick.

"Aren't you proud to be working with a pair of loafers such as us, Miss Green?" asked Edgar with a grin.

"I am indeed."

"Life is less complicated when you loaf," he continued. "No one tries to besmirch you or do all the other things that most likely happened to that poor inventor chap."

"But what about your legacy?" I asked.

"My what?"

"How will your descendants remember you?"

"As a loafer!" Edgar laughed.

"No one remembers loafers, I'm afraid. They remember those who did something remarkable during their lifetime," I said. "That's why I'm so saddened by Simon Borthwick's death. There was so much more for him to do. Just think what he might have achieved! And to think that the opportunity was denied by his own hand. It makes no sense."

"You hold this inventor chap in high regard, Miss Green, yet you know very little of his story," replied Edgar. "Perhaps there was something rather peculiar about him."

"And what if there was?"

"Well, it would change your opinion of him, wouldn't it? Perhaps he wouldn't seem quite so marvellous after all."

"I should like to find out more about him. And about his persecutor, too."

"You suffer from an inquiring mind, Miss Green."

"That's why I'm a news reporter. I'm supposed to have one!"

"I agree in part, but you create extra work for yourself, you see. Why not just concentrate on the work Sherman gives you?"

"Because I sometimes happen upon a newsworthy story by myself."

"Let me quickly solve this inventor suicide for you," said Edgar. "The main reason a chap shoots a bullet into his head is unrequited love. That's all there is to it. There's a woman behind this, I'm sure of it."

"That's rather presumptuous," I said.

The editor of the *Morning Express*, Mr Sherman, marched into the room, allowing the door to slam closed behind him. He wore a dark green waistcoat and his shirt sleeves were rolled up. His hair was oiled and parted to one side, and a pipe was lodged beneath his thick black moustache.

"Ah, Mr Sherman!" said Edgar, quickly removing his feet from his desk. "There's no need to give Miss Green any work to do today, as she's found some for herself."

"Is that so, Miss Green?" asked the editor.

"Not exactly, though I should be interested to find out why the inventor Simon Borthwick has taken his own life."

"He explained it in a letter, didn't he?" replied Mr Sherman.

"He sort of did and didn't. The letter raised more questions than it answered."

"Well, I don't suppose we need to worry ourselves too much about what it did or didn't say. You've written your article about the inquest, have you?"

"It is almost finished."

"Get it done within the hour, please. You'll need to get yourself to St Bartholomew's Hospital. They're finally allowing a few news reporters in there following the death of that chap in the medical school's museum."

CHAPTER 6

The ancient hospital of St Bartholomew's was a brisk fifteen-minute walk from our offices in Fleet Street. By the time I reached the railway bridge at Ludgate Circus my brow was damp with perspiration. Flies rose and settled on the horse manure in the road and an unpleasant miasma wafted up from the drains. I waved a fan in the direction my face as I walked, but it had little effect. The heat was almost too much to bear; even the horses moved more slowly than usual.

I entered the hospital grounds through a stone gateway decorated with a statue of King Henry VIII. The hospital dated from the twelfth century, but today I was to visit one of its newest departments, the medical school buildings, which had been opened by the Prince of Wales five years previously.

All Mr Sherman had told me was that a man named Richard Geller had been found dead in the medical school's museum two days ago. I didn't know where the medical school was and soon found myself in a quadrangle enclosed by four classically styled stone buildings. At the centre was an elegant fountain, and beside it stood a bored-looking police constable.

I approached him and introduced myself.

"I hear the press are allowed to visit the scene of the crime. Where is the medical school's museum?"

He regarded me suspiciously. "Are you sure you're from the press?"

"Yes, I'll show you my card."

I delved around in my carpet bag and found one to hand him. He held it at varying distances from his face, as if trying to focus his eyes on it.

"Perhaps you need spectacles like mine," I suggested. "The card only tells you what I have just told you myself. Please can you tell me where the medical school is?"

"It's behind that building there." He pointed to his left. "Are they expecting you?"

"Yes," I lied, following in the direction he had indicated.

The lobby of the medical school was quiet. Ahead of me was a staircase and to my left was a set of double doors marked Dissecting Room. I climbed the staircase and found myself in a corridor with a polished wooden floor and numerous portraits of medical gentlemen adorning the walls. I walked through a set of doors, passing one room marked Medical Officer and another which said Laboratory. A group of animated young men in stiff white collars and bowler hats passed me. I guessed that they were medical students.

"Excuse me, can you please tell me where the museum is?" I asked.

My question was met with silence, no doubt prompted by the recent tragedy which had occurred there.

"It's on the next storey, madam," one of the students eventually replied.

I thanked him and walked on ahead to find a flight of stairs.

I eventually found the door to the museum and peered inside to discover a large, bright room with sunshine pouring in through the glass roof. The walls were lined from floor to ceiling with cases and shelves. Two galleries ran around the perimeter of the room, one above the other. Both could be reached by means of an elegant spiral staircase.

There seemed to be no one else there.

I slowly walked into the silent room, captivated by the countless jars and display cases. To my right was a skeleton with bowed legs. Next to it was another skeleton with one pair of legs but two ribcages and two heads. I gasped as I tried to comprehend what poor unfortunate being had once inhabited that body.

I was startled by a jar of eyeballs and befuddled at the sight of a skull with an extreme deformity. I quickly looked away, my eyes falling on a row of jars containing human brains floating in a clear liquid. I recalled reading a description of the brain, but never before had I seen one. Its deep wrinkles and folds were surprising, yet strangely beautiful. Some of the brains had been sliced in half to reveal still more surprising structures. The organ appeared almost plantlike. So spellbound was I by the sights before me that I almost forgot why I was there.

"Can I help you?" a sharp voice asked.

I was jolted back to my senses and turned to see a pale-faced chap with dark hair. He looked about twenty-five years of age. The man had a thin moustache and wore a dark suit.

His face grew stern as I explained who I was.

"I thought we'd seen the last of the reporters," he said with a sigh. Then he looked me up and down. "None of them have been ladies, however. Until now."

"Did you know Richard Geller?"

"Of course I did. He was my colleague. My name is Mr Kurtz, and I'm the curator of this museum."

"I'm sorry. This must be an extremely difficult time for you."

"It is."

"Can I ask when and where Mr Geller was found?"

"I suppose you intend to bother me until I reply, don't you? That's the nature of news reporters. However, I don't consider it such a terrible hardship to be bothered by a well-favoured lady such as yourself."

A smile played on his pale lips and I felt a bitter taste in my mouth.

"I have no wish to bother you," I said. "If you'd rather I left I should be happy to do so. I can speak to the police instead if you prefer."

"There's no need. As your manner is quite affable for a news reporter I'll tell you everything you need to know." He walked toward a table on the other side of the room, upon which three skulls had been placed. Next to them I saw a pile of papers, a pen and a pot of ink.

"Everything has been kept as Richard left it. He was carrying out some classification work here when he was attacked."

I removed my notebook from my carpet bag and glanced at what appeared to be a log sheet next to the skulls. My eyes skimmed over the handwriting and I shivered as I considered that this must have been the last duty poor Richard Geller had performed just before he was killed.

"This skull here belonged to the murderer John Bellingham," said Mr Kurtz.

"His name is familiar to me, but I cannot recall why."

"He assassinated Prime Minister Perceval in 1812. Shot

him through the heart with a duelling pistol." His eyes lingered on my face, as if to assess my reaction.

"Goodness."

"It was in the lobby of the House of Commons. 'I am murdered, I am murdered,' cried the prime minister, and then he collapsed to the floor, quite dead."

"How terribly sad." I kept my eyes fixed on the skull and avoided Mr Kurtz's gaze. His presence made me feel uncomfortable. "But why is Bellingham's skull here?" I asked.

"He was dissected at the Royal College of Surgeons after he was hanged. In those days the bodies of criminals who had been sentenced to death were used for the purpose of medical teaching. How else could students learn?"

"Indeed. Those were the days of the body-snatchers as well, I suppose."

"The likes of Burke and Hare, and the London Burkers, you mean?" He chuckled. "They came a little later. In the year 1823 it was decided that fewer offences should carry the mandatory sentence of death. It was good news for criminals but bad news for medical students. We had a shortage of cadavers."

I nodded, wishing I hadn't mentioned body-snatching.

"There was good money to be made from it," he continued. "The London Burkers charged twelve guineas per corpse. Matters worsened when they murdered to order, however, and they were caught before too long. In a strange twist of fate, their own bodies were used for medical teaching after they were hanged!"

The air in the room was warm and I began to feel nauseous. I didn't like the way John Bellingham's skull appeared to be grinning at me.

Mr Kurtz chuckled again. "It is unusual to find a woman who doesn't fall into a swoon at the mention of something so macabre."

"I've experienced quite a bit of unpleasantness in my line of work," I replied, busying myself with my notebook. I could feel his eyes on me still.

"I should think you have, Miss Green," he replied. "These days we are quite civilised about the whole affair, and people donate their own corpses to the medical school."

"Good."

"And as for Bellingham here, he's proved useful to generations of medical students. The chap has been far more helpful in death than he ever was in life."

"If he has helped students become fully fledged doctors that is to be applauded." I felt keen to find out what I could from Mr Kurtz and leave promptly. "Mr Geller was standing here, where we stand now?"

"Yes. And I found him on the floor just behind you."

I turned around to look at the shiny parquet floor, where fortunately there was no sign of the terrible incident which had occurred there.

"*You* found him?" I asked.

"Yes."

"Goodness, how dreadful. I'm sorry."

"I hadn't been out of the room for long. It was shortly before lunchtime. When I returned, he was dead."

"And you think someone came in and attacked him while you were out of the room?"

"That's exactly what happened. He was garrotted with a piece of twine."

"Ugh."

"Exactly. It wasn't pleasant."

"And no one saw the murderer?"

"No. Or perhaps they saw him without realising that he was the murderer. No one suspicious was seen here that morning."

I stared down at the floor, finding it difficult to believe that a poor man had been murdered on that very spot.

"Do you know if anyone had a reason to harm him?" I asked.

"Can there ever be a justification for murdering someone?"

"No, I suppose not."

"Whatever the motive, the murderer always has something to gain by the death, doesn't he? Murder is usually committed in an attempt to either remove a problem or acquire something."

"Perhaps the motive was robbery."

He shrugged. "The only valuable item Richard wore was his pocket watch, and that was left on the body. The police will have a better idea of the motive than I do."

"What was Richard like?"

"He was a pleasant fellow. He'd studied medicine here and had so enjoyed visiting this museum as part of his studies that he decided to work here rather than becoming a doctor himself. I didn't know him socially, but he was an outgoing fellow and had plenty of friends. His father is a rabbi at the West London Synagogue. I cannot imagine how his family must be feeling at this present time."

"Rather devastated, I should imagine. You must find it difficult to remain in this room knowing what has happened here." I shivered.

"Oh, it doesn't bother me at all. I'm accustomed to morbidness."

"I see. Well, thank you for speaking to me, Mr Kurtz. Presumably the City of London police force is dealing with this case."

"Yes. Chief Inspector Stroud, I believe."

As I turned to leave the room a small jar caught my eye.

"What on earth is *that?*" I asked. A tiny white foot floated in the liquid within it.

"The bound foot of a Chinese woman."

I shuddered. "Where's the remainder of her?"

"That's a good question. I'm not entirely sure."

CHAPTER 7

The City of London police headquarters were in Old Jewry, which meant a walk along Cheapside from St Bartholomew's Hospital. I made my way through the bustle of people, many of whom were sheltering themselves from the sun beneath the shade of various shop awnings.

The police station was an attractive red-brick building in a cool, shadowy courtyard. After a conversation with the desk sergeant I was permitted to speak to the investigating detective.

"Do you have any suspects in the Geller case yet, Chief Inspector Stroud?" I asked.

The detective seemed too large for his small, wood-panelled office. Squeezed into a leather chair, he regarded me over steepled fingers. His thick grey whiskers spilled out over his collar.

"None yet," he replied curtly.

"I spoke to his colleague, Mr Kurtz."

"Good."

"Do you consider him a suspect?"

"No."

"Does he have an alibi for the time at which the murder was committed?"

"Our investigation will explore the matter. You consider yourself a detective, do you, Miss Green?"

"No, sir. I'm perfectly content with being a news reporter. Have you considered the possibility that Mr Kurtz could have done it? He discovered Mr Geller's body, and presumably you only have his word that he left the room for just a short while before returning to find his colleague dead."

"Mr Kurtz didn't commit the crime, Miss Green. There's no doubt about that. He's the curator of the medical school's museum, not a murderer."

"But there's something rather odd about him, don't you think? He displayed little emotion when talking to me about his colleague's death."

The inspector replied with a shrug. His manner was so dismissive that I wondered why he had agreed to speak to me in the first place.

"So it's safe for me to report that you have no idea who carried out Mr Geller's murder," I pressed.

"None."

"Have you found out much about Mr Geller?"

"A reasonable amount. He was a clever, sociable young man who enjoyed his work."

"A man with enemies?"

"We have found none so far."

"Was he wealthy? Did he have anything valuable on his person which could have been taken by his murderer?"

"Not that I know of."

"Mr Kurtz told me a pocket watch was still on the body when he was found."

"Yes, it was."

"That would seem to rule out robbery as a motive."

"It does. Thank you for your assistance in the matter, Miss Green."

"What about his marital status? Was he a bachelor?"

"Yes he was, and there is no indication of any courtship."

"So the possibility that he was murdered by a love rival is rather unlikely."

'A *love rival*. Now, I do like that description. Do you read a lot of novels, Miss Green? It sounds like a description from a penny dreadful."

"No love rival, then?"

"There's no evidence of such, no."

"Perhaps he upset someone," I said.

"Perhaps he did." The inspector glanced at his watch, which was pocketed to one side of his ample midriff. "Are you finished with your questions now, Miss Green?"

"I suppose I am," I sighed.

It was disappointing to find that Chief Inspector Stroud wasn't prepared to tell me anything that might be useful. I wished James was investigating the case instead.

"I can't be coping with this heat any longer," said my landlady, Mrs Garnett, when I returned home that evening. "Don't tell anybody, but I've removed my stays. I haven't done that since the summer of 1872."

She wiped the beads of perspiration from her brow with her apron. A childless widow of about sixty, she had arrived in London from British West Africa as a child.

"A sensible idea, Mrs Garnett," I replied. "I'm tempted to do the same. My sister never wears a corset these days."

"That doesn't surprise me a bit. Your sister also rides a bicycle and wears men's breeches beneath her skirts. There has always been something rather unconventional about the woman."

"She no longer wears the men's breeches. She has taken to wearing a divided skirt to preserve her modesty when she's bicycling."

"But if she didn't ride a bicycle she wouldn't have to wear a peculiar skirt, would she?"

"But bicycling is a pleasurable pastime, Mrs Garnett."

"Pleasurable?" She sucked her lip disapprovingly. "She'll end up in an accident one of these days."

"Mrs Garnett! That's not a nice thing to say!"

"It happens all the time. You see these bicyclists colliding with horses, accidentally travelling down basement steps or being upended in ponds!"

"You're exaggerating, Mrs Garnett."

"I am not! There was a man just yesterday who got his wheels stuck in the tram lines on Whitechapel High Street. The horse tram couldn't get through and there were a lot of angry people shouting at each other, let me tell you."

"Eliza is a little more sensible than that."

Mrs Garnett sucked her lip again. "If you say so, Miss Green."

I sat at the writing desk in my attic room with the sash window open in front of me. My cat Tiger was perched on the roof watching the birds roost on the chimney tops. I worked by the rays of the fading sun, as turning on my paraffin lamp always attracted crowds of troublesome flies.

Spread over the desk were my notes from the inquest into Simon Borthwick's death. I simply couldn't comprehend why he had taken his life so publicly.

Surely this meant he had little care for the distress it would cause those around him. Was he selfish in this respect, or had he merely been too distraught to consider other people?

The letter the inventor had written about his suicide was the only form of explanation we had as to why he had chosen to take his life in such a dramatic manner. But although I had read it a number of times I felt frustrated that many questions remained unanswered:

There is so much more for me to do, but I can no longer do it. Instead, I must resort to recognising my accomplishments to date, and I hope that my colleagues will continue my work. I will never experience a world powered by electricity, but I feel proud that I have contributed to the progress of harnessing its power. This invisible, though mighty, energy is day by day becoming more the obedient servant of mankind, whom once it only terrified in the lightning flash.

Although I hold myself responsible for what I have become, I cannot understand why it has become so difficult to live in this world. Everything I held dear has been taken away from me, piece by piece. To Lillian - I am sorry. You no doubt care little for my apology now.

Who was Lillian? I wondered. *His wife? His sister? Had she attended the inquest? She hadn't spoken at it, or I should have remembered her. Was Lillian the cause of his distress? Was there a woman behind his suicide, as Edgar had suggested?*

There was, however, another paragraph which made me doubt such a theory:

My persecutors have finally won. I think it best to die by my own hand rather than theirs.

This final sentence worried me the most. It suggested that Borthwick had been in fear of his life. *But why? And who had been threatening him?*

Although the letter had been read out at the inquest, it frustrated me that nothing had been done to investigate the questions it raised. *How did Borthwick's family and friends feel about it?* I knew that if a close friend or relation of mine had written such a despairing letter I would wish to understand what had led to such a drastic course of action.

CHAPTER 8

"Is this a social meeting?" asked Inspector James Blakely as he removed his jacket in the Museum Tavern. "Or is it work?"

"Work, of course," I replied. "Otherwise we'd have had to organise a chaperone, wouldn't we?"

"Oh yes, so we would. Work it is, then." His blue eyes sparkled as he grinned and took a seat across the table from me. He wore a checked grey waistcoat and a green silk tie. I noticed that the recent spell of sunshine had given his face a warm glow.

I smiled, feeling happy to see him again. A gentle hum of voices and haze of tobacco smoke rose up from the tables around us.

"How are you, Penny?" he asked. "I haven't seen you since we happened upon each other in Hyde Park a few weeks ago."

"That's right." My toes curled uncomfortably at the memory. "How pleasant it was to finally meet the future Mrs Blakely," I lied. "And her mother as well."

"Yes, and her mother as well." He took a large gulp of his stout. "How is Mr Edwards?"

"Very well, I believe."

"You *believe*? You haven't seen him recently?"

"I've been rather busy."

"I see. Well if truth be told I found our chance meeting in Hyde Park rather awkward."

"It was quite awful, wasn't it?"

"I always try not to mix business with pleasure."

"I have heard that is sound advice. But which am I, James? Business or pleasure?" I sipped my East India sherry as I watched him laugh uncomfortably.

"Somehow you manage to be both, Penny!" His face reddened.

"So you do mix business and pleasure after all."

We held each other's gaze and I thought of all the things I would like to say to him but couldn't. I cleared my throat and opened my carpet bag, which sat on the seat next to me.

"You've heard about the inventor's suicide?" I asked as I retrieved the notes I had taken at Simon Borthwick's inquest.

James' face grew serious and he nodded.

"I heard the shot," I continued. "I had just attended his illuminations at the Crystal Palace in Sydenham."

James placed his tankard on the table. "Oh Penny, that's awful!"

"There were a lot of people milling about at the time. And it seems as though that's what he wanted. A letter he wrote before his death was read out at the inquest and I copied it down."

I went on to read the letter aloud to James and shared my thoughts about what it might mean.

"If someone is driven to do such a thing," I said, "then surely it can't be suicide. It's murder, don't you think?"

"That's an interesting point," replied James. "Although there's no evidence that anyone drove him to his death, is there? All you have is the chap's word for it. Letters written by the suicidal often apportion blame to someone or something else."

"But don't you think Borthwick's death requires further investigation? Don't you think the coroner should have requested it at the inquest?"

"He'd already decided on a verdict of suicide, so in his mind the matter is closed. There's no use in trying to find out who may or may not have been persecuting a man who is already dead."

"But the culprit might do the same thing to someone else."

"It's possible, but we don't know exactly what was done to him, do we? Consider the fact that this chap wrote the letter while in a distressed state of mind. And he doesn't provide any facts for us to work with. If Borthwick was truly angry with the people who did this to him, why didn't he name them? That would have been far more useful for the coroner; in fact, the coroner could have requested that those individuals were summoned to appear at the inquest. This Borthwick chap has thrown about vague accusations, but if things were as bad as he said, why didn't he report anything to the authorities while he was alive?"

"Perhaps he was frightened."

"Perhaps he was. But you can see now why the coroner, or the police for that matter, can't go off and investigate something that has been written in a distressing letter of this sort."

"*I thought it best to die by my own hand rather than theirs,*" I read out again. "That's terrible!"

"I agree. It's upsetting to read it. Have you read this sort of letter before, Penny?"

"I can't say that I have."

"It's impossible to do so without feeling saddened or

angered in some way. Suicide is an act with which no one can reconcile themselves. It evokes difficult emotions."

I sighed. "So we should simply ignore his letter?"

"*We?*"

"You and I."

"How am I involved? I thought this evening was merely a social meeting."

"It's work, remember? There's no chaperone."

James gave me an exasperated smile. "Penny, the Yard won't allow me to spend any time working on this, I'm afraid. My job is to investigate crime and there is no evidence that any crime has been committed; only Borthwick's suicide."

"So you think *I* should ignore the letter," I replied sulkily.

"I didn't say that. If what Borthwick says in his letter is true I am concerned about the people who may have done this to him. They could do the same thing to someone else, as you have already suggested. However, in my capacity as a Scotland Yard detective I'm unable to do anything more about it. If you wish to investigate it further I would be happy to help, if required. I wouldn't allow it to take up too much of your time, though, as it's unlikely to lead anywhere."

"Aren't you the least bit interested in the people he refers to in the letter?"

"I should like to know who they are, certainly."

"And Lillian. Who is Lillian?"

James shrugged. "Who indeed? I'm sure you could find out if you're determined enough."

"Perhaps I become too easily attached to things, but having seen Mr Borthwick's wonderful illuminations it was rather a shock to see him pulled out of a cab just an hour later with a self-inflicted gunshot wound to his head..." My voice trailed off as the memory crept up on me.

"I understand, Penny. You have a personal connection

with the whole sorry event. Much like you did when Jack Burton was murdered."

"Exactly! You do understand don't you, James?"

"Of course I do. I know you well enough by now. I understand your need to find out the truth. But do I think it's a good idea? No, I'm afraid I don't. Besides, it's highly likely to come to nothing."

CHAPTER 9

Donald Repton's assistant showed me into a great hall filled with the thundering and hissing sound of a working steam engine. Sunlight shone through tall, narrow windows and smoke curled with steam above Mr Repton's top hat. He wore a dark suit and stood with his back to me inspecting a row of electric lamps, which glowed intermittently.

Wires attached the electric lamps to a larger generator than the one I had seen at the Crystal Palace. A glum man I recognised as Jack Copeland was adjusting something on the front of it.

The assistant left me to wait in the corner of the room. It was too noisy for me to hear what Mr Repton was shouting to Copeland, but it didn't sound complimentary. Copeland walked over to the engine and turned a lever, slowing the pistons a little. More shouting and gesticulating soon followed from Mr Repton, and Copeland leapt back to the generator to adjust its settings.

Then there was a sharp, deafening crack accompanied by a plume of sparks. My heart leapt into my throat as the electric lamps shattered, showering tiny shards of blackened glass across the floor. Both men ducked, shielding their heads with their arms, and the engine's pistons ground to a halt.

The air filled with an unpleasant, acrid smell and I wiped a layer of damp grime from my spectacles. Mr Repton recovered himself and, rather than admonishing Mr Copeland, began to laugh.

Jack Copeland remained bemused as Donald Repton's cackle echoed around the hall. I shifted uneasily from one foot to the other, wondering when to announce my presence. It was Mr Copeland who saw me first. Mr Repton followed his gaze and turned to face me.

"Miss Green!" He grinned. "How good of you to come. Shall we go somewhere that isn't strewn with broken glass?"

Mr Repton's office was a large, untidy room stacked with books, papers and all manner of cogs, cylinders, wires and lamps. Half-constructed pieces of machinery were propped up against the walls, and the air smelled of oil and stale tobacco smoke.

He gestured for me to sit on a worn velvet chair to one side of his desk. He sat on the other side and removed his top hat to reveal a thick mop of white hair. He looked older than I remembered.

"You don't mind if I smoke do you, Miss Green? I require something to calm my nerves after Copeland's demonstration of ineptitude."

"Of course not."

He lit his pipe and lifted a glass decanter of amber liquid from his desk.

"Brandy?" he asked.

"No, thank you."

He filled a filthy glass and took a sizeable gulp of the

drink before sighing with satisfaction. I used the pause to express my condolences regarding Simon Borthwick's death.

He shook his head. "I still can't quite believe it. I keep expecting him to saunter in through that door. In fact, only yesterday I thought I saw him at the far end of the corridor. Grief plays such terrible tricks on one's mind."

"I'm sorry to hear it, Mr Repton."

"You'd think one would become accustomed to grief, wouldn't you?" he said. "One doesn't reach my age without losing a fair few people along the way. However, it never gets any easier, does it? Humans are very resistant to the notion of dying. Our minds refuse to accept it."

My eye was drawn to a small carriage in the corner of the room. It had a boiler and funnel attached to one end.

"That looks interesting," I commented. "What is it?"

"A steam-driven road carriage," he replied. "It's some age now. I built it about thirty years ago."

"There is no need for a horse?" I asked.

"No need at all. It's entirely steam-driven, though a little difficult to manoeuvre once it gets going."

"Will you work on it again?"

"There is no use in my doing so, Miss Green. Times have moved on. Rumour has it that a German chap, Mr Karl Benz, has produced a carriage which runs on an engine powered by petroleum. I have no idea how much petroleum is required for his vehicle; however, I suspect the fuel usage is more efficient with his invention. To travel any reasonable distance my steam car requires a significant volume of coal and water."

"Perhaps you could invent an electric vehicle."

"It has already been done, Miss Green. Mr Thomas Parker of Wolverhampton has built a carriage powered by electricity. His Elwell-Parker Company is also building electrical trams. It's all rather exciting, isn't it? Imagine a world without temperamental horses spilling their cartloads. And no more filth in the road, either!"

"So your interests lie in electrical lighting for the time being?"

"Indeed they do, Miss Green. With the widespread electrical lighting of our cities imminent, it's important to produce the most powerful, reliable and efficient generators possible. That is no easy task. Repton, Borthwick and Company is currently contracted to supply electricity to one hundred new houses which are being built in Kensington. The generating plant will have seven steam engines driving seven generators, and that will power a two-hundred volt, three-wire DC electrical supply."

"That sounds impressive, though I don't quite understand what it means."

"DC means direct current, as opposed to AC, which is alternating current. I shall be happy to explain it in more detail for you, Miss Green, as and when required." He sighed. "But I'm forgetting myself here. I had been enormously excited about the contract to supply the new homes in Kensington Court, but without Borthwick the project will take much longer. He was the reason that our previous projects – King's Cross station, the new law courts and the Lord Mayor's residence, the Mansion House – were such a success." He lowered his voice to a whisper. "Don't mention this to anyone, but we've been in discussion with Buckingham Palace about installing electric lights at Windsor Castle."

"Really?"

He nodded, then shook his head sadly. "But I was relying on Borthwick and his expertise with the incandescent lamp. What will happen now?"

He took another glug of brandy and his eyes grew damp. I struggled to find any words of comfort.

"Anyway, Miss Green. I haven't yet asked what brings you

here, although I do recall seeing you with the other reporters at the inquest. I assume you're here to ask me some questions. Did you bring any fruit jellies with you?"

"I'm afraid I didn't, Mr Repton."

"That's a shame."

"Mr Repton, can I ask what you thought of the letter Mr Borthwick left behind?"

"I thought it rather gloomy. That's to be expected, I suppose, if one is planning to take one's own life. I never had an inkling that he would do such a thing."

"Do you have any idea who the persecutors he alluded to in his letter might be?" I asked.

"No idea at all."

"He didn't mention anyone to you?"

"No, not at all. But then I don't imagine he would have. A chap keeps his emotions private in the workplace, doesn't he? He was a professional gentleman and would never have bothered anyone with his troubles. I suppose that's the nature of suicide, isn't it? These thoughts privately ferment in one's mind and then spill over into some terrible act of personal despair. I must say that it was a shock to hear his words. I don't recognise the man in that letter at all."

"Do you know who Lillian is?"

"Yes. Maynell's wife."

"Jeffrey Maynell? The gentleman I met at the Crystal Palace?"

"Yes." Mr Repton sucked a lungful of air in between his teeth. "Rather awkward, isn't it? I should add that Borthwick and Mrs Maynell had previously courted one another. Prior to her courtship with Jeffrey, of course."

"What was the relationship between Mr Borthwick and Mr Maynell like?"

"What do you mean?"

"Surely there must have been some animosity between them regarding Lillian?"

"No! None at all!" He waved his hand dismissively. "Everything was quite friendly between them."

"That's unusual, given the circumstances."

"Both Maynell and Borthwick are professional chaps. There was absolutely no issue between the two gentlemen regarding their shared affection for Mrs Maynell."

"Perhaps I could speak to Mrs Maynell," I said.

"I'm sure there is no need for that."

"I'm interested because Mr Borthwick specifically mentions her in his letter."

"I wouldn't bother her, Miss Green. The last thing a lady needs to know is that a chap was thinking of her as he considered taking his own life. That would weigh rather heavily on the poor woman's mind. I'm not quite sure what you're trying to achieve with all this. The unfortunate chap is dead."

"But having witnessed his death myself, I'm concerned about the people he has claimed drove him to it."

"I must say that I was rather puzzled to hear of that in his letter. I'm inclined to think that his mind wasn't functioning normally when he wrote it. In fact, it can't have been given the fact that he committed self-murder."

"Perhaps his mind wasn't in good form at the time, but I still find his words extremely concerning," I said.

"Have you mentioned your concerns to the police?" asked Mr Repton.

"Actually, I have. I discussed it with a good friend of mine who is a detective at Scotland Yard."

"And what are his thoughts on the matter?"

"He doesn't think there is anything about Borthwick's death which requires investigating."

"That is interesting to hear indeed. It seems the detective and I are in agreement. It's a terribly sad incident, and we are all struggling to accept that it has happened." He refilled his glass. "It must be particularly difficult for you, Miss Green, having witnessed the aftermath. But there isn't a great deal any of us can do about it, is there? Simon Borthwick was my protégé, and I had great affection for the chap. His talent was precocious and I'm immensely saddened when I think of the many things he might have contributed to advancements in the use of electricity. And to think that while he was setting up the illuminations that glorious summer evening he was secretly carrying a revolver about his person and had already written a letter saying goodbye to the world!"

"Those are my thoughts exactly, Mr Repton, and that's precisely what compels me to investigate. There has to be more to his actions. His letter certainly suggests as much."

"But what if there isn't? Perhaps the supposed threat to Borthwick was merely in his mind. He had an extremely active brain and was prone to wild imaginations."

"But don't you think there may be a chance that the threat to him was real?"

"He never mentioned the threat while he was alive. But there's a possibility, I suppose, that his letter tells the truth. And if it does I am deeply saddened for him, as he must have suffered terribly."

"Was he close to any of his colleagues? Is there anyone else who works here in whom he may have confided?"

"You could try Jack Copeland. I suppose he might know something. It's unlikely, though. The contents of Borthwick's farewell letter have certainly come as a surprise to me. I had no inkling that he was under such strain. I wish now that he had spoken to me. I feel sure that I could have talked him out of it." Mr Repton's voice wavered. "It's a terrible loss."

CHAPTER 10

The air in the British Library reading room felt stifling. Sunshine poured in through the windows of the great dome above me and the red-whiskered man sitting opposite kept pulling at his tie. My corset and blouse felt damp with perspiration.

"Here you are, Miss Green. I found this book by Mr Donald Repton," whispered Mr Edwards. "*The Maintenance of Electric Currents*."

His keen, green eyes were fixed on me through the thick lenses of his spectacles, and his sandy hair hung limply against his forehead.

"Thank you, Mr Edwards. I'm not sure I'll be reading it from cover to cover, but I appreciate your bringing it to my attention."

He chuckled. "It's one of many he has written. I can show you the location on the second gallery if you wish."

"I hope there's rather more air up there," I replied, fanning myself.

I followed Mr Edwards up a narrow flight of steps to the

first gallery. He was being his usual helpful self as a clerk of the reading room, but I felt increasingly uncomfortable in his company.

We had enjoyed several walks in Hyde Park together with my sister Eliza as chaperone, and I felt concerned that he hoped our friendship might develop further. Each time I saw him I felt my shoulders become tense as I wondered whether he was about to spring an awkward question or invitation on me. It wasn't that I didn't like Mr Edwards, but more that I didn't like him enough to consider a courtship. As each day passed I feared that we were nearing the moment when I would have to politely decline him.

We climbed the iron staircase up to the second gallery. I enjoyed the view of the reading room from up there, with the long desks radiating out from the head librarian's dais at the centre of the room.

Mr Edwards took hold of a ladder which was leaning up against the book shelves.

"I'm afraid this will be required to reach Mr Repton's works," he said as he moved it along the shelving racks so that it was in line with the required section. "Would you like me to climb up and fetch them for you? It can be quite dizzying up at the top."

"I'm happy to look myself. Thank you, Mr Edwards."

I climbed the ladder and surveyed the leather-bound works of Donald Repton. His writings were more prolific than I had realised. The air felt even warmer up there, closer to the windows. Next to Mr Repton's books was a slim volume written by another author.

"A book by Simon Borthwick!" I exclaimed. It was on the far right of the shelf, I leaned out to take hold of it.

"Careful, Miss Green," warned Mr Edwards. "Please don't fall."

I managed to pull the book out with one hand, but it was heavier than I had thought. My hand couldn't hold on and it slipped from my grip.

"Watch out!" I called down to Mr Edwards.

But he had already stepped forward and caught the book in his arms.

"That was a close one, Miss Green!"

"I do apologise. What a fine catch, Mr Edwards."

"I was an excellent short leg, Miss Green."

"Is that something to do with cricket?"

He nodded as I climbed down the ladder. Once I was standing on the narrow walkway beside him, I had the distinct impression that he was about to ask me something before handing me back the book.

"May I say how much I have enjoyed our perambulations with your sister in Hyde Park, Miss Green."

"Thank you, Mr Edwards. I have also enjoyed them."

I looked expectantly at the book. It was titled *A Practical Treatise on Electric Illumination*.

"I wondered if you would perhaps like to visit another location with me. With your sister as chaperone, of course. After all, we live in this wonderful great city with so many sights to admire!"

"We do indeed."

"Where would you like to go?"

I paused. "Mr Edwards, would you mind terribly if I were to suggest an idea next week? It is rather too hot to consider anything much at the moment and I have quite a lot of work to occupy me at the present time."

He quickly hid the disappointment on his face with a cheery smile.

"Of course, Miss Green! You're right. It is terribly hot, and I understand that you have a lot of work to do. You certainly keep me busy here in the reading room with all the different areas of research required for your news articles. One week it's Egypt and the next it's French authors, and then there are the maps of Colombia. Did that explorer chap, Mr Fox-Stirling, have anything useful to say about his search for your father in Colombia? I forgot to ask how your meeting with him went."

My father had been a plant-hunter but had disappeared in Colombia nine years previously. I was attempting to write a book about his life and had recently met with Mr Fox-Stirling, who had conducted an unsuccessful search for my father.

"Not anything particularly useful, but he was rather pushed for time. He has invited Eliza and me to have dinner with him and his wife."

"That's wonderful. He may have some interesting titbits of information about your father for the book. How's the book writing going, by the way?"

"Slowly, Mr Edwards."

He laughed. "You always say that, Miss Green!"

"Probably because it's the truth." I forced a smile but was beginning to feel rather irritable. "Thank you for helping me find this book, Mr Edwards. I must go and look through it as I need to be back at the office shortly to meet my deadline."

"Of course, Miss Green." He stepped aside to allow me to pass. Although he was smiling, the look of disappointment still lingered in his eyes.

Back at my desk, I leafed through the pages of Simon Borthwick's book. The text was rather detailed and dense, so I chose to browse the illustrations of galvanometers, drum armatures and various types of generators. There were countless pictures of arc lamps and incandescent lamps; lamps which could be used for industrial purposes and others which could be used at home. Each turn of the page fanned the air under my chin slightly.

Then I came across a folded piece of paper tucked into the centre of the book. I opened out the stray sheet and saw that it was a letter. It was undated and unsigned.

Dear reader

Observe if you will that this book lacks any expertise which can be attributed to Mr Simon Borthwick. The man has been credited for his work on the incandescent bulb and successfully filed a British patent for a lamp utilising carbonised cotton thread as a filament. This idea, however, was stolen directly from the Scottish inventor Mr Hugo Bannister, who recently died in ill-deserved poverty and obscurity in New York.

For how much longer will Mr Borthwick hoodwink the scientific community, the establishment and the great British public with his supposed innovations? Sadly, only time will tell.

And so, my dear reader, consider yourself enlightened with regard to the true identity of Mr Simon Borthwick. The man is not an inventor; he's a thief.

I read the letter through a second time just to be certain that I had read it correctly. *Was there any truth to what it said? How long had the anonymous letter remained hidden within the pages of this book?*

I stared at the words in their sloping black ink and tried to understand the motive behind the letter. *Was this the sort of thing to which Mr Borthwick had been referring when he wrote that someone had been trying to besmirch his name?*

I flicked through the pages of the book looking for another letter but found nothing more.

"How are you finding the book, Miss Green?"

"Very enlightening, thank you, Mr Edwards."

"Is there anything else I can assist with?"

"You may like to look at this."

I showed him the letter and explained that I had found it inside the book.

"Have you noticed anyone placing pieces of paper inside any of your books, Mr Edwards?"

"Certainly not." He scowled. "It's an abuse of library property, and when I find out who did this I shall report them to the head librarian and ensure that their reading ticket is confiscated."

"That sounds like a good idea. I should very much like to find out who wrote it. Have you ever heard of a Hugo Bannister?"

"No."

"I haven't either until now. Perhaps the person who wrote this was a friend of his. Or even a family member."

"I will have a look through our reader records and see if I can find anyone who shares the same surname."

"In the meantime, I will have to try to find out more about him."

"Would you like me to do that?"

"Thank you, Mr Edwards. I should be very grateful if you could. Do you mind if I keep this letter for the time being?"

"I'm not sure about that, Miss Green. I really need to show it to the head librarian."

"I understand, but I will keep it safe. Do you mind if I hold on to it for just a few days? I should like to see if I can have the handwriting analysed."

"I'm not sure where you would begin with that, Miss Green, but very well. Please ensure that you hand it back to me, however, as this is evidence of a crime against an asset of the library."

"I certainly will, Mr Edwards. We both need to find out who the culprit is."

I folded the letter carefully and slipped it into my carpet bag.

CHAPTER 11

"Why did you decide to work with electricity?" I had asked Simon Borthwick during our first and only meeting.

"My grandfather took me to one of Michael Faraday's Christmas lectures at the Royal Institution when I was fourteen. Faraday was a fascinating speaker and I remember his demonstration as clearly as if it were yesterday. I was amazed at the way he could generate static electricity by rubbing a glass rod with a piece of silk, shuffling his feet on the carpet and combing a lock of hair with a tortoiseshell comb. To demonstrate the electricity he was creating he used a gold-leaf electroscope. Do you know what that is?"

"I don't."

"I have one right here."

He had walked over to one of the shelves and brought back a glass jar.

"Look, it has a circular brass plate on top of it. A rod descends from the plate into the jar and suspended from the rod are two pieces of gold leaf. See them there?"

I nodded.

"When a charge is applied to the plate these two gold leaves separate, rather like an upside-down letter V. When I saw what Faraday did, I knew that I wanted to become an electrochemist. My grandfather also had an interest in electricity, although his interest was more associated with magic. He often practised his own conjuring tricks, but he was no good at them." Borthwick laughed. "He enjoyed magic shows and went to see the French magician Robert-Houdin at the St James's Theatre in 1853. Robert-Houdin used electromagnetism in his tricks, and in those days few members of the audience had any understanding of electricity at all. They believed that what they were seeing was true magic."

"What about your parents? Did they have an interest in electricity?"

"They may have done, but I wouldn't know. They died within a year of each other. My father succumbed to rheumatic fever when I was eight years old and my mother never recovered from his death. My grandmother maintained that she had died of a broken heart, but I'm not sure that is strictly possible. My younger brother went to live with an aunt and uncle in Wales. I don't see much of him. They didn't want to take on two boys and they preferred the younger one. They felt I would be too much work for them. I'm grateful for the time my grandparents devoted to me. It's a shame that neither of them is around to see my work."

"I'm sure they would be extremely proud, especially of your patent for the light bulb."

"Perhaps, but I didn't manage it alone. The work I did merely built upon the travails of others who had gone before me: Davy, Yablochkov, de Moleyns, Sprengel and Bannister among them. Then in Canada you have Woodward and Evans, who sold their light bulb patent to Edison. And the Sawyer-Man incandescent lamps have been around for a few years now."

"And Thomas Edison?"

"There's no doubt that his light bulb patent in America infringes upon the work of others including mine, but I am leaving that to the lawyers. I prefer not to involve myself in legal discussions." His amenable mood vanished and his expression swiftly darkened.

"But Mr Edison's lightbulb must differ from yours in some way, does it not?"

"I don't wish to discuss it, Miss Green," snapped Borthwick. "Legal matters make me angry."

"While you're at the typewriter, Miss Green, I don't suppose you fancy typewriting my article on the Belgian elections, do you?" asked Edgar Fish. "It's only four hundred words."

"I can't, Edgar. I'll miss my deadline."

"I'm going to miss mine, too! Sherman's told me he wants my articles typewritten now because it hastens the editing process."

"Have you asked his secretary, Miss Welton?"

"She isn't speaking to me at the present time."

"Why not?" I stopped typewriting and turned to look at him over my shoulder.

"I don't know."

"It's because you called her an old lady," said Frederick Potter.

"I said it in jest!" exclaimed Edgar. "It was supposed to be humorous."

"Miss Welton isn't the humorous type," I replied.

"No, she's not," said Edgar. "And neither am I when I have no one to do my typewriting for me."

"You could try learning it yourself," I said.

Edgar snorted. "I have no patience for that. It requires

perseverance, which is something the fairer sex possesses in far greater measure than us men. Those little keys you press down are no match for my great fingers. I feel sure they'd snap! And besides, my fingers don't have the dexterity."

"You play the piano, don't you, Fish?" asked Frederick.

"Yes, but what's that got to do with anything?"

"It means your fingers must have dexterity."

"It's entirely different, Potter. That's music. There's an ebb and flow to it, which causes one's fingers to dance. They could never plod, plod, clatter, clatter on the keys of that infernal typewriting machine. It's as if one's hands become machines themselves!"

"I think a chap needs to invent a typewriter which plays music when you press the letters on it," said Frederick. "What do you think to that, Fish?"

"I think it's a capital idea. We just need to wait for some fellow to invent it. In the meantime, Miss Green, please can you typewrite my article for me?"

"No," I replied firmly.

Mr Sherman entered the room, the door slamming behind him once again.

"I regret to report, sir, that I am unable to have my article typewritten," said Edgar. "Miss Welton won't do it, and neither will Miss Green. I feel utterly abandoned."

"Abandoned, eh?" Mr Sherman removed his pipe from his mouth. "Miss Green, please typewrite Edgar's article for him when you've finished whatever it is you're doing there."

"But I don't have enough time, sir!"

"Make some time, then. It won't take you long. You're quite an expert on that machine now. I refuse to edit spidery handwriting any longer. I want it all typewritten."

"Thank you, sir," said Edgar. "Women don't seem to appreciate the genuine advantage they have over men in the operation of typewriter machines, do they?"

"They don't, Fish. They're blessed with far more patience than us."

I felt my teeth clench.

"Exactly, sir," said Edgar. "And, as I mentioned to Miss Green just now, perseverance."

"A trait naturally found in women," responded the editor. "As well as tolerance."

My fingers jabbed angrily at the typewriter keys.

"And an overall sanguinity," added Frederick. "And calmness."

"Not to mention feminine serenity and a gentle acceptance of menial tasks," said Edgar.

"Enough!" I snarled, ripping my completed article out of the typewriter.

"Miss Green?" asked Mr Sherman. "Are you all right?"

"I apologise, sir. Perhaps I don't possess the patience that nature was duty-bound to bestow upon me."

"How are you getting on with the murder at the medical school?"

"Chief Inspector Stroud of the City of London police is working on it."

"Is there a suspect yet?"

"Apparently not. I think there's an obvious one, but the chief inspector disagrees with me."

"They need young Blakely on the case," said Edgar. "The schoolboy inspector. That would put a smile on your face, wouldn't it, Miss Green?"

I glowered at him.

"There has been much speculation regarding the medical school murder down at the Turkish baths," said Mr Sherman. "I spoke to a chap who knew Mr Geller, and he couldn't possibly imagine why anyone would wish to harm such a pleasant young man."

"I'll tell you something you might be interested in, Miss

Green," said Edgar. "It's regarding that inventor chap who shot a bullet into his own head."

"Yes?"

"It turns out that Mrs Fish has a schoolfriend who once courted him. She's terribly upset, apparently."

"Lillian Maynell?"

"I don't know. It might be. In fact, I think perhaps it could be. The name Lillian does sound rather familiar."

"Thank you, Edgar."

"I'll tell you what, why don't you go and ask Mrs Fish yourself? We're in Brunswick Square, number twenty-six."

"Thank you, Edgar. I will."

"Is there a story in this, Miss Green?" asked Mr Sherman.

"Yes, there may well be. I think that Simon Borthwick was driven to his death."

"You *think* he was? Or he *actually* was?"

"I don't know yet. That is what I'm trying to find out."

"Well, don't spend too much time on that. It sounds rather flaky to me," said my editor. "And don't forget to typewrite Edgar's article. I need it in one hour."

CHAPTER 12

"Goodness, Penelope! Your lodgings are stifling," Eliza commented as she fanned herself. "I don't know how you manage to breathe properly in here."

Even in the evenings the heat of midsummer showed no sign of abating.

"Keeping the window open helps to cool the room," I said.

"Even worse! Just think of all the disease carried in the air!" Eliza marched over to the sash window and pulled it shut with a loud slam.

"But I often keep the window open," I protested. "I haven't fallen foul of any disease as yet."

"Not yet, but there's always a chance. You don't want to be getting yourself Asiatic cholera. That terrible epidemic in the south of France may well spread to our shores. Have you read about it in the newspaper? Of course you have; you work for the newspaper."

"There's no outbreak of cholera in London at the moment, Ellie."

"Not at the moment, but it's likely to reach us very soon. They say it's happened in the south of France because of the heat. Well, it's also hot here! They need to start disinfecting the streets as a precaution."

"How's Fenella?" I asked. "I hope she wasn't upset over that unpleasant business with Simon Borthwick after the fair."

"She's absolutely fine. We didn't see or hear anything about it. Thankfully, the cab had whisked us away before he committed the heinous act. I haven't mentioned it to her, either. Children don't need to hear about such things."

"I'm pleased to hear that she was unaffected," I said.

"Why would the man do such a thing? And so publicly, too?" said Eliza. "Perhaps it was an accident. Perhaps he was sitting in the cab inspecting his revolver when it accidentally went off."

"No, it was suicide," I replied. "He planned it and left behind rather a despondent letter."

"Oh dear. Perhaps he had a weakness of the mind," said my sister. "Perhaps his brain was prone to episodes of sudden paroxysm. It can happen, you know. A neighbour of Cousin Agatha's suffered the same affliction and shot himself because he could withstand the symptoms no longer."

"That's very sad. I'm not sure how a mind as brilliant as Simon Borthwick's could be affected by an impairment such as that."

"Oh, that's where you're quite wrong, Penelope. It is generally considered that a mind with genius capability actually possesses a higher incidence of flaws."

"How do you know that, Ellie?"

"I read it somewhere. Anyway, I can't stop here for long discussing such morbid matters. I came to ask if you'd like to join our meeting of the West London Women's Society this evening. We're discussing the sad news that the Clause for the Enfranchisement of Women has been rejected. I had such hopes for Mr Woodall's proposed amendment to the Reform Bill. We had the support of seventy-nine Liberal MPs, and yet it came to nothing."

"That's sad news."

"Well it is, and I cannot foresee when the next opportunity will arise for women's suffrage. But there's no use in bemoaning what has happened. We plan to formulate our next plan of action at this evening's meeting."

"Miss Green!" Mrs Garnett knocked at my door. "There's a gentleman here to see you."

Eliza's eyes widened with sudden interest. "A gentleman, Penelope? Were you expecting someone?"

"No, I'm not expecting anyone. I wasn't even expecting you this evening."

Was it James?

I quickly repinned my hair and smoothed out my cotton dress.

"Miss Green! Can you hear me?"

"I'm on my way, Mrs Garnett!" I called back as I skipped over to the door and opened it.

"He's waiting in the hallway," said my landlady as I followed her down the narrow wooden staircase and then descended the wider carpeted stairs. Eliza followed close behind me.

It wasn't James in the hallway; instead, it was Mr Edwards. Wearing a pale grey suit, he held his hat in one hand and a leather document case in the other. He greeted me with a wide grin.

"Miss Green! And Mrs Billington-Grieg, too! What a delightful surprise."

"It's a surprise to see you here this evening, Mr Edwards," said Eliza. "Are your visits here a regular occurrence?"

"No, Ellie. This is the first time Mr Edwards has visited," I said swiftly.

"Hugo Bannister!" he announced as he held up the case. "All the notes I've made about him are in here."

"Oh, thank you, Mr Edwards. That's extremely kind of you," I said. "And rather quick work as well. There was no need for you to go to the trouble of delivering the notes to my home. I could have collected them from you during my next visit to the reading room."

"It was no trouble at all. It's a good excuse for a stroll on a pleasant summer's evening."

"You're not worried about cholera, then?" I asked.

"Cholera?" His face grew concerned. "Has there been another outbreak?"

"It is spreading in the south of France," I replied.

"That's rather far away," he said. "I shouldn't think you need to concern yourself about that at the present time, Miss Green."

"Thank you for the reassurance, Mr Edwards. If you're not worried about it then neither am I." I glared at my sister, still mindful of the window she had slammed shut.

"If it were to reach Paris that would be a different matter," said Mr Edwards. "I think we should need to be on our guard then."

"Is it going to reach Paris?" asked Mrs Garnett.

"We don't know," said Mr Edwards. "I wasn't aware that it was prevalent in the south of France."

"I don't want it getting to Paris," said Mrs Garnett. "If it gets there it won't be long before it ends up in London. I don't want any cholera here again. I remember it back in '66. Awful times. Dreadful times. It was exactly like hell on earth."

Her lower lip began to wobble, and I wished I had never mentioned the disease.

"Don't worry, Mrs Garnett," I said breezily. "I'm sure it won't return."

"With this heat you can never be too sure," said Eliza.

"The heat brings it on, does it?" asked Mrs Garnett, her eyes wide with fear.

"No, it doesn't, Mrs Garnett. There is no need for unnecessary concern," said Mr Edwards. He handed me the leather case and I thanked him again.

"The pleasure is all mine, Miss Green," he replied. "I enjoyed finding out about Mr Bannister, although it's a rather sorry tale."

"Is it?"

"Yes. He was an extremely clever man by all accounts and worked on early prototypes of the electric lamp, but he died poor and alone."

"I worry about that happening to me," said Mrs Garnett.

Eliza rolled her eyes.

"You won't be alone, Mrs Garnett," I said. "I'll be here."

"Will you, Miss Green?" asked Mr Edwards. "You won't have moved somewhere else by then?"

"Why should I move anywhere else?" I asked.

"Your circumstances might change," said Eliza.

"I have no plans to change my circumstances in the immediate future," I replied curtly, aware that my sister was hinting at marriage.

"Mr Edwards," said Eliza. "Has Penelope mentioned to you that we are due to dine with the celebrated plant-hunter Mr Fox-Stirling and his wife?"

"She has indeed. I hope he has some more useful information to impart about your father."

"Has she not invited you to join us?" asked Eliza.

I felt a sinking sensation in my chest and saw a flush of colour spread beneath Mr Edwards' spectacles.

"Invited me? Oh, I see... Well, I don't recall Miss Green mentioning an invitation."

"That was rather remiss of her," said my sister. "Would you like to join us?"

"I should be delighted to," said Mr Edwards. "But only if Miss Green is acquiescent." He gave me a half-worried, half-expectant look.

"I acquiesce," I said with a forced smile. The alternative was that I would be the only person without a companion for the evening.

A wide smile spread across Mr Edwards' face.

"Wonderful! Well, I must say I am looking forward to it immensely. Thank you, ladies."

He took his leave of us and departed.

Mrs Garnett shook her head once she had closed the door behind him. "Now there's a lovesick man if ever I saw one."

"What do you mean?" I asked.

"It's in his eyes, Miss Green. The way he looks at you. Lovesick."

"Exactly, Mrs Garnett," said my sister. "You and I don't often agree, but I'm pleased that you are also able to see it."

"Nonsense," I retorted. "He's merely a chap who works in the reading room. He helps me with my research."

"And why does he help you so much with your research?" asked Eliza.

"Because he's naturally helpful."

"Does he help many other people with their research?"

"Probably. Anyway, I need to get on and take a look at these notes."

I wanted to rebuke Eliza for inviting Mr Edwards to dinner without my permission, but it would have been impolite to do so in front of my landlady.

"So he's replaced the inspector, has he?" asked Mrs Garnett.

"No!" I replied. "Absolutely not. And I don't know what you mean by *replaced*. In what capacity would Mr Edwards *replace* Inspector Blakely? One is a clerk from the reading room and the other is a detective."

Mrs Garnett wagged her finger at me and grinned, her teeth flashing white against her dark skin. "But we know better, don't we? You don't think we can see through your insouciance, but I've been around for a long time. I've seen it all before. I was married once myself, you know."

"Mr Edwards and Inspector Blakely are merely gentlemen I have encountered in the course of my work," I said. "People always speculate on these matters because I happen to be a spinster. If I were married no one would pay any attention whatsoever."

"You're right, Penelope," said Eliza. "They wouldn't. Married women escape such speculation. That is why most women follow the sensible path and become wives at their earliest opportunity."

CHAPTER 13

Mrs Georgina Fish was a young, pleasant, horse-faced woman with soft curls of dark hair. She wore a pale green linen day dress and received me in her parlour with three of her cats.

"Edgar and I always joke about our name and the fact that we have so many cats," she giggled. "Cats catch *fish*, don't they?"

I smiled politely. "They do when they have the chance. My cat lives on the rooftops and catches pigeons."

"A rooftop cat? Goodness. Perhaps you should marry a man with the name Pigeon!"

I feigned laughter. Mrs Fish's jokes were as poor as her husband's.

"I must say that it's extremely admirable of you to pursue a profession," she continued. "I don't possess the brains for such work. And I certainly don't know how you put up with Edgar every day!"

"Me neither!" I laughed again.

"He's very fond of you, I can tell. He often comes home with a story about what Miss Green has been up to."

"Does he indeed?" I began to feel concerned. "Such as?"

"Oh, little things. Such as the way you like to poke fun at tubby Frederick and the manner in which you talk back to your editor."

"Well, I must say that tales such as those make me sound rather rude."

"Oh no, not at all." She waved a delicate hand dismissively. "Edgar always talks about it in such an amusing way. He says you'd like to speak to me about my friend Lillian."

"Yes. Lillian Maynell, isn't it?"

"The very same!" she clapped her hands together with glee, startling the white cat on the sofa next to her. "Isn't it funny how these things transpire?"

"Isn't it?"

"Especially when you think how big London is! What are the chances of it happening?"

"Indeed. The chances are very slim, I suspect."

"Would you like some tea, Miss Green?"

"Thank you. Do call me Penny."

Georgina summoned a maid and asked her to fetch some tea.

"Lillian is married to Mr Jeffrey Maynell, an engineer with Repton, Borthwick and Company. Is that right?" I asked.

"Yes. He does something to do with electricity and that's all I know, I'm afraid. He's extremely clever, though."

"I understand that, previous to her marriage, Lillian courted Mr Maynell's colleague, Simon Borthwick."

"The one who shot himself? Yes." Georgina's face fell and became solemn.

"Did you ever meet Mr Borthwick?"

"Yes, I did. A few times in fact. I didn't ever get to know him well, as he was always so busy. I think he was more interested in his work than marriage, and I suspect that was why Lillian turned her attentions elsewhere."

A ginger cat jumped up onto my lap and stared at me, its face inches from mine.

"Just push her off," said Georgina. "It's because you're sitting in her favourite chair."

I tried to remove the cat, but she twisted her head around and tried to bite my hand. Georgina hissed at her and she jumped down.

"Does Lillian know that Simon Borthwick mentioned her in a letter which he wrote just before his death?" I asked.

"Did he?" Georgina's mouth hung open. "Goodness! I didn't know that, and I shouldn't think she does either. What did he say about her?"

"He apologised to her, but said that she no doubt cared little for his apology."

"Did he really?" I saw tears appear in Georgina's eyes. "That is quite a surprise."

"Why do you find it surprising?"

"Because it suggests that he cared for her after all. I had assumed he was rather indifferent to the courtship. She grew tired of waiting for him to propose."

"That is why the courtship ended?"

"Yes. Lillian was rather saddened by it, and I cannot deny that she was also receiving the attentions of Jeffrey Maynell. He seemed to possess more enthusiasm for marriage than Simon Borthwick. But it seems that Simon must have cared for her if he mentioned her in his letter in such a manner." Georgina paused and wiped her eyes with a lace handkerchief. "I think she would be saddened to know that he had written that."

"Do you think it would be appropriate to tell her?"

"I really don't know. She's happily married now, you see, and it wouldn't do to stir up a hornet's nest."

"Simon Borthwick's letter concerns me because he

suggested that he was persecuted to the point where he had no option but to take his own life."

"Oh, that really is dreadful." A tear trickled down Georgina's cheek. "I had no idea he had suffered so much."

"You're not aware of anyone persecuting him?"

"No."

"Do you think Lillian would know?"

"I don't think she would."

"Do you think she might be happy to speak to me? I would be very tactful about the matter."

"She's already had quite an upset hearing about his suicide. A sudden and untimely death is one thing, but suicide..."

"It's not at all pleasant, is it? If I were to meet her you would be more than welcome to accompany me. If you were happy to, of course."

"Can I please think about it, Miss Green?" She wiped away her tears. "I feel as though I'm having to consider so many things all at the same time, and I don't have the brains for thinking, I can assure you."

"Nonsense, Georgina. You seem like a woman with plenty of brains to me."

"You think so?" She smiled.

"Apart from marrying Edgar. Perhaps you didn't use your brains properly when you made that decision."

"Oh, Miss Green!" She laughed and clapped her hands together. "You are so terribly funny!"

CHAPTER 14

"I'm not sure why you're here again, Miss Green. I have nothing further to share with you about the murder of Mr Geller."

Chief Inspector Stroud did not admit me to his office this time. Instead, he spoke to me while leaning with one elbow on the desk of the main lobby. His thick grey whiskers were damp with perspiration.

"That's a shame, Inspector. How many people have you interviewed?"

"There is no requirement for me to disclose that information to you."

"Would it be helpful if I wrote an article in the *Morning Express* appealing for witnesses who may have seen a person acting suspiciously in or near the medical school on the day that Richard Geller was murdered?"

"If, at some later date, I consider that to be a useful course of action I shall inform you then."

"Do you have an alibi for Mr Kurtz yet, for that brief period of time when he says he left the museum and Mr Geller's murder took place?"

"It would not be customary for me to share that information with a news reporter."

"I understand, Inspector, but don't you think the public would like to learn more about the investigation? It was an extremely shocking attack on an innocent man, and I would like to write an article which reassures our readers."

Chief Inspector Stroud made a derisory snorting noise. "I think the good people of London instinctively put their trust in our police force. There is no need for supposed reassurance from the newspapers."

"I'm afraid I disagree, Inspector. When a terrible crime occurs gossip spreads misinformation and people can become disproportionately concerned. The ability to read and digest certain facts about the case will put the public's mind at rest."

"This is the City of London police force, Miss Green, not the Metropolitan. I'm well aware that my colleagues in the Met are happy to share every detail of their investigations with the scribbling race, but that is not the case here. We have a certain way of doing things, and we have done them most successfully for forty-five years now."

"My editor has asked me to write about any progress that has been made with Mr Geller's case," I said. "Shall I return to the office and tell him that there has been no progress?"

"Tell him that the Richard Geller case is of no concern to the press."

It was my turn to emit a derisory snort.

"Times are changing, Inspector Stroud. You cannot exclude the press from a case such as this."

"I can and I will."

"I shall return to my editor and tell him there has been no progress whatsoever."

"That would be a lie, because there has been."

"Such as?"

"I'm not at liberty to say."

"Then I shall report that no progress has been made."

"It would be misleading to report such a thing."

"There hasn't been any progress, has there?"

"Yes, there has."

"If there had been I think you would share it with me, Inspector. Detectives often feel a sense of pride when they make a breakthrough in a case and usually cannot resist sharing their news."

"Detectives in the Metropolitan Police, perhaps."

"So you are no closer to catching Mr Geller's murderer than when I spoke to you last?"

"I haven't said that."

"But I have, and I shall commit it to paper in our next edition."

❧

"You need to march into Old Jewry and take charge of that medical school museum case," I barked at James, still fuming. "I don't think I've ever met a police inspector as cantankerous as Chief Inspector Stroud!"

"You know that it's impossible for me to do so, Penny," said James, sipping his stout. We were seated at our usual table in the Museum Tavern. James' shirt sleeves were rolled up and his tie pin was topped with a small gold star.

I removed my spectacles and rubbed at my eyes, which felt dusty from the warm streets that day.

"Inspector Stroud hasn't made any advances with the case," I said. "That is why he's refusing to share any information with me. He's done nothing about Richard Geller's murder. I wish I could place an infernal machine beneath his chair to inflame his languorous derrière!"

"Mind your French, Miss Green."

"Does it not anger you?"

"Perhaps not quite to the extent to which it angers you, Penny, but yes it does disappoint me when a case appears to be floundering."

"It's more than floundering. I don't think the inspector particularly cares about it. A poor fellow has lost his life! Can't you do anything about it?"

"No, I can't. The City of London police force is an entirely separate entity from the Metropolitan."

"But it makes no sense! Why should the City of London have a separate police force? The Metropolitan force looks after all of London, spreading from... how big is it?"

"Approximately fifteen miles in each direction from Charing Cross."

"It's enormous! And then there is a tiny little bit in the middle, the City of London, which has its own separate force! It's nonsensical and also rather inconvenient. What's so funny?"

James quickly removed the smile from his face. "I'm sorry. Nothing's funny."

"But you were laughing. What were you laughing about?"

"You."

"Me? Why?"

"I don't know why. It's funny seeing you so angry sometimes."

"Oh, is it now?"

"Penny..." He tried to adopt a soothing tone. "The world is full of geographical anomalies, largely born of tradition or a historical conflict of some sort. Take Jerusalem as an example."

"*Jerusalem*? What does Jerusalem have to do with the City of London police?"

"Very well, let's forget about Jerusalem."

James took a large gulp of stout and allowed his eyes to linger on mine. I smiled, feeling sure that he preferred to see me without my spectacles for a change.

"Your telegram requesting this meeting suggested you had a letter to show me," he said. "What's that all about?"

"Oh, it's here." I pulled the letter out of my bag and handed it to him. "I found it inside Simon Borthwick's book in the reading room."

James read it through with interest.

"This implies there is some truth to Borthwick's claim that someone was attempting to undermine his work," I added.

"Do you know if there is any truth to what the letter says?" asked James. "Who is Hugo Bannister?"

"He was a Scottish inventor who pioneered work on the vacuum lamp."

"Which is what?"

"The electric lamp. The vacuum keeps the level of oxygen low enough so that the filament glows. Too much oxygen would cause it to catch fire."

James raised his eyebrows. "You're quite the scientist, Penny."

"I'm afraid not. Fortunately, Mr Edwards explains it all quite well in his notes. It appears that Simon Borthwick used Mr Bannister's work in the patent for his incandescent lamp. Apparently, the carbonised cotton filament was a particular feature of Mr Bannister's lamp, and Mr Borthwick supposedly stole it. I prefer to think of him as having borrowed it because I recall him telling me that his work built upon the work of others. A number of them have been working to the same end so I imagine conflict over their work is common. Mr Borthwick was involved in legal action against Thomas Edison."

"It seems that someone felt aggrieved by what Simon

Borthwick had done," said James. "Perhaps Bannister can tell you more."

"He died in New York last year having gone to work for Edison."

"A natural death?"

"It would seem so. The letter said that he died penniless, doesn't it? I can imagine him living a pauper's life in a miserable part of the city."

"It can't have gone well with Edison, in that case."

"It doesn't appear to have done. Donald Repton didn't mention any of this Hugo Bannister business to me. Surely he must be aware of any such feud."

"It's difficult to know without asking him directly."

"So the question is, what do we do now?"

"You're using the word *we* again, Penny. I cannot involve myself in this. No crime has been committed other than suicide."

"And you can't investigate Richard Geller's murder either."

"You know I can't. I should like to help you, but..."

"There's no need to explain. I understand. At least I know who the mysterious Lillian is that Borthwick mentions in his letter. She's married to Borthwick's colleague, Jeffrey Maynell. I'm awaiting a possible meeting with her. I also wish to speak to another colleague of Borthwick's, Jack Copeland. I have met him briefly a couple of times."

"Goodness, you're quite determined about all this, aren't you? You're putting Chief Inspector Stroud and his languorous derrière to shame."

"That wouldn't be difficult."

James finished off his stout. "I cannot directly involve myself in these cases, Penny, but if you need someone to listen and suggest ideas I am always happy to help you."

"Thank you, James. I appreciate you helping me. And thank you for coming to meet me here this evening."

"Try keeping me away," he replied with a smile.

CHAPTER 15

Upon enquiring at the works in Southwark, I was told that I would find Jack Copeland at the construction site in Kensington. The area was filled with scaffolding, carts and men in caps and dirty shirts. Walls of red brick rose up from the chaos and I made my way toward one of the few completed buildings I could see: the Electric Lighting Station.

It was a relief to enter its shade. Within it was a staircase, which led down to basement level. I struggled to see the steps as my eyes slowly accustomed to the gloom.

A man in an oil-streaked work coat was examining a steam engine in the large subterranean room by the light of a paraffin lamp. Another man was hammering away at the boiler.

"Mr Copeland?" I called out.

The man in the work coat turned slowly to look at me with his bulbous eyes. His dark, drooping whiskers gave him a morose appearance.

"Good morning, Miss Green. Have you come to marvel at our generating station?" His speech was muffled by his long moustache. "It's one of the first in the world to supply domestic premises."

I didn't correct him with my true reason for being there, but instead displayed a look of keen interest in the hope that this would make him amenable to my questions when the time came.

"It's a very exciting project, Mr Copeland. This here is one of the engines?"

"Yes. One of seven which will be installed here. As you can imagine, it's quite a task getting the parts down the steps and into this room. Seven engines for seven generators."

"That sounds like it should be a popular rhyme, doesn't it?" I commented cheerily.

He gave me a blank look.

"The generators will be positioned here." He gestured toward one end of the concrete floor. "And we'll have belts running from the engines on this side to the generators on that side. It'll be quite a spectacle when they're all running at full power."

"And they'll make quite a din, too, I should imagine."

"We're putting in a three-wire DC electrical supply."

"Direct current? Mr Repton explained that to me."

He glanced at my hands and frowned. "Don't you need a notebook to write everything down in?"

"Ah yes, it's just here." I pulled a notebook and pencil out of my carpet bag.

"Mr Repton told me the number of volts employed, but I'm afraid I have forgotten it," I said.

"Two hundred."

I wrote this down.

"You'll probably want to see the pump house next," said Jack Copeland. "It's being constructed by the London Hydraulic Power Company to power service lifts."

"Service lifts? How interesting."

"I understand the water pressure will be supplied at four hundred pounds per square inch."

I wrote this down, unsure of what it meant and reluctant to ask for an explanation.

"It's rather saddening, isn't it, that Mr Borthwick is not here to see the progress on this pioneering project?" I said.

"It is," Mr Copeland replied.

I waited for some further words, but none came.

"How long did you know him?" I asked.

"We met as undergraduates at Imperial College."

"How long ago was that?"

He sighed. "It would be over twenty years ago now."

"And you were personal friends as well as colleagues?"

"Not particularly. But I'd rather discuss the Kensington Court project. That's why you're here, isn't it?"

"Well yes, it is. There's just one small matter I would like to ask you about if it's not too much trouble."

He scowled. "Is it about Kensington Court?"

"No. It's about this letter." I retrieved the page I had found in Simon Borthwick's book from my bag and passed it to him.

"It was written by an anonymous writer who accuses Simon Borthwick of stealing the ideas of Hugo Bannister," I said. "I found it in Mr Borthwick's book, *A Practical Treatise on Electric Illumination.*"

Jack Copeland's brow furrowed as he read it. "How peculiar," he remarked. "It was just sitting in the book, was it?"

"Yes. Is the author of the letter correct? Did Simon Borthwick steal Hugo Bannister's ideas?"

"Well, I'm not sure they were Bannister's ideas to begin with. Many people are working independently on the light bulb, and it's natural that comparable ideas should occur to similar minds."

"So the carbonised cotton filament in Mr Borthwick's

patent for his incandescent lamp wasn't stolen from Mr Bannister?"

Jack Copeland raised an eyebrow. "*Stolen* is the wrong word."

"So your view, Mr Copeland, is that Mr Borthwick did nothing wrong?"

"We're all working with the same science, Miss Green, and the materials which could be used for an effective filament are limited. It's rather difficult to prove whether someone did or didn't steal ideas from another. However, egos are fragile, and some chaps grow resentful while others become downright angry."

"Do you know anyone who might have been angry with Mr Borthwick?"

"No, I don't. I tend to stay well away from it all. I don't have the temperament for disagreement or confrontation."

He handed the letter back to me and I stowed it safely in my bag.

Mr Copeland had given little away, and I was struggling to ascertain what his relationship with Borthwick had been like.

"It's a rather calculated act, isn't it, to put a letter criticising Mr Borthwick inside a copy of his book in the British Library?" I said. "The author of that letter must bear him a great deal of resentment. I don't suppose Mr Borthwick ever knew about it. Did you hear what he wrote in his letter before he died?"

"Yes, I've heard the gist of it. It sounds as though he was rather embittered."

"I think he sounded fearful."

"No, Simon wasn't the sort to be frightened."

"He said he would rather die by his own hand than by someone else's."

"Ah, now that's melodrama. He was terribly melodramatic."

"So he was exaggerating the perceived threat?"

"Not purposefully, I wouldn't have thought. After all, the man took his own life. But Simon had been known to make much ado about nothing. Sadly, he didn't have anyone to talk some sense into him on this occasion."

"You believe he could have been talked out of the suicide?"

"I think so. Somehow he was seized by a fit of irrationality and caused a fatal wound to himself." Jack Copeland seemed remarkably composed as he discussed the death of his colleague.

"Do you think the persecution he describes in his letter was less serious than he believed it to be?"

He wiped his hands on an oily rag. "Success is a double-edged sword, Miss Green. While one can expect praise, one must also expect criticism. Now I've already said too much on the matter and you'll get no more from me, I'm afraid. Instead, let me tell you a bit more about the copper strip distribution system we're installing here. You'll need all the details for your article in the *Morning Express*."

CHAPTER 16

"Mrs Fish has taken quite a shine to you, Penny," said Edgar. "She described you as a humorous and clever woman."

"That's very kind of her. She is too flattering by far."

"She would like to invite you to dinner with us one evening. The only problem I can foresee with the plan is that we don't know who to invite as your guest. Your mother, perhaps?"

"Thank you, Edgar. My mother lives in Derbyshire and cannot abide trains. It's been some years since she travelled to London."

"Wasn't there that chap who worked in the reading room?" asked Frederick.

"Oh yes, him!" said Edgar. "The bookish fellow. I forget his name. Come on, Miss Green, help us out. You're courting him, aren't you?"

"I believe you're referring to Mr Edwards, and no, I'm not courting him. He is merely an acquaintance."

"Who else could accompany you?"

"My sister, perhaps."

"The one with the bicycle?"

"Yes."

Edgar pulled a sceptical face. "I'm not sure that she and Mrs Fish would hit it off."

"Did your wife mention whether she had heard from her friend Lillian Maynell about the possibility of my meeting her?"

"Oh yes, that was the other thing. She has indeed, and I think Lillian would like to meet with you. There needs to be a bit of secrecy involved because the husband, Maynell, might not like his wife discussing her previous suitor."

"I respect her need for privacy; husbands can be terribly overprotective. It's the reason I haven't taken one."

Edgar laughed. "But doing so would make it rather easier to invite you to dinner parties!"

"Perhaps, but I consider that a small price to pay."

"Anyway, Miss Green, I take offence at your suggestion that husbands are overprotective. I can't say I'm an overprotective man at all," said Edgar.

"I am," said Frederick.

"Perhaps I could meet Mrs Maynell and your wife for lunch somewhere," I suggested. "I can recommend The Holborn Restaurant."

"I'm sure that will do very well," said Edgar. "I shall ask her to confirm the arrangements. Oh, look! I've just had another idea as to whom we can invite as your guest to our dinner party!"

I heard the newsroom door close and turned to see James walking towards us.

"A dinner party, Mr Fish? That sounds excellent," he said, taking off his bowler hat. "Good morning, Penny."

I returned his smile.

"Capital! I shall make the arrangements," said Edgar.

"Inspector Blakely cannot be my companion at your dinner party," I said. "It would be highly inappropriate."

James gave me a downcast glance.

"Oh yes, I forgot!' said Edgar. "You are engaged to be married, aren't you, Inspector? Never mind, Miss Green. Perhaps it will have to be that chap from the library after all. What can we do for you, Inspector?"

"I'm here to ask Miss Green if she would like to accompany me to the medical school at St Bartholomew's Hospital."

My heart skipped. "Has there been a development?" I asked.

"The Yard has been approached to assist."

"I thought Mr Geller's murder was a matter for the City of London police," I said as we left the *Morning Express* building and made our way towards Ludgate Hill. The bright sunlight made me squint. "Has Inspector Stroud relented and asked for your help?"

"No, but Richard Geller's father has," replied James. "He is Rabbi Geller of the West London Synagogue. He's friendly with the commissioner, and is understandably upset and frustrated that no progress has been made with regard to his son's dreadful murder."

"And the commissioner has asked you to investigate? That's excellent news, James."

"It is for us, but I don't think Chief Inspector Stroud will take kindly to my involvement."

We found Chief Inspector Stroud and Mr Kurtz waiting for us at the medical school museum. The inspector scowled as we entered the room, while pale-faced Kurtz gave me a libidinous smile, which I ignored.

"I'll be surprised if you spot something I've missed, Blakely," said Chief Inspector Stroud. "I can't tell you how many times we have been over the events of that day and searched this room."

The chief inspector mopped his perspiring face with a large handkerchief. By contrast, Mr Kurtz seemed unaffected by the heat.

"A fresh pair of eyes will do no harm, I'm sure," replied James.

"There are plenty of eyes in this room already," said Mr Kurtz with a macabre grin.

I wanted to warn James not to look too closely at the contents of some of the jars.

"I see no need for a news reporter to attend," said Inspector Stroud, glaring at me.

"Miss Green and I have worked together a number of times in the past," said James. "She has a knack for spotting important details."

"Perhaps she does, but it is not appropriate for her to be present." He sighed. "Unfortunately, this is indicative of how the Metropolitan Force conducts itself these days."

"I don't mind Miss Green being present," added Mr Kurtz with a grin.

James ignored both comments and readied himself with a notebook and pencil.

"Mr Geller was found murdered on Tuesday the seventeenth of June," he said. "How was his mood on that morning, Mr Kurtz?"

"The same as on any other morning. He was perfectly pleasant and busied himself as usual. I've already answered more questions than I care to recall, Inspector. Must I answer more?"

"I'm afraid so," replied James. "What did Mr Geller's work entail that morning?"

"Now just a moment, Blakely," interrupted Inspector Stroud. "You've begun your questions and this reporter is still in the room. I want her out!"

"You can rely on my discretion, Chief Inspector Stroud," I said. "I won't report on anything Mr Kurtz tells Inspector Blakely."

"Then why the devil are you here?"

"Miss Green's editor has asked her to report on this case," said James. "Therefore, it's important that she knows the details. You can trust her not to report on anything which would compromise the investigation."

"It's not right," huffed the chief inspector. "Not right at all."

Mr Kurtz wearily explained to James the work Mr Geller had been doing that morning and which table he had stood at.

"Mr Geller was standing where you are now when you left the room for a short while. Is that right, Mr Kurtz?" asked James.

"Yes." Mr Kurtz loitered beside the table where the skulls had sat during my last visit.

"And what time was that?"

"About a quarter to twelve o'clock."

"How can you be sure about that? Did you look at your watch or a clock just before you left?"

"I often look at the clock up there," Mr Kurtz pointed to a large timepiece near the spiral staircase. "I can't say I checked it just before I left, but I glance at it regularly throughout the day because I like to keep an eye on the time."

"Is it possible that it could have been half-past eleven o'clock when you left the room?"

"No, I'm certain that it was after that."

"Could it already have been midday?"

"No, because I returned to the room shortly after midday."

"So is it safe to assume, Mr Kurtz, that you were out of the room between, shall we say twenty minutes to twelve and five minutes past twelve? Is that a reasonable suggestion?"

"Yes."

James wrote the times down.

"And what were your parting words to Mr Geller?"

"Something along the lines of 'I'm going to see Mr Daly for a few minutes.' Words to that effect."

"Did he reply?"

"He acknowledged me with a nod."

"And that was the last time you saw him alive?"

"Yes." Mr Kurtz nodded solemnly.

"And when you left the room you had no concerns about him or the situation whatsoever?"

"No, why would I? It was an entirely normal situation. It was an ordinary morning."

"Where did you go?"

"I went to see Mr Daly."

"And who is he?"

"The assistant surgeon. I wished to speak to him about the curriculum for topographical anatomy so that Mr Geller and I could make the relevant specimens available to the students."

"And Mr Daly can vouch for having seen you, can he?"

"Sadly no, as he wasn't in his office."

"You knocked at the door and there was no reply?"

"Yes. I even opened the door and peered in, but the room was empty."

"Did anyone see you visiting his office?"

"I don't think so."

"Who did you encounter on your way to and from his office?"

"I honestly don't think I can remember." Mr Kurtz scratched his temple. His previously pale face now had some colour to it.

"You didn't stop to talk to anyone on the way there or back?"

"I don't think so."

"Did you encounter anyone at all?"

"Yes, I must have passed people in the corridor."

"And some of them would have been familiar to you?"

"Yes, I should think many of them would have been. I don't necessarily know everyone's names, but I would recognise their faces."

"There was no one who looked out of place? No one appeared suspicious?"

"You mean the murderer?"

James shrugged. "Anyone who didn't look quite right to you."

Mr Kurtz shook his head.

"Chief Inspector Stroud," said James. "Was the ligature present on Mr Geller's body when he was found?"

"Yes. It was a length of thick twine."

"Do you have any idea where it came from?"

"How should I know where it might have come from?"

"It wasn't from somewhere inside this room? Or somewhere else on the premises?"

"No, I don't think so. I suspect the murderer was carrying it on his person," Chief Inspector Stroud said.

"That suggests a strong degree of premeditation," said James. "So at some time during the twenty-five-minute window while you were out of the room, Mr Kurtz, someone came in and strangled Richard Geller with a thick piece of twine."

"That appears to be what happened."

"Where does that door behind you lead to?"

"It's the storeroom, Inspector."

"Is any twine kept in there?"

"No. I didn't recognise the twine around Richard's neck. The murderer must have brought it with him, as Inspector Stroud said."

"Chief Inspector Stroud, have you spoken to anyone who witnessed Mr Kurtz on his journey to and from Mr Daly's office?" asked James.

"Not yet."

"How long does it take to walk from here to Mr Daly's office?"

"I don't think I have ever paid attention," replied Mr Kurtz.

"One minute? Ten minutes?"

"Somewhere between the two."

"And you went straight there and came immediately back again?"

"Yes."

"We've already determined that you were out of the room for about twenty-five minutes, Mr Kurtz. That suggests the walk to Mr Daly's office takes a little over twelve minutes. Is that right?"

"A twelve-minute walk? That's quite a distance," I said. "About half a mile, I should think."

"It must take less time than that," said Mr Kurtz. "Perhaps I have my timings wrong. Perhaps I returned to the room just before midday."

"We'll walk the route in a moment and time it for ourselves," said James.

Mr Kurtz rubbed his hand over his chin nervously.

"Chief Inspector Stroud, at what time were the police summoned here?" asked James.

"We first heard of the incident at twenty minutes past midday."

"I ran down to the lobby as quickly as I could," explained Mr Kurtz. "I asked the man at the desk to summon the police."

"Mr Kurtz, did anyone visit this room while you and Mr Geller were working here on that fateful morning?"

"Some students came in, I think."

"And what time was that?"

"I struggle to remember precisely. About ten o'clock, I should think."

"If it was ten o'clock, as you suggest," James continued, "and we can find the students to confirm it, that leaves us with more than two hours between their visit and the police being alerted. During that time we have only your word for what occurred."

Mr Kurtz's eyes widened. "I hope you're not suggesting that I had anything to do with this, Inspector. I've just told you everything that happened and it's the truth. Upon my honour!"

CHAPTER 17

"I believe the man," said Chief Inspector Stroud defensively. "He is not responsible for the murder of his colleague."

"Good," replied James. "And there is nothing to suggest at this moment that Mr Kurtz is a dishonourable man who caused his friend some mischief. However, what you're lacking, Mr Kurtz, is a corroborated alibi. Let me suggest that you re-enact the walk you took that morning and think extremely hard about anyone you may have encountered on the way to Mr Daly's office, and on your return journey. Those people could be extremely helpful for you, and they may also have seen the culprit without realising it. We also need to find out which students visited this room and what time they were here. And anyone else for that matter. Please think as hard as you possibly can, Mr Kurtz, otherwise you may find yourself in hot water."

"It's a bit rough, isn't it, Blakely, to treat the man in this way?" said Chief Inspector Stroud. "He found the body of his colleague on the floor!"

"You don't need me to tell you that we must be as thorough as possible, Chief Inspector Stroud. Can you show me where Mr Geller's body was found?"

"In the place where Mr Kurtz is standing now."

"So Mr Geller died in the place where he was working?" asked James.

"Yes."

This struck me as odd.

"Surely if a man entered the room with murderous intent Mr Geller would have tried to get away," I interjected.

"You'd think so, wouldn't you?" said James. "He would have made an attempt to either defend himself or escape. Perhaps he knew his assailant."

"Even so, there must have been an altercation of some sort shortly before the murder," I said. "I can't imagine that Mr Geller would have remained standing exactly where he was."

"Perhaps he didn't notice the intruder," suggested Chief Inspector Stroud.

"But he was standing facing the door," said James. "I take it this door offers the only way in and out of the room?"

"It does," nodded Mr Kurtz. "Perhaps he was too engrossed in his work."

"Too engrossed to notice a man enter the room and move close enough to strangle him with a length of twine?" asked James. "Did he often get that caught up with his work, Mr Kurtz?"

Mr Kurtz sighed. "Probably not. That would be rather difficult to miss, wouldn't it?"

"If you were moving around the room, Mr Kurtz, Mr Geller presumably wouldn't have paid you too much attention. You would have been able to sneak up close to him without him flinching."

"I didn't do it, Inspector!" His face coloured again. "Why should I kill Richard?"

"I don't know," replied James. "But can you see how imperative it is that you find people to confirm your alibi and ask them to speak to Chief Inspector Stroud or myself? I'm sure Chief Inspector Stroud and his men are happy to look for anyone who might have seen you that morning. Isn't that right, Chief Inspector Stroud?"

"If it's to help him escape the clutches of the Yard, then yes, I am!" said Inspector Stroud defiantly.

"Good. Now then, Mr Kurtz, please show us the route you took to Mr Daly's office that morning," said James.

Half an hour later, James and I left the hospital and walked down to Cheapside. We passed a cab driver sloshing a bucket of water over his horse to cool it.

"Do you agree that this case seems rather odd?" said James. "Two minutes! That's how long it takes to walk to Mr Daly's office from the medical museum. What was Mr Kurtz doing for twenty-five minutes?"

"What was he doing in general that morning? He has no one who can vouch for him at all."

"Exactly. That gives us an even longer period of time during which we have no idea what happened. And Richard would surely have moved from his position when the murderer entered the room. I cannot see why he would have remained standing there. If he fell where he was standing someone must have surprised him, and the only person I can think of who could have got close enough to him without arousing his suspicion is Mr Kurtz."

"Unless the murderer had an accomplice," I suggested.

"How would that have made a difference?"

"Perhaps one man kept him talking and the other managed to sneak up on him."

"But both would have had to walk through the door, and then he would have seen them," said James. "This case is rather confusing, and I'm sure that Mr Kurtz is hiding something from us."

CHAPTER 18

As I walked toward The Holborn Restaurant to meet Mrs Fish and Mrs Maynell, I reflected on my conversation with Jack Copeland a few days' previously. He had been surprisingly calm while discussing his colleague's death. In fact, I had detected very little emotion at all. *Could it be possible that he had written the letter tucked into Simon Borthwick's book?* I wished I had asked him more about Hugo Bannister. *Perhaps the man had been a friend of his.*

Mr Edwards had told me that a search of the reading room's records had revealed a few members with the surname Bannister. However, it wouldn't be easy to ascertain whether any of them had a connection with the late inventor.

"Miss Green!" Georgina Fish greeted me warmly as I met her inside the restaurant, her dark curls bouncing around her face. "How lovely to see you again. Please meet my good friend, Lillian Maynell."

Lillian smiled warily. She was several years my junior and

wore a pale rose dress made of silk. Her hair was pinned beneath an elegant cream-coloured summer hat with silk flowers on it.

"It's a pleasure to meet you, Mrs Maynell," I said. "I met you briefly with your husband in the engine room at the Crystal Palace."

"Oh yes, I recall that now," she replied with a smile.

"Thank you for agreeing to meet me," I said as I sat down.

"Do call me Lillian. I must say I'm not keen on the idea of speaking to a press reporter, but George persuaded me."

"George?" I asked.

"That's me!" replied Georgina with a laugh. "Lily has always called me George."

"You're not going to publish anything I say, are you, Miss Green?" asked Lillian.

"No, of course not."

"That's reassuring."

"Edgar tells me you know each other from your school days," I said.

"Yes," replied Lillian. "Charlbury Gate School, wasn't it, George? It was a school for the daughters of clergymen run by Miss Hobhouse, who was terribly strict. I didn't like her at all."

"No one did," added Georgina. "We tried to liven the place up a bit, didn't we?"

Lillian chuckled. "Oh, I don't know about that."

"There were a few pranks." Georgina giggled.

"Miss Green doesn't want to hear about pranks!" scolded Lillian with a smile on her face. The two women appeared to have regressed into giggling schoolgirls.

"You, me and Catherine Preston," said Georgina.

"Oh, Catherine was the worst of the three," said Lillian. "Let's blame her because she isn't here to defend herself!"

"Do you remember putting a spider in Mary Baring's desk?" said Georgina.

"That was because she kept tripping me up in ballet class."

"And you splashed ink all over Elizabeth Turner's dress!"

"That was Catherine, not me."

"She did it because you asked her to. Catherine always did everything you asked."

Lillian laughed. "I suppose she did, didn't she? Perhaps it was her motherless upbringing. But I had to have my revenge on Elizabeth Turner because she started the rumour that I had six toes," said Lillian. "Even today some people believe I have six toes." Lillian turned to me. "My apologies, Miss Green. I worry that you have altogether the wrong impression of me now."

"Miss Green should know that you always did well in your school work, Lily. You were a good scholar," said Georgina. "I learned nothing at all during my schooling."

"I wasn't that much of a scholar."

"Now you're being modest, Lily. Of course you were. You were the only one who could commit all those French verbs to memory."

"My mind has always been good at retaining useless information," replied Lillian.

"My mind is no good at that," said Georgina. "In fact, I'm not sure mine does anything much at all. Ask Lily about her capital cities, Penny. She still knows all her capital cities."

"Miss Green has better things to do than ask me about capital cities George."

"You remind me of a friend of mine who works in the British Library, Lillian," I said. "He has a great memory for facts."

"Now that's a job I should like to do," said Lillian.

"Working in a library would be far more interesting than being a wife, don't you think, George?"

"No, I don't think it would," replied Georgina. "Libraries are dull places. Besides, you'll be kept very busy when you have children."

"I'm not sure that I shall be blessed with children," said Lillian. "And that's something I'm rather happy about."

"But children are dear little things!" protested Georgina.

"There's nothing dear about my nieces and nephews. They are noisy and time-consuming," said Lillian. "Would you like to have children, Miss Green?"

"I'm not sure that my mind is made up on the matter," I replied. "But I think I've probably made the decision not to now. I chose to become a news reporter instead."

"I wish I'd made the same choice," said Lillian.

"Perhaps so," I said. "But it's difficult to know if we've ever made the right decision, isn't it? Although I enjoy my work, there are times when I find myself wishing there was someone to share certain moments with."

"I expect those times are quite fleeting, though, aren't they?" asked Lillian. "Oh, how I would enjoy the freedom of living by myself and doing whatever I please!"

"Miss Green can't do whatever she pleases," said Georgina. "She must work for a living and she's responsible for every penny! There is no man to provide for her. Imagine what that must be like!"

"I am imagining it, George, and I quite like the idea," replied Lillian.

"Oh, no. I don't at all." Georgina shuddered. "I would find it quite frightening. I'd much rather leave the work to Edgar."

"Do you mind if I ask you about Simon Borthwick, Lillian?" I asked, keen to move the conversation on.

"Oh, yes," replied Lillian. "I almost forgot that was why you wanted to meet."

"I wished to speak to you from personal interest more than anything else," I said. "I was close by when Simon Borthwick administered that fateful gunshot."

A forlorn expression flickered across Lillian's face, but she maintained her composure well.

"That terrible moment has remained with me," I continued, "and I should like to understand why he did it, especially after creating such a wonderful spectacle at the Midsummer Fair. Have you heard about the letter he wrote?"

Lillian nodded. "George mentioned it to me."

"He accused nameless people of persecuting him," I said. "And he also..." I glanced at Georgina briefly and saw that her expression was encouraging. "He also mentioned you," I said, turning back to Lillian.

She raised an eyebrow. "He said that I was persecuting him?"

"No, no. His meaning was quite different regarding you. I hope you won't feel too upset if I say that he apologised to you but said that you no doubt cared little for his apology."

I noticed that her lower lip wobbled slightly as she retrieved a handkerchief and dabbed at her eyes. A waiter asked if we wished to order our meals, but Georgina waved him away.

Lillian took a deep breath before speaking. "That's an odd thing for him to write," she said.

"Why do you say that?"

"Because he didn't particularly care for me while we were courting!"

"Perhaps that's why he was apologising."

"Perhaps."

"You were the one who ended the courtship?"

"Yes, I was."

"May I ask why?"

"I felt rather overlooked, to tell you the truth. He was

always at his laboratory in Southwark, and even when he was home he was often too busy to see me. He would be working late into the evening on designs for something or other."

Georgina Fish wiped her eyes with a handkerchief.

"Oh, Lily," she said. "Don't you think it rather emotional that he apologised to you? Perhaps he loved you after all."

"I think it is rather a shame that he left it until after his death to express it," replied Lillian. Her jaw was clenched, as if she were struggling to maintain her composure.

"It is a shame. It's a huge shame, isn't it, Lily? Just think what might have been."

"I would prefer not to," replied Lillian, tearing a small piece of bread from the slice on her plate.

"If only he had told you how he felt, Lily!"

"He would have been an unbearable person to live with, George. He may have loved me, but on a day-to-day basis it would have been inordinately frustrating. I cannot say that I regret putting an end to our courtship. I'm not sure why he wrote something like that in his letter. It's rather embarrassing."

"I am more concerned about the people he believed to be persecuting him, Lillian," I said. "Can you think of anyone who has made malicious comments about him?"

"No, I didn't encounter anything of the kind."

"A colleague of his said that he was prone to melodrama. Is that an accurate description?"

"I wouldn't describe it quite like that, but he was certainly a sensitive person. He took things to heart and he took offence rather easily."

"The wording of his letter suggests that he was driven to his death by people he refuses to name."

Lillian laughed sadly. "He names me but refuses to name them."

"Do you know whom he might have meant?"

"I don't, I'm sorry. Jeffrey might know, but you'll struggle to speak to him about Simon. Jeffrey didn't care for him because he was once my suitor. It's a rather delicate situation, as I'm sure you can appreciate."

"I understand. Are there any other colleagues who might know more?"

"Donald Repton and Jack Copeland. You may find it useful to speak with them."

"I have already done so, as a matter of fact."

Lillian shrugged. "Then I don't know of anyone else."

"And your husband wouldn't know who might have been persecuting Simon?"

"I daren't ask him, and neither would anyone else. It is a cause of some embarrassment that I once courted Simon Borthwick, and it simply wouldn't do to discuss it. My husband doesn't know that I am meeting you to discuss him. You'll keep this meeting secret, won't you? I shall be in terrible trouble if he finds out."

Lillian's eyes grew wide and I felt sure there was fear behind them.

"You have my word that I shall be discreet."

"You must be, because it's dreadfully important that he doesn't find out. He has quite a temper."

Georgina nodded. "He does."

"Please don't be offended by what I'm about to say, Penny," said Lillian, "but I don't understand what your intention is with all this."

"I wish to find out what, or who, drove Simon Borthwick to his death. Having met him and then witnessing his wonderful illuminations at the Crystal Palace, I cannot understand why he should shoot himself on a busy street. What did he seek to achieve in doing so?"

"We shall never know," said Lillian. Her demeanour had

changed considerably from the one I had seen when she was joking about schoolgirl pranks just minutes earlier.

"Did he strike you as someone who might take his own life?" I asked.

Lillian paused for a moment as she considered this. "No, I didn't think he could ever do such a thing."

"Was he impulsive?"

"No, not really. I've no doubt he planned it. He planned everything."

"Jack Copeland suggested that he might have been consumed by a fit of madness."

"Did he? I never saw Simon consumed by a fit of madness. He only ever seemed to be consumed by his work. It's odd, because I always got the impression that he didn't care much for what others did or said. He tended to ignore people, so this idea that he was somehow persecuted is a strange one. Still, I don't think you will find any answers in this situation, Penny."

"A few people have said the same to me."

"They are probably correct. I certainly wouldn't hold much stock by what Simon wrote in his letter. I don't believe that he ever truly cared for me."

"Did he even write it?" queried Georgina.

"He must have done," I replied. "The letter was found in the case he was carrying on the night he died, and it was presumably signed and identifiable as his handwriting, otherwise the inquest wouldn't have considered it. It's an interesting thought though, Georgina. I have come across forged suicide notes before."

"Do you mind if we change the subject?" asked Lillian. "I have a tendency to become rather gloomy when I talk about Simon, and I should like to cheer up a little. Tell me more about being a woman on Fleet Street, Penny. What a fascinating profession! I hear you have to work alongside George's Edgar."

"I'm afraid I do," I replied.

"Tell Lily what you think of him, Penny!" chuckled Georgina.

"He's the most irritating man I've ever met," I said.

Georgina shrilled with laughter.

CHAPTER 19

Mr Sherman's secretary, Miss Welton, approached me as I worked at my typewriter in the *Morning Express* newsroom. Despite the heat, she wore her usual woollen dress, which was buttoned up to her throat. A pair of pince-nez was clipped to the end of her nose, and in her hand she held an envelope.

"It's not a very nice letter, I'm afraid, Miss Green," she said apologetically.

"Please don't worry, Miss Welton," I replied, taking the envelope from her. "It isn't the first time someone has sent me something unpleasant!"

I opened the envelope to find a newspaper cutting inside. As I took it out I saw that it was an advertisement for the Crystal Palace Midsummer Fair from the seventeenth of June.

"That's strange," I said.

"There's a piece of paper inside as well," added Miss Welton.

I reached inside the envelope again and found it. There were only four words scrawled upon it:

Stay away, Miss Green.

"Stay away?" I said to Miss Welton. "From what, exactly? I've already attended the fair."

Her face paled. "How horrible of someone to write such a thing. I wouldn't want to do your job and receive notes like that. It's cowardly, too, isn't it? Notice how the person doesn't write his name."

"It is nothing to worry about at all," I said. "Thank you, Miss Welton. I'm sure this is someone's idea of a prank."

CHAPTER 20

"Many of the Spanish gold mines in Colombia have been abandoned or lost," said Mr Isaac Fox-Stirling as we dined on roast guinea fowl at his home in Chelsea. Tropical plants sprouted from pots by the windows, and lithographs of African hunting scenes hung on the walls.

"The natives are doing their best to rediscover the mines," he continued. "During one of my trips to the country I heard an amusing story about the pinnacle of gold. In fact, I refer to it in Volume Two of my book, *Travels, Trials and Adventure in the Andes*, don't I, Margaret?"

His silver-haired wife responded with a proud nod.

Eliza was accompanied by her husband, George, while I was accompanied by Mr Edwards. Mr Fox-Stirling had dominated much of the conversation thus far. He was a stocky, fair-haired man of about fifty, with suntanned and freckled skin.

"There is a pinnacle in the mountains of San Lucas which was said to have been made entirely of gold," he continued. "This great tower of gold could be seen from a great many miles around, gleaming brightly from the time the sun rose every day until it set again. For years, men had tried to reach the pinnacle, but not a single one had made it there. A legend grew that the mountain was inhabited by a race of pigmy gold-diggers, who mined the gold and had riches beyond the imagination of any man. Some even claimed to have encountered the gold-digging pigmies. It was said that they spoke a language so loud and strange that a man's ears would be deafened for the rest of his life upon hearing them!

"I forget who it was now. I think it was a group of Germans. Anyhow, this was the first group of men to ever reach the golden pinnacle. After a long, arduous journey, they returned with disappointed faces. They reported that not only was the mountain devoid of pigmies, but that the golden pinnacle was nothing more than a large grey rock!" He slapped the table and threw his head back with laughter.

"Those poor Germans!" said George. "It is fortunate that no Englishman wasted his time trying to reach the golden pinnacle."

"Oh, I'm sure there must have been an Englishman who set out on the fool's errand at some point or another," said Mr Fox-Stirling, wiping tears of mirth from his eyes. "Some men even lost their lives trying to get to it!" He laughed some more.

"I've heard that two Colombian merchants are doing a good job of exploring the Spanish gold mines," said Mr Edwards.

"Indeed," replied Mr Fox-Stirling. "Lopez and Navarro own a number of them now. It's a prosperous business to be getting into. Perhaps I should abandon my plant-hunting and open a few gold mines instead, Margaret."

"But then I should see even less of you, darling!"

"Sadly, that's the life of an explorer and plant-hunter, my dear. We are a rare breed indeed. I remember discussing the gold mines of Colombia with your father, ladies," Mr Fox-Stirling said, glancing at me and Eliza in turn. "We were attending a gathering at Kew Gardens together when he told me that he had stayed at a gold mine for a few days while he was searching for epidendrum in the Bolivar region. The miners were very hospitable, by all accounts, and he was permitted to share their huts. However, I think he only returned home with plants, not gold!"

"I would very much enjoy the life of an explorer," said Mr Edwards.

"And you can!" replied Fox-Stirling. "There's nothing to stop you. One merely needs to be hardy, resourceful and think quickly on one's feet."

"There must be more to it than that," replied Mr Edwards.

"You need a patron, of course; a chap who is willing to pay you to travel overseas to discover or fetch something for him. You're a librarian, aren't you?"

"A clerk at the British Library's reading room, to be exact."

"That is rather different from exploring," said Mrs Fox-Stirling. "One is an indoor profession and the other all about the outdoors. In fact, the two couldn't be more different!"

She laughed, but Mr Edwards seemed disappointed.

"You must have missed your father, ladies, when he travelled," Mrs Fox-Stirling said, appearing not to notice.

"Very much so," replied Eliza. "He was often gone so long that we forgot what he looked like, didn't we, Penelope?"

"Yes, we did. And he always looked so different when he returned. His face would be thinner and his skin darker. I felt each time as though we had to get to know him as our father all over again."

"And he always gave us rather odd gifts, didn't he? What

was that strange little bowl he gave you that time? He had a particular name for it. A cala something."

"A calabash shell," corrected Mr Fox-Stirling. "A calabash is otherwise known as the 'bottle gourd', and when hollowed out it serves as a useful cup. If I close my eyes now I can picture a calabash of steaming coffee sweetened with raw sugar. Very pleasant at breakfast with a roasted banana."

Mrs Fox-Stirling spoke again. "Although you must have missed your father a great deal, there can be no doubt that he contributed enormously to the collections of tropical plants we now enjoy on these shores."

"Absolutely," said Mr Fox-Stirling. "There are even a few cases of his work in the natural history department of the British Museum in Kensington. That's more than they've ever done for me, isn't it, Margaret?"

"Perhaps that's because you're not dead yet, darling." Her comment was met with silence. She flung a hand over her mouth. "Oh, goodness! I didn't mean to offend Mrs Billington-Grieg and Miss Green. It was only supposed to be in jest! Oh, I do apologise, I..."

"Please don't worry, Mrs Fox-Stirling," said Eliza. "This dinner has been entirely good-natured, and we take your comment in jest as it was intended."

"Oh, thank you, Mrs Billington-Grieg," said Mrs Fox-Stirling with a sigh of relief.

"Margaret often talks before she thinks, don't you, dear?" said Mr Fox-Stirling.

"A common trait of the fairer sex," George added. "It's as if the route from their minds to their mouths is a river in full flow. Men, on the other hand, have several sluice gates in operation, and only open them when they deem it appropriate to do so."

"What twaddle, George!" said Eliza scornfully, pushing her lips together into a thin line.

"In response to your earlier comment, Mrs Fox-Stirling, there is no doubt that Mr Frederick Brinsley Green did a great deal of good work," said Mr Edwards. "Particularly with orchids. I know that modesty prevents Miss Green from boasting about his achievements at the dinner table."

"She should go ahead and boast, I say," Mr Fox-Stirling insisted. "How's your book about his life progressing, Miss Green?"

"Rather slowly," I replied. "It takes a long time to write a book, doesn't it?"

"It does, I'm afraid," replied Mr Fox-Stirling. "I found it rather easier as everything I wrote about was already in my head. You, on the other hand, have the unenviable task of collating and reading everything before you can commit anything to paper."

"I have been helping wherever possible," Mr Edwards chipped in.

"Very admirable of you," said Mr Fox-Stirling.

"I think the most pressing matter for me," I said, "is to decide on how the book should end. The uncertainty about Father's fate prevents me from making any decision about it. That's where I hoped you could help us, Mr Fox-Stirling."

"Indeed, and I'm more than happy to. When we last met I told you about my visit to that little place on the banks of the Funza. I cannot remember what it was called."

"El Charquito," I replied.

"That's the one. Yes, and as I explained to you I could find no evidence of any final resting place for your father. The natives of that country may have simple ways but, to give them their dues, they do treat the death of a foreigner respectfully. There is scarcely a corner of the world these days that doesn't contain the well-tended grave of an adventurous European."

"True," said George, nodding proudly in agreement.

"I think if your father had a grave I would have been directed to it," continued Mr Fox-Stirling. "Which, my dear ladies, leads me to speculate on a possibility."

"Which is what?" I asked.

"That your father is still alive."

His knife and fork remained poised above his plate as he awaited our response.

"No," I said slowly. "He can't be."

"Why not?" asked Mr Fox-Stirling.

"Because he would have come home," said Eliza. "Or he would have written to us, at the very least."

"But suppose that he has been unable to."

"For nine years?" said Eliza incredulously. "I think he would have found a passage home or at least a method of sending a letter during that time. Unless he has been imprisoned."

"Perhaps he has."

"Did you ask around at any prisons?"

"No, but then I didn't come across many."

"Why would our father have been imprisoned?" I asked.

I thought back to the massacre he had described in his diaries. I looked down at my plate and pushed a piece of guinea fowl around it with my fork. I felt Mr Edwards' sympathetic eyes on me.

"Is this theory mere speculation?" asked Eliza. "Or do you feel certain that he might still be alive, Mr Fox-Stirling?"

"Perhaps he was kidnapped," suggested George.

My stomach began to twist into knots and I felt unable to eat anything more. I couldn't bear the thought that my father might have been held hostage by someone for all this time. *Surely death was preferable to nine years of suffering.*

"It can only be speculation," I said. "I would like to think that he is still alive, but if he is I am worried about what must have befallen him."

"I think the lack of a grave site for your father means that you should remain hopeful," said Mr Fox-Stirling. "I knew him to be a brave and courageous man, and I feel certain that he is able to look after himself wherever he is."

"You really think he's still alive?" I asked.

"I like to think he is, yes. And there is no evidence to the contrary, is there?"

CHAPTER 21

The four of us left Mr Fox-Stirling's home in a carriage. I sat next to Eliza, while George and Mr Edwards sat opposite us.

"Thank goodness that's over," said George. "What an irritating man. He is only ever happy when talking about himself."

"He has some interesting things to say," said Eliza.

"Such as suggesting that your father is still alive? That's one way to upset the dinner guests!" laughed her husband.

"I feel pleased that he said it," Eliza replied. "Although the possibility raises many questions, it gives me hope."

"That's the problem with these flippant comments; they do just that. Why make people hopeful when they're only likely to be disappointed?" said George.

"But perhaps Miss Green and your wife will not be disappointed," said Mr Edwards. "Suppose Mr Brinsley Green truly is alive."

"The chap's not been seen for nine years!" scoffed George.

"No one heard anything from David Livingstone for six years," argued Mr Edwards.

"Which is not as long as nine years, but I see your point, Edwards," said George. "Has the Fox-Stirling chap got you living in hope as well, Penelope?"

"Living in hope sounds rather desperate, George," I said. "However, he has encouraged me to rethink Father's disappearance. It's nice to imagine that everything is not lost after all."

We said goodbye to Mr Edwards as he got out of the carriage at his home in Devonshire Street.

I was lost in my thoughts about Father as we continued on to my home in Milton Street. A flash of white in the gloom caught my attention and I saw that Eliza had taken an envelope out of her bag. I could just about see George resting against the side of the carriage. Now and then he emitted a loud snore.

"This rather odd letter arrived for me yesterday morning, Penelope," whispered my sister. "You won't be able to read it in this light, of course, but when you do please remember that it's just some silly nonsense."

"What is it, Ellie?"

"Someone making disparaging remarks. I don't know why they have chosen to address it to me. And I don't know how they know that I am your sister. You've encountered this sort of thing in your work before, haven't you? There really are some strange people about. Who do you think you might have upset on this occasion?"

"No one intentionally! But I suppose it's inevitable that someone will always take exception to the work I do."

Eliza held the envelope out towards me. "Promise me you won't take the contents of this letter to heart, Penelope. It's nothing more than the words of a foolish person."

"Of course I won't!" I said, laughing it off. "I've received plenty of strange notes before, haven't I? I'm used to it."

"Are you sure?"

"Yes. I'll show it to James as well. I know I can rely on him to help me if there is any real threat."

I took the envelope from her outstretched hand.

"He will help you, Penelope. I know that."

Once I was back in my room, I lit my paraffin lamp and sat on my bed with the envelope. A warm breeze drifted through the open window, as did a number of flies, which proceeded to buzz around the lamp.

The sender had written Eliza's correct address on the front. *How had its author known where she lived?* I thought to myself with a shiver.

The letter read:

As you are not only a valued sister to Miss Penelope Green but also her friend and confidante, I suggest that you advise her to resign from her work as a news reporter. You are no doubt aware that the profession is a rather insalubrious one and is especially unsuitable for a lady.

You must also be aware that it is a rather dangerous profession to follow. Miss Green has discovered this herself on a number of occasions, yet she persists in her work. No doubt you care for your sister very much and would encourage her to follow a safer path. With no father or husband to advise her, you really are her only hope.

My first reaction was to laugh. It was as though the author of the letter considered me a child who required looking after. But then I began to feel angered by its patronising tone. *What was the writer's aim in involving Eliza in my work life?*

Perhaps by sending the letter to Eliza he or she sought to demonstrate a far superior knowledge of me than I could show in return.

I walked over to my writing desk and opened out the brief note which had been sent to me at the *Morning Express* offices. The handwriting on the two pieces of paper was quite different. Next, I found the letter which had been hidden in Simon Borthwick's book and laid it next to the other two. I could see no match between the three pieces of handwriting.

Surely the person who wrote to Eliza had something to do with the person who had sent the note to me at the Morning Express *offices. Perhaps the author was simply adept at disguising his or her handwriting.*

I examined the envelopes the two letters had been sent in and saw that the postmarks were different, though both had been posted in London.

Who could have sent them? I mulled over a list of people I had spoken to in recent days: Donald Repton, Jack Copeland, Mr Kurtz, Chief Inspector Stroud, Georgina Fish and Lillian Maynell.

Perhaps one or more of these people had been angered by my questioning. Perhaps Lillian Maynell's husband had found out about our meeting and sent the letters. Perhaps the future Mrs Blakely had somehow discovered that I harboured feelings for her husband-to-be and was writing the letters herself; maybe with her mother's help.

I slumped down into the chair at my writing desk. Tiger jumped up and sat on the letters, her face just inches from mine.

"You're after sardines again, are you Tiger? Even though it's almost midnight."

I opened a tin for her, changed into my nightdress and sat on my bed without any blankets over me. It was too warm to sleep, and I felt a nervousness in my stomach at the prospect of the next letter I might receive if I were to continue my investigation.

CHAPTER 22

"I must say that I enjoyed our evening immensely," Mr Edwards whispered to me in the reading room the following day.

The red-whiskered man sitting opposite kept glancing over.

"And what a thought that your father may still be alive, Miss Green! You must be encouraged by that."

"Perhaps I could be," I whispered in reply, "but if he is then it raises the question of why my sister and I have never heard from him. That's what truly bothers me."

"There might be a simple explanation," said Mr Edwards. "Doctor David Livingstone spent a significant portion of his missing years suffering from ill health, which prevented him from getting in touch with those he loved. Perhaps that is also the case with your father."

"But what a horrible thought," I said. "I don't like to think of him suffering from illness for nine years!"

Mr Edwards seemed rather taken aback. He had probably hoped I would be happy about the possibility that my father was still alive. But in truth the thought had only served to cause rather more complicated emotions to rise to the surface.

Mr Edwards cleared his throat and moved closer to continue his whispering. His breath felt hot and ticklish on my ear and I wanted to lean away from him.

"Miss Green, I really must ask you something. I hope it's not too presumptuous of me to do so, but I think I need some idea from you about—"

A movement near the door caught my eye and I was relieved to see James walking towards us. I smiled at him.

"Oh, it's the inspector," said Mr Edwards flatly. "What could he possibly want with us now?"

"Good morning, James," I whispered.

"She has two chaps fussing over her now," the red-whiskered man muttered to his neighbour.

I glared at him then gathered up my papers and tucked them into my carpet bag.

"Must you leave so soon, Miss Green?" asked Mr Edwards, his brow furrowed.

"I'm not getting any work done here, am I?" I replied. "And I also appear to be disturbing the other readers in the library." I stared at the red-whiskered man as I said this.

"Perhaps we can arrange another meeting soon," said Mr Edwards. I felt a twinge of annoyance in my chest. "With your sister—"

"As a chaperone, of course," I interrupted.

"Are you all right, Miss Green?"

"I'm rather tired if truth be told, Mr Edwards. I found the weather too warm for sleep last night."

He seemed relieved by this explanation. "Yes, terribly hot, isn't it? Good morning, Inspector Blakely."

"Good morning, Mr Edwards," replied James. "There's no need to leave, Penny. My visit will be a quick one."

"I do need to leave, James. It's rather stifling in here."

"What's the matter?" asked James as I marched ahead of him down the steps of the British Museum.

I could feel tears pricking the backs of my eyes.

"I don't know," I replied in a small, tight voice.

"Wait for me!"

I slowed my step and he caught up with me.

"Penny?"

I turned to face him, and his concerned eyes met mine.

"It's too hot in the reading room," I replied, trying to blink away the tears. "And I didn't sleep last night, and Mr Edwards keeps asking me..."

James touched my hand gently. "What does he keep asking?"

"I'm not sure exactly. But I feel as though he wants to clarify the status of our relationship and I'm absolutely terrified that he might ask me to marry him."

"Really?" James' eyes widened.

"I have no wish to be married."

"Then that's your answer to him. Perhaps you should let him know sooner rather than later so that he doesn't keep upsetting you by trying to ask. It's not right, Penny. You should be able to work peacefully in the reading room without feeling harassed by the clerk."

"He doesn't harass me, as such. In fact, he doesn't really upset me at all. I'm fairly indifferent to him, I would say."

I noticed that James smiled in response to this.

"I think what's actually upset me is the thought that my father might still be alive."

James scratched his chin. "Alive? Is there new information about his disappearance?"

"Not as such. It's just something the plant-hunter Isaac Fox-Stirling said at dinner last night."

"I think the Museum Tavern may have just opened. Let's go in there and you can tell me all about it."

"Thank you, James. I'd like that."

❦

James sipped his stout and listened patiently as I told him about the dinner with Mr Fox-Stirling.

"I can see why you find these thoughts upsetting," he said. "It has presumably taken a long time to accept the idea that your father was most likely dead. That's what most people believed for a while, wasn't it? And after a certain length of time I suppose you begin to believe the same. But to be asked now to consider that it's not the case at all... that's rather difficult, isn't it?"

"Have you ever stirred a deep pool with a stick?" I asked.

"Not recently, no."

"When you do so all the silt which has lain undisturbed at the bottom is brought up to the surface again. That's similar to how I feel at the moment."

"It's not really surprising, Penny. Does your sister feel the same way?"

"I haven't had a chance to discuss it with her yet. On the way home in the carriage she wanted to discuss a letter which had been sent to her. In fact, I have it here."

I pulled the letter addressed to Eliza out of my carpet bag and handed it to him, watching his face intently as he read it. Once he had finished he sighed and dropped it onto the table.

"Some people!" he hissed.

"It's not the first time I have received such a letter. Although it is the first occasion when something like this has been sent to a member of my family."

"That's even worse!" said James. "It's a cruel, calculated,

malicious thing to do. How I wish I could get my hands on that person!"

"Perhaps you will," I said.

"I hope so," he snarled, thumping his fist against the table.

"Don't be angry, James. This is a common occurrence for news reporters. People don't like us asking questions. I must have got close to something which someone wishes to conceal. That's encouraging news, isn't it?"

"I wouldn't be so sure."

"If I had any idea who had sent the letter I should know which situations to avoid."

"That's the problem though, isn't it? You simply don't know. Threatening letters are rarely explicit, are they? Their authors are cowards who are purposefully vague so they can instil fear into every aspect of your life."

"The tone isn't particularly threatening, though, is it? It's more of a warning."

"Either way it's unpleasant, Penny, and I wish I could advise you to ignore it, but I know that would be useless. You don't know what you're getting yourself into here. Who have you met with recently?"

I told him the list of people I had met with and interviewed.

"So it could be something to do with the work you're doing on Simon Borthwick or Richard Geller."

"If it was Mr Kurtz or Chief Inspector Stroud you would surely have received threatening letters yourself."

"Not necessarily. In the eyes of a malicious person you're an easier target. You're female for a start. A coward is likely to think it easier to scare off a female."

"Two cowards."

"What do you mean?"

"I received another note." I took it out of my bag and

gave it to James. "They were written by two different people. I can find no similarity between them."

James glanced from the letter to the note and sneered. "Perhaps you're right. Sadly, I think one thing is certain."

"What's that?"

"You will receive more of these. I have no doubt about it."

I picked them up from the table, folded them and put them back in my bag.

"That's enough about my woes," I said, finishing off my sherry. "Talking to you has made me feel a bit better."

"That's good news," said James. "If only I could do something about them."

"What did you come to see me about in the reading room?" I asked. "We've become so distracted that I forgot to ask why you wanted to find me."

"Oh yes. I spoke to Mr Daly, the assistant surgeon at St Bartholomew's Hospital. He's the chap who Mr Kurtz claimed he went to see. It turns out that Mr Daly was in his office for the entire morning of the seventeenth of June. And what's more, he neither heard nor saw any sign of Mr Kurtz!"

"So Mr Kurtz is lying?"

"Yes, just as we thought. His story always seemed rather suspicious."

"Has Chief Inspector Stroud found anyone to provide an alibi?"

"Only the medical students who visited the museum at about ten o'clock that morning, so Mr Kurtz wasn't lying about that. And the students can vouch for the fact that Mr Geller was alive and well at that time."

"But no one saw Mr Kurtz on his way to or from Mr Daly's office?"

"No. Presumably he didn't go that way at all. So where was he? Did he ever leave the room?"

"Oh dear. Mr Kurtz didn't think his explanation through

at all, did he? Surely he must have known you would ask Mr Daly about him. I think you should instruct Chief Inspector Stroud to order his arrest."

"I must say that I'm not far away from doing so, Penny. The man has to find someone who can verify his story."

"I don't believe he can. I think it is quite obvious that he murdered his colleague."

CHAPTER 23

"Was Mrs Maynell of any help?" asked Edgar.

"She was indeed. Please thank Georgina for arranging our meeting." I hadn't found the meeting with Lillian particularly useful, but I had no wish to admit that to Edgar.

"Jolly good. Well, you must hurry up and decide who will accompany you to dinner at our place. I know Georgina would be delighted to see you again."

"Thank you, Edgar."

As I returned to the article I was writing about the Metropolitan District Railway Bill I heard the newsroom door slam behind me. It could only mean that Mr Sherman had entered the room.

"Miss Green! In my office now, please."

It was unusual to be called into the editor's office for a conversation.

"Of course," I replied, my heart thudding in my chest.

The editor's office had greasy, yellowing walls and smelled of pipe smoke. Piles of books and papers were stacked on top of the desk and all over the floor.

Mr Sherman sat down behind his desk. "Do take a seat," he said, gesturing toward the chair opposite him.

Conversations in Mr Sherman's office always made me nervous, as they usually involved the breaking of unpleasant news. Mr Sherman picked up an envelope from his desk.

"I've received a rather unusual letter," he said.

"Oh no." I closed my eyes and groaned.

"What's the matter, Miss Green?"

"Is it anonymous?"

"As a matter of fact it is, yes. Have you also received one?"

"Not a letter. I received a short, rude note and someone sent my sister a letter telling her that she should advise me to stop working as a news reporter."

"Ah. Oh dear. Well this one is rather similar in tone, I'm afraid. There's no need for you to read it. I don't wish you to be upset by it."

One of the speaking tubes next to his desk whistled.

"Excuse me a moment." He turned to bark into it. "Yes?"

"What page is the Tonkin War story going on, sir?"

"Page eight. Tell Byers it needs the sketch map to accompany it!" Mr Sherman moved away from the speaking tube and shook his head. "Compositors," he tutted. "There's little more than empty space between their ears. Now, where was I?"

"The letter, sir."

"Ah yes." He pulled the letter out of its envelope and pushed his spectacles up onto the bridge of his nose. "Let me just give you an idea of what it says... *Inept... Should not be employed by such a reputable newspaper... Misguided... Reporting on the news is not a suitable profession for a woman... Weak-minded...*"

"I think I have a general idea of what's in it now. Thank you, Mr Sherman. May I take a look at it?"

"I don't think that is a good idea, Miss Green."

"I wish to look at the handwriting and see if it resembles the writing on the note and the letter I already have in my possession." I reached into my carpet bag and pulled them out.

"I suppose that is a good idea. But don't dwell on the contents, Miss Green. It has clearly been written by someone with a vendetta against you."

He passed the letter over to me and I could see that the handwriting was different yet again.

"This person is playing games," I said. "There cannot possibly be three people who wish to discredit me!"

"They're simply adept at adapting their handwriting, is that what you're saying?"

"They have to be! Why would three separate people suddenly bear me ill-will, sir? I cannot think of anything I have done wrong."

"That was to be my next question. Are you sure of that?"

"I'm certain. I have visited a few people recently and asked them about Simon Borthwick. Each was perfectly civil and I didn't publish any of our conversations. And then there is the medical school murder. I suppose Mr Kurtz and Chief Inspector Stroud were rather grumpy to see me in attendance with Inspector Blakely. But there's quite a big jump from being grumpy to writing vindictive letters, isn't there?"

"I suppose there is. Although you never quite know the thoughts which run deep in a man's mind."

"No, you don't, and it's probably just as well. Please may I keep this letter, sir?"

"Absolutely not, Miss Green! You'll only go upsetting yourself over it."

He reached out his hand for the letter, but I held on to it.

"I am perfectly capable of coping with the situation, Mr

Sherman. I know that it's nothing but the scribblings of a madman."

"You are sure you can handle this? You won't lie awake tonight worrying about unpleasant missives? I know it's rather personal of me to say this, but I know that you live on your own. It's not as though you have a husband or someone who can keep an eye on you."

"There are plenty of people who can keep an eye on me, sir."

"Are there? Well, that's good to hear. I'm not saying we all need spouses. I'm a bachelor myself, but I do have a trusty housekeeper who looks after me. Perhaps us men need looking after more than women, eh?"

"Perhaps." I smiled. I didn't often see the gentler side of Mr Sherman.

"Right, well you keep that letter for now, but don't torture yourself by reading it over and over. And perhaps have a mind to tell your friend Inspector Blakely about these unpleasant notes. Usually the writing of a barbed letter is enough to satisfy the anger of the aggressor; rarely does it come to anything more than that. But we don't know who we're dealing with here, do we? You must be careful, Miss Green."

"I will, Mr Sherman. I can hardly stop working on my stories, though, can I?"

"That is true, but if you encounter any more unpleasantness you will let me know, won't you? As your editor I feel rather responsible for you."

"That's thoughtful of you, sir. I shall be fine, I feel sure of it."

CHAPTER 24

"I asked the headmaster of Wilstead School if he would like me to carry out some demonstrations for the schoolchildren," Borthwick had told me when I had visited him in his laboratory. "I feel enormous gratitude to Faraday for his dedication to the Christmas lectures. He did them for more than thirty years! I could never equal Faraday's expertise, but if I can inspire just one child to become an electrochemist I would consider my work complete."

"Are your demonstrations at the school to be a regular fixture?" I had asked.

"Yes, I visit them once a month. And another school has asked me to do the same."

"I think that's extremely honourable of you, Mr Borthwick."

"No, not honourable. All I wish to do is share my enthusiasm and encourage the next generation. That's my only aim. Just think of what the future holds, Miss Green! The possibilities are almost unimaginable."

It occurred to me that the children of Wilstead School must have been greatly upset by Simon Borthwick's death. I hoped he had inspired some of them as he had wished. I stood under my parasol outside his home in a pleasant street of terraced houses close to Swiss Cottage station. This was number eleven, Adamson Road: the address which had been given at the inquest. It was a four-storey home with a dozen steps leading up to the portico. Curtains had been pulled across the large bay windows on the ground and first floors.

When I rang the bell, the front door was opened a short distance by a woman in a simple black mourning dress. The bunch of keys at her waist indicated to me that she was the housekeeper. She looked about thirty with thick brown hair swept back from her face.

"Yes?" she asked.

"Good morning. My name is Miss Green and I'm a news reporter for the *Morning Express*. Is there someone I can speak to about Mr Borthwick?" I saw her open her mouth to reply, but before she could speak I quickly added, "I was there on the night he died."

The door opened wider once I had relayed this piece of information, as I had hoped it would.

"You were there?" asked the housekeeper.

"Yes. I attended his illuminations at the Crystal Palace and as I was leaving his cab passed me. I heard the gunshot and ran over to the cab with some other people. They got him out and... well, that's when I saw what he had done to himself. This was his home, I believe."

The woman nodded in reply.

"Then please accept my condolences. You must be extremely shocked and saddened."

I handed her my card.

"Thank you, Miss Green. However, in answer to your

question, there is no one here to speak to you about Mr Borthwick. He lived alone."

"With staff?"

"With staff, yes, but he had no family in London."

"Perhaps I can speak with you for a short while. I'm sorry, I don't know your name."

"Miss Blight. I don't think there's anything much I can tell you. Besides, I shouldn't be speaking to news reporters."

"I won't publish anything about our meeting, Miss Blight. You have my word."

She stared at me for a little while longer.

"I can only talk for a few minutes," she said eventually, widening the gap behind the door so that I could step inside.

"Thank you, Miss Blight."

I folded up my parasol and followed her into the cool, gloomy interior. Mr Borthwick's home already had an air of abandonment about it. I felt a shiver run down my back.

"You'll have to forgive the state of the house," said Miss Blight as she closed the door behind me. "I've covered the furniture in dust sheets. Would you mind holding our conversation in the kitchen? It's one of the few rooms we still use."

"Not at all," I replied, wondering who the other people in the house might be. "Is this place to be sold?" I asked as I followed her down a flight of stairs to the basement kitchen.

"Yes, it's to be auctioned. The butler has already left and it's just me and Kitty here now. We leave at the end of this week."

"Have you found another position?"

"Yes, in the country. That's where I'm from, so I'm looking forward to returning. Here's Kitty."

A young maid with a round face sat at the kitchen table. Miss Blight introduced us, then occupied herself with filling a kettle.

I sat down on a wooden chair and felt reminded of the

brief time I had worked undercover as a maid in the house of Mr Glenville.

"Did you work for Mr Borthwick for very long?" I asked the housekeeper.

"Almost three years; the duration of the time he lived here."

"And you saw him on the day he died?"

"Yes, in the morning."

"What was his mood like?" I asked. "Was there any indication that something was bothering him?"

She placed the kettle on the stove. "If truth be told, he was in rather a foul mood and had been for some days, hadn't he Kitty?"

The maid nodded.

"It wasn't unusual. He often suffered from a bad temper," the housekeeper added.

"Did he ever take his temper out on you?"

"It was never directed at me personally, but he could be rather rude and dismissive. Of course, he was mostly a well-mannered man, and he could be amusing and entertaining when it pleased him. He struck me as someone who always had something weighing on his mind."

"Did he give any idea of what that something might have been?"

She shook her head. "No. I can only assume it was to do with his work because that's what he did most of the time. He spent a lot of time in his laboratory."

"Did he socialise with friends?"

"Occasionally, but his work was what he loved to do more than anything else."

"It's interesting you should say that, because it concurs with what Mrs Lillian Maynell told me last week when I met with her. She and Mr Borthwick once courted, didn't they?"

"You've spoken to her? You seem to know quite a bit

about him already. Yes, but she called off the courtship. I could tell that it upset him a great deal."

"Did he talk about her much?"

"He did for a little while when she first ended it. In fact, he seemed to blame a third person for it. I remember him saying, 'They've taken her away' or something similar."

"Who did he mean by *they*?"

"I have no idea. I was wary of asking too much as he seemed quite upset at the time."

"Are you aware of the letter he wrote just before his death?" I asked.

"Yes, I heard it read out at the inquest."

"What do you think he meant when he said that his persecutors had finally won?"

Miss Blight shook her head. "I have no idea."

"He said that he would rather die by his own hand than theirs. Did he ever discuss anything of this kind with you?"

"No, never. But then I was his housekeeper. It would have been unusual for him to discuss such matters with me. Have you asked his friends and colleagues about it?"

"I haven't found any friends of his yet. I've spoken to a few colleagues, but they know little more than you do. They do say, however, that Mr Borthwick tended to be rather melodramatic."

"He certainly could be."

"Do you think there was a valid reason behind his so-called melodrama?"

"I certainly detected some discord surrounding his work, although I couldn't tell you exactly what it was. He took offence easily. If someone said or did something unpleasant he would be terribly upset about it."

"To the extent that he might take his own life?"

"I can only imagine that's what must have happened. I hope you don't mind me saying this, Miss Green, but you're asking a lot of questions and I've been answering them without giving any thought to what you plan to do with the information. Why do you need to know all this if you don't intend to publish it in your newspaper?"

"That's a good question, Miss Blight. My interest in Mr Borthwick has become a personal one because I admired his work and I saw him on the night he died. And having listened to his letter being read out at the inquest, I'm keen to find out who these people were who supposedly persecuted him. I suppose I have an inquisitive nature."

"Rather essential for a news reporter!"

"It is, isn't it? Although I'm finding it rather frustrating trying to get anywhere with this. I've come across a malicious note which was left in one of Mr Borthwick's books in the British Library, but other than that no one seems to have any idea about who might have born him resentment. I confess that I'm at rather a loss as to who I could speak to next."

"I'm not sure you'll find the answers to all your questions, Miss Green. None of us could ever know what his true thoughts were."

"Perhaps not. But I'm inclined to think that the letter provides the most clues."

"But with him no longer being here there is a lot that cannot be explained."

"That is true, and you probably feel I'm wasting my time with this. You wouldn't be the first to say so."

Miss Blight sat down at the table and smiled politely.

"Are there any friends of Mr Borthwick's I could speak to?" I asked.

"I can only think of his colleagues. There's Donald Repton and Jack Copeland."

"I've spoken to them, thank you."

"There were a few friends he invited here occasionally, but

I forget their names now. I think they were something to do with his work."

"Was he a member of any clubs you know of? Any favourite restaurants or other places he would go to regularly?"

"None that particularly spring to mind. I'm sure I remember somewhere in Covent Garden he used to go to. Do you recall it, Kitty?"

The young maid pursed her lips in thought.

"Can you remember what it was called?" Miss Blight asked her.

"The Ha'penny I think," replied Kitty.

"The Ha'penny public house. There you go, Miss Green. That's the best we can come up with between us, and he probably only went there a handful of times, didn't he, Kitty?"

The name of the public house sounded familiar, but I couldn't think why.

"If you recall anywhere else he went or someone else he knew could you let me know?" I asked. "You can write to me at the *Morning Express* offices. The address is on the card I gave you."

"I will do. Thank you, Miss Green. I'll be interested to hear if you find out the answers to your questions. Mr Borthwick did have his bad tempers, but he could also be a pleasant and charming man. I miss him very much."

"There's just one other matter," I ventured. "Do you think it would be possible to view Mr Borthwick's private papers?"

"Oh, I don't know about that." The housekeeper folded her arms. "I would have to check with his family. I can ask them for you, but I'm not sure they would allow it."

"They probably wouldn't." I sighed. "I suppose I was rather hoping for a quick, informal look at them. The sort of quick look which the family needn't know about."

"I'm afraid I couldn't allow it, Miss Green. I feel responsible for the care of his house and belongings until everything is sold or passed on to his family. It would be remiss of me to neglect that duty."

"Of course. I understand, Miss Blight. I won't make the request again."

"Perhaps Mr Repton will allow you to look at the papers of Mr Borthwick's they hold at the Southwark works."

"That's a good point; I'll ask him. Thank you, Miss Blight."

CHAPTER 25

"Good morning, Miss Green," whispered Mr Edwards in the reading room the following day. I noticed that he wasn't smiling as much as usual.

"Good morning, Mr Edwards. Is everything all right?"

"Of sorts. I'm wondering if I could speak to you at a convenient moment. It doesn't have to be now, and I realise you're busy. I would ensure that the matter was dealt with as quickly as possible seeing as we don't have your sister present as a chaperone. Perhaps we could take a quick stroll in Russell Square."

A bead of perspiration rolled down the side of his face and he mopped at it swiftly with his handkerchief. I glanced down at my notes on the Congo Treaty and decided that if I were to put off our conversation I should be distracted from my work wondering what it was that he wished to discuss.

"Shall we get it over with now?" I suggested.

"That's probably for the best." He seemed relieved at the suggestion. "I'm sorry, Miss Green. I hope to only interrupt your work for a short while."

"It's fine, Mr Edwards," I replied, picking up my carpet

bag. "I have plenty of time to finish it before my deadline later today."

We walked down the steps of the British Museum and turned left into Montague Street, which was lined with large terraced houses. The air felt warm and oppressive, but the sky was a heavy grey.

"I fear this glorious weather we've been having will shortly come to an end," said Mr Edwards. "I sense a storm brewing, do you?"

"I do, and it's much needed. I'm looking forward to some cooler air again."

I hoped that our conversation would remain focused on the weather. *Surely Mr Edwards wasn't about to choose this moment to propose to me. What would be the best way to politely decline him?*

As we walked, I pondered on how our relationship had progressed to this stage. It had begun when I had asked him to help me find a map of Colombia in the reading room, and then I had been too polite to turn down his request to meet in Hyde Park. His requests had been made respectfully and he was such a pleasant, well-mannered man that I had struggled to find a reason to say no to him.

But I had to say no, otherwise I was likely to find myself engaged to a man I did not love. I recalled how Eliza had described her early days with her husband:

There only needs to be a glimmer of interest in the beginning. That's how it began with me and George. In fact, I quite disliked George when I first met him, but true love takes time. You need to nurture it and allow it to grow. It doesn't happen in the way it's described in poems.

Was that how all marriages began? I didn't want to believe it, but perhaps my expectations were too high.

I thought of James and how my heart performed an excitable flip every time I saw him. Much as I liked Mr Edwards, the sight of him never stirred the same emotions.

Could I avoid marriage for the rest of my life? Did I even want to? I knew that many day-to-day matters would have felt easier had I been married, and it would stop people speculating with regard to my availability. *Perhaps some people felt threatened by an unmarried woman*, I mused.

As we approached Russell Square I steeled myself for the uncomfortable conversation ahead. I decided to use my profession as an excuse. I would tell Mr Edwards that it kept me far too busy to be an attentive wife.

"I've managed to speak to a couple of the men who go by the name of Bannister," said Mr Edwards. "However, both assured me that they had no familial relationship with the inventor Bannister, so I'm still no clearer on the identity of the person who vandalised our book in that manner. I will keep working on it."

"Thank you for making these enquiries, Mr Edwards."

We crossed over the road and walked into Russell Square, where neat pathways criss-crossed the lawn and a breeze gently rustled the trees.

"Russell Square is rather pleasant on a summer's day, don't you think, Miss Green? Shall we walk the circumference?"

I nodded.

Mr Edwards reached into the pocket of his jacket and brought out an envelope. As he did so, I felt a combination of sentiments: relief that he wasn't about to propose and concern about what the envelope might contain.

"This was the matter I wished to speak to you about Miss Green. I don't know how to begin to explain it, but—"

"You've received an anonymous letter which says unpleasant things about me."

"Yes." He stopped and stared at me. "How did you know?"

"Because Eliza and Mr Sherman have received similar notes," I replied. I walked on, and he strode alongside me.

"But why on earth would someone do such a thing?" he asked.

"I have no idea, Mr Edwards. It happens from time to time."

"You make it sound as though it's perfectly acceptable!"

"It's not acceptable, but it isn't the first time it has happened. What angers me this time is that my family, friends and acquaintances are being bothered by the anonymous letter writer when they should be left well alone!" I held out my hand toward the envelope. "May I read it?"

"Oh no, Miss Green. You mustn't!" Behind his spectacles, his olive-green eyes were wide with concern. "No! You would find it too upsetting."

"That's what my editor, Mr Sherman, said, but he allowed me to read the one he received. I know the person sending these letters is simply trying to be vindictive and I refuse to allow such a person to frighten me."

"I don't understand what you could possibly have done to deserve it."

"Neither do I! I can only imagine it has something to do with one of the stories I'm working on. I've upset someone and they're not brave enough to tell me in person. Instead, they write these cowardly letters to people who are of no concern to them whatsoever."

"How does this person know that I have any connection to you? How does he know where I live?"

"I don't know. People who write such things like to think they're rather clever. Please can I look at the letter, Mr

Edwards? I would particularly like to see if the handwriting matches that of the others."

He tucked the envelope behind his back.

"Mr Edwards," I pleaded. "I am not a young woman any more. I have experienced hurtful comments before and I can assure you that I am quite at ease with reading a malicious letter. The person who wrote it doesn't know me. He is simply trying to think of hurtful things to say so that I will stop doing my work."

"Why have you chosen this profession, Miss Green?"

"Because the events which happen in this city are rarely what they seem. I like to find out the facts and communicate them to the general public, so that when they read the newspaper they are better informed on these matters. For hundreds of years the everyday working person has had to live in ignorance, relying only on hearsay and gossip to develop an understanding of the world."

"That's true. And what the church told them."

"Yes, and the information passed on to people by the church was usually only what the church wanted them to hear. That's all changed, Mr Edwards! For more than ten years now almost all children have been able to go to school, regardless of their wealth and status. That means more people than ever can read! And what was it Francis Bacon said? Knowledge is power."

"Ipsa scientia potestas est," said Mr Edwards. "The phrase appears in Bacon's most famous work, *Meditationes Sacrae*."

"Well, my Latin isn't as good as yours, Mr Edwards. But you and I agree with Bacon's sentiment, don't we? It's an exciting time to be a reporter and a writer. I can help people discover what is going on in the world around them."

"All the 'Arrys and the 'Arriets out there."

"Exactly."

Mr Edwards smiled. "You've persuaded me now, Miss

Green. I fully understand why you have chosen this profession. It is a noble calling."

I laughed. "There are far nobler callings, I'm sure!"

We held each other's gaze for a moment. I found myself quite impressed by his proficiency with Latin. Perhaps there was more to Mr Edwards than met the eye.

"Please may I read the letter now?"

"If you must." He handed it to me. "But please don't—"

"Become upset about it? I won't."

I examined the handwriting on the envelope and could see that it was different again from the other letters. I opened it out and began to read.

Mr Edwards

I am writing to suggest that you reconsider your association with Miss Green. She regards herself as a proficient and able news reporter, but she suffers from an inquisitive nature that is leading her into trouble. She is reliant on the advice of those around her and I would urge you to ask her to refrain from investigating matters which don't concern her. I'm sure you would agree that only the police and judicial authorities have the right to investigate matters of supposed wrongdoing, and questions asked by anyone else should be treated as nothing more than an intrusion.

You are the person who is best placed to become her husband. If you were to marry her it would be easy to prevent her from putting herself in danger. It will only be a matter of time before someone forcibly stops her, and I'm sure you agree that it would be undesirable to reach that stage.

I can understand the predicament of any man who is interested in proposing to Miss Green. Her friendship with Inspector Blakely must, I am sure, raise as many questions in your mind as it does in everyone else's. By marrying her, however, you would not only be able to remove her from Fleet Street but also from her influence at Scotland Yard. I don't suppose you realised how powerful a position you were in until you read this letter!

I had been able to read the letters which had been sent to Eliza and Mr Sherman without too much difficulty, but this note seemed more offensive than either of them. I looked up at Mr Edwards and wondered what he must have made of the mention of marriage, and of James. It felt embarrassing, almost shameful, to see such things written down on paper, particularly as they had been written by someone who was supposedly a stranger. *How did this person know so much about me?*

Mr Edwards had watched me read the letter and was slowly shaking his head.

"I knew I shouldn't have allowed you to read it." He held his hand out for the letter and I returned it to him.

"I think it would be best if you burned it," I said, my voice shaking.

"Don't you want to show it to the police?"

"What could the police do about it? They have no way of finding out who wrote it. All this person wishes to do is cause as much offence as possible."

"Why would someone do this?" asked Mr Edwards.

He looked down sadly at the letter in his hand and I felt a surge of tears rush into my eyes. I couldn't show him that I was upset, especially not after persuading him that I wouldn't be. I strode off toward a large statue and tried to compose myself.

CHAPTER 26

"Miss Green!" I heard Mr Edwards call out from behind me.

I stood in front of the statue, removed my spectacles and wiped away my tears as quickly as I could. My throat felt tight with anger at the person who had written these things. Had the letter been sent to me directly I would likely have been less upset. But to offend me so publicly by writing to the people closest to me was a cruel trick indeed.

I heard Mr Edwards' steps behind me.

"Miss Green, I'm so sorry."

"Don't be," I said. "Please don't be."

I stared ahead at the statue of a man resting his hand on a plough with sheep and cherubs at his feet.

"I asked to read the letter, didn't I?"

"But I should have refused. I shouldn't have given in. And now you're upset."

"Not upset, just angry. I'll be fine. I just need a moment to calm myself."

Mr Edwards joined me but maintained a respectful distance and didn't look directly at me. He passed me a neatly pressed handkerchief, and his gesture of kindness brought fresh tears to my eyes.

"Ah yes, the fifth Duke of Bedford," he said, looking at the statue in front of us. "Francis Russell. He commissioned many of the buildings which surround this square. He was responsible for building most of Bloomsbury, in actual fact."

He talked quickly, as if trying to distract me from the cause of my upset.

"He wasn't just a man of the city, however. He also had a farm and bred sheep at the family seat, Woburn Abbey. Which is why you see him with a sheep here and some sort of..." He paused to inspect the statue. "Is that a plough?"

"I think so," I replied.

"He was a Whig and was most upset when the government introduced a tax on hair powder."

"Hair powder was taxed?"

"Yes. Those who wished to use hair powder had to buy a certificate each year at the cost of one guinea."

I laughed. "How silly."

"Bedford decided he'd do without, and instead wore his hair short and un-powdered. It was a hairstyle which caught on and became known as the Bedford Level."

"How do you know these things, Mr Edwards?"

He shrugged. "I work in a library and I read a lot Miss Green. Speaking of which..." He checked his pocket watch. "Oh goodness! I shall be in terrible trouble with the head librarian if I don't return to work right away. I shouldn't even be here."

He turned to face me. "Are you all right, Miss Green? Do you require more time to compose yourself?"

I put my spectacles on again and smiled. "I'm fully composed, thank you, Mr Edwards. Let's get back to the reading room before the head librarian notices you're missing."

"Oh, he will already have noticed." He grimaced. "Never mind."

"You mustn't pay that letter any attention, Miss Green," said Mr Edwards as we hurried back to the reading room. "There isn't an ounce of truth to any of it."

"I will do my best to ignore it. Would you mind giving me the letter so that I can keep it with the others?"

"I thought you wished to have it burned?"

"I was upset. It's important evidence and needs to be kept."

"But you mustn't read it again."

"I won't."

"I'm sorry that you read it at all. But I know that you would never have allowed me to keep it from you."

He handed me the envelope and I slipped it into my bag.

"Thank you for telling me about it," I said. "I will find out who is sending them eventually. It can't have been easy for you to read, either."

"Oh, but I know that it's all nonsense!" he replied dismissively.

I thought about the mention of my friendship with James and wondered whether Mr Edwards had dwelt on that matter at all.

"And I also know that any man who married you would stand no chance of stopping you from pursuing your profession."

I laughed. "He wouldn't at all! I think you know me quite well by now, Mr Edwards."

"I do." He stopped at the bottom of the museum steps and pushed his fringe away from his spectacles. "I wish to make it clear, Miss Green, that I would never stop you."

"Well, it would be rather unreasonable of you if you did, wouldn't it, Mr Edwards?"

"If you were my wife, I meant to say. I would never expect you to stop being a news reporter." His cheeks coloured, and he looked down at the ground. "I'd better go," he added hastily, before dashing off up the steps.

CHAPTER 27

Mr Edwards' parting words continued to act as a distraction the following day as I tried to typewrite an article about the Panama Canal. It was the closest he had ever come to suggesting that he would like me to become his wife. I had found his company surprisingly comforting after reading the contents of the anonymous letter, and the thought of courting him no longer felt as unpalatable as it had before. *Was it possible that I could develop some sort of affection for him?*

"A penny for your thoughts, Miss Green," said Edgar.

"I'm sorry?" I replied.

Edgar sat with his feet on his desk, fanning himself with a sheaf of paper. Outside it was another hot, overcast day. The storm which was supposedly brewing hadn't yet arrived.

"I don't think you've pressed a key on that typewriter for the past minute," he said. "What are you thinking about?"

"Not a great deal, really." I quickly changed the subject. "Edgar, does The Ha'penny public house in Covent Garden sound familiar to you?" I asked.

"It does for some reason. I'm trying to remember why," he replied.

"The fancy dress ball and the police, do you remember?" said Frederick.

"That's it!" I said. "That's how I know the name."

Edgar laughed. "That fancy dress ball where everyone there was a chap, with half of them dressed up as ladies?"

"The police arrested a fair few that night, as I recall," said Frederick. "What a sight the police cells must have been!"

Both men laughed.

"Why are you asking about it, Miss Green?" asked Edgar. "I don't think they're fond of ladies down at The Ha'penny."

"They're certainly not!" laughed Frederick. "They're only fond of men dressed as ladies!"

My colleagues laughed again.

"I think Simon Borthwick sometimes drank there," I said.

"The inventor chap?" said Edgar. "Well, well, well. The plot thickens."

"Please don't mention anything about it to your wife," I said. "She might tell Lillian Maynell, and then matters could become quite awkward."

"It would be awkward indeed," said Edgar.

"I don't know for certain that Borthwick went to the place," I continued. "I need to find someone there who might have known him."

"No, don't!" said Edgar. "There is no need to begin investigating such unsavoury matters. Some stones are better left unturned."

"Which unsavoury stones are we talking about, Fish?" asked Mr Sherman, who had stridden into the room without us noticing. The door slammed closed as we turned to face him.

"The Ha'penny in Covent Garden, sir," said Edgar. "The

place where the police raided the fancy dress ball and discovered that the ladies were, in fact, chaps."

"I remember that well," replied the editor. "What of it?"

"Miss Green says the inventor who shot himself frequented the place."

"Did he indeed?"

"I can't be certain, sir," I said, "but his housekeeper told me that he sometimes went to that establishment."

"The chap should have chosen a more discreet housekeeper," said Mr Sherman.

"I wonder if he was one of the chaps who dressed up as a lady!" laughed Frederick.

"That's enough, Potter." Mr Sherman glared at him. "Miss Green, perhaps you can get on with the work I have asked you to do rather than pursuing a wild goose chase after an inventor who decided that enough was enough."

"I'm working on it in my own time, Mr Sherman."

"I find that hard to believe. My preference would be that you didn't work on it at all."

"I can't help but feel intrigued about the people who were persecuting him."

"There are many things which intrigue me, Miss Green, but I don't have the time to go dashing about London trying to answer every possible question, and neither do you."

"But perhaps I could find someone at The Ha'penny who knew him."

"That's enough, Miss Green! Stay well away from The Ha'penny!"

Mr Sherman's stern tone silenced me.

"Please forget all about the inventor," he said. "I know you witnessed the man's death, but you can't change what has happened. What I want is an update on the medical school murder. Has Inspector Blakely made any progress with it?"

"Yes. He established that an important witness has been lying."

"Good. The arrest needs to be made now so that we can report on it. And don't forget that your article on the Panama Canal needs to be one thousand words."

"I can't understand why someone would write something like that about you, Miss Green," said Mrs Garnett as we stood in her hallway. In her hand was the anonymous letter she had received that morning. "Why would they tell me that you're about to be dismissed from your job and won't be able to keep up with your rent? Are you about to lose your job again?"

"Not to my knowledge, though my editor was rather grumpy with me today. However, I have managed to amass some savings, Mrs Garnett, so I shall be able to pay my rent even if I did lose my job. You can be assured of that. Please ignore the letter. It seems everyone I have any association with has received one."

I had examined the handwriting in the letter sent to Mrs Garnett, but it was different again from the previous letters. Although I had tried my best to create the impression that the letters didn't bother me, each one I read wore me down a little. On every occasion I had to explain to the baffled recipient that it was nothing to worry about and pretend it was something to which I was accustomed, but in reality I was tiring of it all. I wished I knew what I had done to provoke the ire of the letter writer.

"Do you want me to throw this letter away?" she asked.

"I'll keep it for now, Mrs Garnett. It may prove useful in helping me discover who sent it."

"I don't know how. The sender didn't put a name on it."

"Nevertheless, I shall find out who it is, Mrs Garnett."

She sucked her lip disapprovingly and handed the letter over. "You get yourself into some scrapes, Miss Green. I still can't forget the time when you got shot. And the time you were nearly strangled to death!"

"Yet I have lived to tell the tale, Mrs Garnett." I forced a smile and began to make my way up the stairs to my room. "You'll let me know if you receive any more, won't you?"

"I will. And you be careful, Miss Green. You need to stop going around upsetting people."

Tiger was desperate to be let in at my window, as fat raindrops had begun to splash onto the rooftop around her. I heard the distant rumble of thunder as I opened a tin of sardines for her.

I laid the malicious letters out on my writing desk and examined them for any signs of similarity. In each case the handwriting was different, as were the ink, writing paper and postmark on each envelope. I folded them up and placed them in a drawer. I knew that I would become saddened if I looked at them for too long. This thought angered me, as that had presumably been the very intention of the person who had written them. Tiger was some comfort as she jumped up onto my lap and began to clean her face.

I tried to distract myself by compiling some notes for the book about my father. If Isaac Fox-Stirling was right there was only one thing for it. Someone would need to go back to Colombia and search for my father again. Perhaps they would even need to rescue him. The only reason I could imagine for his failure to send a message home was that he was being held there against his will.

I was disturbed by a knock at the door.

"Miss Green! A telegram has arrived for you!" called Mrs Garnett. She pushed a small envelope under the door.

The envelope was damp from the rain, and the telegram within it was brief and anonymous:

Meet me at Lincoln's Inn Fields. Seven o'clock tomorrow evening.

CHAPTER 28

Despite the shelter provided by the large tree in Lincoln's Inn Fields, the evening rain poured off the umbrella I stood beneath with James. The pleasant scent of his eau-de-cologne mingled with the smell of fresh, damp grass.

"What's the time?" I asked him.

"About a minute later than when you last asked me," he replied with a smile. He glanced at his pocket watch. "Two minutes to seven o'clock."

I scoured the pathways and lawns looking for the person who had asked to meet me here. A few men scurried through the square, their heads bent low under umbrellas, but there was no one who appeared to be waiting for me. The columned portico of the Royal College of Surgeons stood on one side of the square and at the far end stood Lincoln's Inn, one of the Inns of Court, with its attractive red and cream brickwork and stained-glass windows.

"The wonderful British summer, eh?" said James, surveying the grey sky. It had been raining ever since the storm broke during the night.

"I suppose we had it coming," I said.

"That's the problem. We always do, don't we? It can't be warm and sunny without a prolonged spell of pouring rain afterwards. Are you all right?"

"Not really," I replied. My heart was pounding quickly in my chest. "I'm nervous. You do have your revolver with you, don't you, James?"

"Absolutely. I'll look after you, Penny. There's no need to worry."

"Do you think he'll harm me?"

"I think he is unlikely to in a public space such as this. And if it's the person who's been sending the letters he'll hopefully explain himself."

"He'll need to. I don't want anyone receiving further missives of this kind. I try not to let these things bother me, but of course they do."

"You'd have to have a heart of stone not to be bothered by them."

"Hopefully we'll find out who is behind them this evening."

"Just be careful when you speak to him, Penny. He may want something from you in return for agreeing to write no further letters."

"Presumably he'll want me to stop doing my work. That's what he said in the letter sent to Mr Edwards. He wants to keep me away from news reporting altogether."

"He may well suggest something of that sort, and you'll make things much easier for yourself if you simply agree to it."

"I will never agree to it!"

"*Pretend* to agree to it, I meant. Just tell him what he wants to hear and then he's unlikely to cause any more trouble. Although I have my revolver with me, I don't particularly want to be given an excuse to fire it here this evening."

"I don't like telling people what they wish to hear, especially when I strongly disagree with their sentiments."

"I realise that, but sometimes you have no choice. You don't want to go putting yourself in any more danger."

"But surely it will make him even angrier if I tell him I intend to cease my work and then continue doing it."

"Possibly, but you'll also know the identity of the person by then, so we can take measures to stop him. All we need to find out this evening is who is causing you trouble. Whatever you do, don't get yourself into an argument with the chap."

The bell on a nearby clock chimed seven.

"He's late," I said.

"Why don't we have a stroll around?" suggested James. "He may be sheltering under a tree somewhere."

We began to trace the perimeter of the square.

"Has Chief Inspector Stroud arrested Mr Kurtz yet?" I asked.

"No, and I don't think he will do."

"Why not? It's already been proven that he was lying about his whereabouts at the time when Mr Geller was murdered. He didn't go to see Mr Daly at all!"

"But that doesn't mean he is the murderer."

"He must be! Why else would he lie? Besides, he has no alibi."

"Actually, he does."

"He does? Who provided it?"

"Well, it took Mr Kurtz a while, but he eventually confessed to us that he went to meet a young nurse on the morning of Mr Geller's murder. It was a regular arrangement between them, apparently."

"A romantic liaison?" I pictured Mr Kurtz's pale, unattractive face and suppressed a laugh. "Why didn't he mention it earlier? I know it's not what he should have been doing while he was working, but if he'd been honest sooner he would have saved us all some trouble."

"It's certainly not something he should have been doing while he was working. Perhaps more importantly he's a married man, so I can understand his reluctance to tell us about it."

"He obviously thought a lie would serve him better, then realised it made him appear guilty of murder."

"We know he's telling the truth this time because Chief Inspector Stroud has spoken to the young lady in question and she has confirmed it. With great embarrassment, I should add. Neither seemed happy to admit to the liaison."

"I cannot say that I am surprised."

"However, this has proven an interesting development, because they have both told us that they met regularly, which means Mr Kurtz's absence from the museum that morning may have been anticipated."

"The murderer knew he wouldn't be there at that time?"

"Exactly."

"But that still doesn't explain why Mr Geller didn't put up a struggle or try to escape his attacker."

"No, it doesn't. Do you remember how Mr Kurtz demonstrated where Mr Geller had been standing that morning? He had his back to the storeroom, didn't he?"

I nodded.

"That may mean the attacker was hiding in the storeroom, then leapt out and attacked Geller while Kurtz was missing from the museum."

"But how did the attacker get into the storeroom without anyone noticing?"

"Perhaps he broke in overnight."

"If that's what happened the killer went to great lengths to plan the attack."

"It certainly appears as though he did. He knew when Mr

Kurtz would be away and brought that length of twine with him. The question is: why?"

We had almost walked the full circumference of the square.

"It's ten minutes past seven o'clock," said James. "I don't see any sign of our man, do you?"

I glanced around. The square was deserted due to the inclement weather.

"No. Perhaps he doesn't like the rain." Then I jumped. "Or perhaps it was a trick! Perhaps he asked me to meet him here so that something could be done elsewhere?"

"Such as what?"

"I don't know. Maybe he's breaking into my lodgings."

"Your landlady would soon see him off," said James.

"We cannot be too sure on that front," I replied, shivering. "Oh, James, I don't like this. I don't like it at all."

CHAPTER 29

Thankfully, my room had been left alone while I was out that evening and Tiger was pleased to see me when I returned. I looked around, checking and rechecking that everything was as I had left it. I felt sure that Tiger would have shown signs of distress if someone unknown had snuck inside my room. She hated strangers.

Early the following morning another telegram arrived for me:

Meet me at Lincoln's Inn Fields. Seven o'clock this evening. WITHOUT THE INSPECTOR.

So the sender of the letters had been there after all! And what's more, he had recognised James. My fingers trembled as I returned the telegram to its envelope. *Was I brave enough to meet this person without James by my side?*

I closed my eyes and tried to recall all the people I had seen at Lincoln's Inn Fields the previous evening. There had been very few people about; certainly no one I had recognised.

❦

The rain had stopped by the evening and my legs felt weak with nerves as I walked around Lincoln's Inn Fields searching for the person who had sent the telegram.

I told myself to remain calm and heeded the advice James had given me the previous evening. I had to pretend that my intention was to co-operate. I couldn't put myself in danger, especially without James by my side. I knew he would be angry when he found out I had come here without his protection.

I was reassured to see that there were more people milling around than there had been the previous evening. *Surely someone would heed my cries for help if anything went terribly wrong.*

I had walked a full lap of the square before I heard the bell chime seven o'clock again. I began a second circuit, more slowly this time, scrutinising everyone who walked past me. A young lawyer appeared quite uncomfortable in response to my glare.

I still couldn't see who might wish to meet with me. *Was the letter writer playing games? Did he plan to request that I meet him here every evening?*

A man of about my height approached. He wore a bowler hat and a dark-coloured suit, and as he drew nearer I could see a pipe hanging beneath his thick black moustache.

I knew him.

"Mr Sherman? What are you doing here?" I asked.

"Just walk with me, Miss Green, and we will find somewhere quieter to talk," he muttered.

"I'm afraid I can't, sir. I've arranged to meet someone here."

"You've arranged to meet me. I am the person who sent the telegrams. Now walk."

I felt my mouth open and close again as I turned around and walked beside him. *Had Mr Sherman sent the anonymous letters? Had he even written one to himself?*

My head felt dizzy with the many questions I wished to ask, but I remained silent until he was ready to talk.

We crossed the road and walked onto Gate Street before taking a sharp right into a narrow street called Whetstone Park. Mr Sherman glanced around, as if to ensure that we were alone. We passed a small public house and a row of cramped little houses. Several horses poked their heads at us out of stable blocks.

"This is the rear of the Soane Museum," said Mr Sherman, looking up at a tall brick edifice.

"I don't understand," I said. "Are you the one who has been sending the letters?"

Mr Sherman stopped and removed his pipe from his mouth. "Absolutely not! Whatever gave you that idea?"

"Your telegrams were anonymous, so I assumed they were from the same person who sent the letters."

"You assumed incorrectly. I have no idea who has been sending you those letters, Miss Green." He pushed the pipe back into his mouth and walked on at a slow pace.

"But why ask to meet me here? And why didn't you want James to come too? I asked him to accompany me yesterday because I feared for my safety."

"You're quite safe with me, please don't worry. I asked you here because I wish to speak to you in confidence about something. It's important that you don't mention our conversation to anyone, not even to Blakely. Do you hear?"

I nodded solemnly.

"Good. I need to have this conversation with you, Miss Green, before you go committing an enormous faux pas. This work you insist on doing with regard to Borthwick is rather tricky, as you are no doubt beginning to discover. I didn't mean to warn you off The Ha'penny public house so sternly, but I needed to make myself clear at that moment. I hope you will appreciate why I was unable to explain anything further at the time."

He lowered his voice so that it was barely audible. "The long and short of it is that I have visited The Ha'penny a few times myself, and this information must only ever be shared between us. Do I make myself clear?"

He paused to look at me and I nodded. His face held its familiar stern expression, but I felt sure that I saw fear in his pale blue eyes.

"I have encountered that inventor fellow in The Ha'penny a few times," he continued. "But I didn't know him particularly well. However, I have discovered a few things about him which should not be repeated anywhere. Do you hear me, Miss Green? It is very important that you never breathe a word of this to anyone. I could lose my livelihood."

"I understand perfectly, Mr Sherman."

"I mentioned that the medical school murder had been discussed quite widely in the Turkish baths. The reason is that Richard Geller was known by quite a few people there. Although I care little for idle gossip, I do like to pay attention to some of the discussions as the editor of a newspaper. That makes sense to you, doesn't it?"

"It does indeed. What have they been saying about Richard Geller? Is it something which would help with the police investigation?"

"Well, possibly." He scratched his chin. "But we have to be careful. Extremely careful."

"I'm not sure I follow, Mr Sherman."

"It's the police we need to be careful of. You understand that, don't you, Miss Green? Of course, a number of men knew Richard Geller, but they won't speak to the police about him as they would risk their own arrest by doing so."

"Risk their own arrest? But why should they be arrested if they have done nothing wrong?"

"The Ha'penny, Miss Green," he whispered impatiently. "Just think about the sort of establishment The Ha'penny is."

The police raid on the fancy dress ball came back to my mind. I stared at Mr Sherman, struggling to comprehend what he was revealing to me.

"Did you know Richard Geller, sir?" I ventured.

"Not well, although I spoke to him once or twice, I believe. I occasionally saw him at the baths, but I don't think I ever saw him at The Ha'penny."

"Is there a connection between Richard Geller and Simon Borthwick?"

"Yes!" He smiled, appearing relieved that I finally understood what he was saying. "Yes, there is. I wasn't sure how to express it in clear terms, but Richard Geller and Simon Borthwick were close friends. I only discovered this three days ago. Up to that point I felt sure you were wasting your time trying to investigate who might have been persecuting Borthwick, but now I realise there is a great deal more behind it. You still mustn't tell anyone about this. You understand that, don't you?"

"Yes, I understand, Mr Sherman. Do you think the deaths of Simon Borthwick and Richard Geller could be connected?"

"As for that, I don't know."

"But they must be!" I rummaged through my carpet bag to find my notebook and flicked through it. "Here we are," I said, finding the right page. "Borthwick took his own life on Tuesday the seventeenth of June. I'm quite sure that Richard Geller was found dead on that same day."

I continued flicking through my notebook. "Yes! It was the morning of Tuesday the seventeenth of June. So Richard Geller was murdered that morning and Simon Borthwick took his own life that evening."

I stared down at the cobbles beneath my feet, trying to comprehend what this could mean.

"Do you think it's possible, Mr Sherman, that Borthwick knew about Geller's death before he shot himself?" I asked.

"It's possible, but you'd need to find out, and I don't know how you would go about making such enquiries."

"It might explain what Borthwick wrote in his letter," I said. "It's no wonder he was fearful if the people he believed to be persecuting him were behind Geller's death. Perhaps he was worried that he would be next."

"He may well have been. We can only speculate at the moment."

"*I thought it best to die by my own hand rather than theirs.* That's what he wrote! Someone murdered his friend and he felt sure they would attack him next. I will have to ask James what he thinks about it."

"No! You must not, on any account, tell the police about this."

"But there is new evidence here, Mr Sherman. Richard Geller and Simon Borthwick were friends. I can tell James that, can't I?"

"There's no need. It won't help him find the culprit."

"So why have you told me about it?"

He paused to think. "I suppose I felt the need to explain the situation. And I certainly didn't want you sniffing around at The Ha'penny. The regulars there must be left well alone."

"I think James needs to know about Richard Geller and Simon Borthwick's friendship," I said. "At the very least it might explain why Borthwick took his own life. What if the people who bullied Borthwick also murdered Richard Geller?"

"There are many possibilities, Miss Green, but I don't think you can involve the police too much in this one. No one will speak to them, anyway."

"But won't the police make allowances if someone has valuable information for them?"

"I don't know, but I strongly doubt that anyone would take the risk."

"Mr Sherman, I promise that our conversation will remain completely confidential. I realise you have taken a great risk by confiding in me. But I think the police need to know about the connection between Richard Geller and Simon Borthwick. No more harm can come to them now. And if I tell James about it I promise I shall never reveal the source of my information. You have my word, sir."

Mr Sherman watched me for a moment, then put his pipe back in his mouth. "You've worked under me for a long time now, Miss Green. I know that I can trust you, otherwise I would never have asked to meet you here. But you do realise that my career will be at an end if you tell anyone it was me who spoke to you about this, don't you?"

"I know that, sir. You can trust me. I promise."

He began to walk on and I followed, still rather stunned by his revelations.

"Tell Blakely the relevant information, then," said Mr Sherman. "I know you work well together. But you must never let my name come into it."

We reached the end of the narrow street.

"Walk on, Miss Green, and I'll see you tomorrow. We never met here. Do I make myself clear?"

"Yes. Completely."

CHAPTER 30

"Simon Borthwick and Richard Geller were *friends*?" asked James. "That is an interesting development indeed."

We were sitting at our usual table in the Museum Tavern, and as I relayed this new piece of information I hoped James wouldn't ask me too many questions about its source.

"Yes, it seems they were," I replied. "Borthwick was a regular visitor to The Ha'penny. You know of The Ha'penny, don't you? It was raided by the police a few years ago."

"I remember. And knowing what sort of establishment The Ha'penny is, I can hazard a guess as to the nature of the friendship between the two men. Am I correct?"

"I cannot be certain; however, I believe Simon Borthwick might have taken his own life because Richard Geller had been murdered that morning. Perhaps he was worried that he would be next."

"But can we be sure that he found out about Richard Geller's murder that day?" asked James. "How would the news have reached him? Presumably he would have been at the

Crystal Palace making final arrangements for the illuminations."

"His work colleagues might know whether or not he had received a message."

"But they haven't mentioned him receiving bad news that day?"

"Not to me, no."

"Who told you about the relationship between the two men?"

"I can't say."

"He won't be in any trouble with the law."

"I told him that, but he doesn't believe it. He's too fearful."

"That's understandable, I suppose. I need you to reassure him for me, though. I should like to speak to him."

"James, I made a promise that I would never reveal his identity. I'm sorry. I know I can trust you to do the right thing, but if you knew who it was and someone such as Chief Inspector Cullen found out there would be huge trouble, I feel sure of it. It's too risky. He's frightened, James. It is someone I have known a while, but I have never seen him frightened before."

James scowled. "Genuine evidence would help us greatly with this case."

I was still trying to comprehend the secret life Mr Sherman had revealed to me. He was taking quite a risk in pursuing such a lifestyle. I wondered what it must be like to constantly live in fear of being found out. I was beginning to understand some of Simon Borthwick's mental torment.

"I have an idea with regard to evidence," I said. "I visited Borthwick's home and I know that his private papers are still kept there, but they're about to be passed to his family. Perhaps you could request access to them? There may be letters between himself and Richard Geller which would confirm the nature of their relationship. And there might be something else that could be of use to us. I did try to sneak a look at his papers when I visited, but his housekeeper wouldn't allow me to do so without his family's permission, which was the right thing for her to do of course."

"That's a good idea; I'll make some enquiries. It will be easier to request access to his papers now we know that the two men knew each other. But what I still don't understand is the motive behind Richard Geller's murder. It was well planned."

"Perhaps it was someone who had a grievance against men like him," I said.

"It's possible."

"Maybe Geller and Borthwick had both been threatened," I said. "The difficulty we have is that many men who knew them will be reluctant to co-operate with the police for fear of incriminating themselves."

"That's true. Perhaps they would speak to you."

"I'm not sure they'll speak to anyone on the subject unless they know them well. The risk is too great."

"But we need to get to the bottom of this. You'd think they'd be willing to do so to help us find Richard Geller's killer."

"You'd think so, but perhaps they're frightened of the people who did this to Richard. Perhaps some are worried they could be next."

"I'm still trying to understand the motive of the culprits here," said James. "Were Geller and Borthwick targeted because of who they were or what they did?"

"That's what we need to find out."

"And something else has occurred to me," said James. "What if Borthwick murdered Richard Geller?"

"Why should he do that?"

"I don't know. But it's possible, isn't it? Borthwick could

have murdered Richard and then, filled with remorse, taken his own life later that day."

"If that's what happened, Richard's murder is solved."

"But I suspect it isn't as simple as that," said James. He took a sip of his stout. "Did you ever hear again from the anonymous letter writer who wished to meet you at Lincoln's Inn Fields?"

"No, strangely enough I didn't," I said, busying myself with my sherry. I hated lying to James.

"How odd," he replied. "I wonder if it was because I was there."

"It might have been," I said. "Or maybe he just wanted to waste my time. I've no doubt he'll try again soon."

"You'll let me know if he makes contact again, won't you?" asked James. "We need to find out who has been sending you those letters."

"I suspect it's all connected, isn't it?" I said. "Now we know that Borthwick and Geller were acquainted, surely it's all part of the same investigation."

"Yes, I think it is. And we certainly don't want Chief Inspector Stroud leading it, do we?"

CHAPTER 31

"Scotland Yard?" asked Jack Copeland when James and I arrived at his laboratory within the Southwark works. "Why is Scotland Yard now involved in Simon's death?"

He occupied himself with a large glass jar on the table in front of him, as if he hoped we would go away. The laboratory had an acrid smell to it, as though something had recently been burnt there. James and I watched closely as Copeland inverted the glass jar over a small wired contraption.

"May I ask what you're doing Mr Copeland?" he asked.

"Experimenting with a new type of filament." The reply was muffled by his drooping moustache.

"Would it be a terrible inconvenience to pause your experiment and speak to me for a moment?" asked James.

Mr Copeland sighed and turned the switch on a small metal box close by. The wire contraption lit up with a bright light before immediately extinguishing. Mr Copeland sighed again.

"Is that box a battery?" I asked.

"Yes," he replied curtly. "I suppose you're both going to keep bothering me until I answer your questions." He fixed us with his bulbous eyes.

"We are, I'm afraid," replied James. "We believe Simon Borthwick's death is connected to another incident which occurred on the same day. We need your help."

"How? What incident?"

"Were you with Mr Borthwick at any time on the day he died?" James asked.

"Yes, of course I was," replied Copeland irritably before turning to me. "I've been buying the *Morning Express* hoping to see your article about Kensington Court in there, Miss Green, but I confess that I must have missed it. Has it been published yet?"

"Not yet, Mr Copeland."

"Perhaps you'll have the courtesy to inform me once it is, so I can stop wasting my time searching through the newspaper every day to find it."

"I will do, Mr Copeland," I replied, thinking it best not to add that the article hadn't yet been written.

"Was Mr Borthwick in this building for the entire day on Tuesday the seventeenth of June?" asked James.

"No."

"Do you know where he was?"

"At Sydenham setting up the illuminations for the Crystal Palace."

"So he wasn't here at all that day?"

"I think he might have been here in the early morning, but then he went off to Sydenham."

"Did you see him before he went there?"

"I can't remember now, but it's fairly likely that I did."

"And you saw him that evening at the Crystal Palace?"

"Yes, we all did."

"Who do you mean by *we all*?"

"Myself, Donald Repton and Jeffrey Maynell."

"Your colleagues?"

"Yes. Why are you asking me these questions, Inspector?"

"I'm trying to understand Mr Borthwick's movements on his final day," replied James. "Can you recall what his mood was like?"

"He was his normal self."

"Not upset or distressed in any way?"

"No."

"Grumpy? Short-tempered?"

"Well, he was prone to that, yes. But there was nothing in his mood to suggest anything out of the ordinary. That's why I can only guess that his shooting himself was a spur-of-the-moment decision."

"Are you aware of Mr Borthwick receiving any unwelcome news that day?"

"What sort of unwelcome news?"

"He didn't mention anything to you?"

"No. Are you referring to the other incident which you mentioned earlier?"

"Yes."

"I don't recall him mentioning an incident of any sort. It would help me, Inspector, if you were able to elaborate on what that incident was."

"I'll explain in due course, Mr Copeland. Thank you for answering my questions. Where might I find Mr Jeffrey Maynell?"

"What a peculiar fellow," commented James as we walked along a whitewashed corridor which was giving off a strong smell of chemicals. "I wonder if he knows more than he's letting on. It's rather difficult to understand what he says through those thick whiskers, isn't it?"

I laughed.

"Have you spoken to this Maynell fellow yet?" James asked.

"Only briefly," I replied. "I spoke to his wife Lillian, but he's not to know about that."

"Very well." We reached a door marked with Maynell's name. "Here we go," he said, knocking briskly.

"Miss Green!" said Jeffrey Maynell once James and I were standing in front of his desk. "I wondered when you'd finally come and find me." He had a square, handsome face, but his pale eyes were cold.

"I'm not sure I quite understand what you mean, Mr Maynell," I replied.

"You've already visited Copeland and Repton, I hear, and you have also met with my wife." He got to his feet and pulled himself up to his full height.

My stomach turned uncomfortably. *How had he found out about my meeting with Lillian?*

I realised there was no use in keeping up any kind of pretence.

"Yes, I did," I replied. "It was very pleasant. Mrs Fish, the wife of one of my colleagues, also joined us."

"Very nice indeed. The purpose of the lunch was, I believe, to discuss Simon Borthwick?"

"I wouldn't say that was the sole purpose of our lunch. However, I have been trying to find out more about Mr Borthwick."

I hoped I wouldn't land Lillian in any trouble by saying this. I could only imagine that he had already discussed the secret lunch with her.

"So you discussed him with my wife?"

"Not in any great detail, Mr Maynell. She merely told me why their courtship had ended."

"And what was her explanation?"

"Mr Maynell, there is no need to be quite so confrontational," said James.

"I don't take kindly to my wife being asked questions about a former suitor!" retorted Mr Maynell. "Can you understand my ire, Inspector?"

"I appreciate that you may feel angered by it, but there is no need to speak to Miss Green in this curt manner."

"What was my wife's explanation?" Mr Maynell asked me again, ignoring James' interjection.

"She told me that Mr Borthwick had seemed more interested in his work than in her, and that she felt he had been rather indifferent to her."

"And that was all?"

"Yes. Please don't worry, Mr Maynell. Your wife harbours no sentiment for Mr Borthwick."

I noticed that his face softened slightly in response to this comment.

"Did you know Mr Borthwick well, Mr Maynell?" James asked.

Mr Maynell turned his nose up at the question. "Of course!" he replied. "He was my colleague for some years."

"Do you know who might have been persecuting him?" I asked.

My question drew an unexpected laugh from Mr Maynell. "You think he was persecuted?"

"That's what his letter suggests."

"Ah yes. Now I've heard about that letter, and I've also heard that my wife receives a mention in it. I should like to read it for myself. Do you know where I can find a copy, Inspector?"

"You would need to contact the coroner," said James.

"I see."

"So you don't believe that Mr Borthwick was being persecuted?" I asked.

"Of course not!"

"How was your own relationship with Mr Borthwick?" asked James.

"We were not unfriendly with each other, but neither were we close. You must remember that he had once been a suitor of Lillian's. Nevertheless, I had no truck with the man. We stayed out of each other's way. Anyway, I think we've rather strayed off the point here. Did I give you permission to question me, Inspector?"

"No. You simply began answering."

"The point I wished to make was to you, Miss Green." He glared down his nose at me. "I don't want you speaking to my wife again about this Borthwick character. Do you understand me? To be honest, the matter upsets her a great deal and must be dropped."

"How did you find out?" I asked.

"Find out what?"

"That I met with your wife."

"She told me! She knows better than to keep secrets from her husband. Stay away, Miss Green. Do you hear me?"

"There is no call for you to speak to Miss Green in such a way," said James, glowering at Maynell.

"And there is no need for her to speak to my wife again!" snarled Maynell. "Good day to you both. I have work to do."

"As have I," retorted James, taking a step closer to Maynell's desk. "I advise you to calm your temper or I shall deem it necessary to interview you down at Southwark police station rather than here in your comfortable office."

Maynell's lip curled slightly.

"Another serious incident has been linked to Simon Borthwick's death," continued James, taking out his pencil and notebook. "I have a few questions for you if I may, Mr Maynell. You were with Simon Borthwick on the day he died, I believe?"

"You know I was. Miss Green will have told you that."

"Was he at the Crystal Palace for the entire day? He didn't leave and go anywhere else at all?"

"No. He was there throughout the day."

"And you were with him for all of that time?"

"Most of it, yes."

"It's possible that Mr Borthwick might have received some bad news that afternoon or in the early evening. Were you aware of anything of the kind?"

"Bad news? What sort of bad news?"

"Something happened to a friend of his that day, but we cannot be sure as to whether he found out about it before he died."

"What happened?"

"If I understand you correctly, you don't recall Mr Borthwick either receiving or discussing any bad news?"

"None. Though it would help if I knew what sort of bad news you happen to be referring to."

"A death, Mr Maynell."

"Another death? No, I didn't hear anything about a death that day. Only Simon's, of course."

"A friend of Mr Borthwick's, Richard Geller, was murdered inside the museum of the medical school at St Bartholomew's Hospital."

Mr Maynell's face lost its sneer and grew solemn.

"I read about that."

"So, to your knowledge, Simon Borthwick received no news about his friend's death before he took his own life?"

"I don't know, Inspector. He may have done, but if so he

did not discuss the matter with me. That's rather rough about Mr Geller, though. Has the murderer been caught?"

"Not yet, sir. Is there anyone else who might have known whether Mr Borthwick heard about his friend's death that day?"

"Only Repton."

CHAPTER 32

"I think we can be fairly certain that Borthwick was at the Crystal Palace for most of the day on the seventeenth of June, and therefore couldn't have been responsible for Richard Geller's murder," said James as we made our way through the corridors to Donald Repton's office.

"Unless he paid someone else to murder Richard Geller."

"That's a possibility, I suppose. But why would he do that? It seems they were good friends. If we can find any evidence of discord between them that would be something to consider."

"This is Inspector James Blakely from Scotland Yard," I said to Mr Repton as we sat in his large, cluttered office. "He is investigating the death of Richard Geller inside the medical school museum at St Bartholomew's Hospital."

"Ah yes, dreadful business. Can I offer either of you a brandy?"

The white-haired engineer hovered a decanter above a filthy glass. We both declined.

"Mr Geller was friends with Simon Borthwick," I continued. "And Inspector Blakely would like to ask you a few questions, if possible."

"I will only reply to questions once Miss Green has paid me in fruit jellies," said Mr Repton, pouring out his brandy and immediately drinking a large mouthful. "I'm only joking, of course. Ask away! I must say, this rings a bell now."

"Rings a bell how?" asked James.

"Simon told me he had received some bad news that day. He seemed rather shaken by it."

"This was while you were both at the Crystal Palace?"

"Yes."

"Did he elaborate on the subject of the bad news?" asked James.

"No, but I'm assuming it was the death of this chap at the hospital or whatever it is. Am I right?"

"Yes. Do you know how he found out about it?"

"I don't, I'm afraid. Perhaps someone had a telegram sent down to the Crystal Palace."

"Did you tell the inquest into Mr Borthwick's death that he had received bad news on the day of his death?"

"Do you know what, Inspector? I didn't. I made no mention of it because I didn't know the nature of the bad news, and in all honesty he often made a big fuss about something or other that had occurred. Or hadn't occurred."

He took another gulp of brandy. "It wasn't out of character. I did try asking him about it on this occasion, but he said that he couldn't dwell on it for the time being because he had the illuminations to prepare for and needed to clear his mind of all else."

"Do you think the news of his friend's death might have driven him to take his own life?" asked James.

"It's difficult for me to say. I didn't know the man personally enough to speculate. But it's possible, isn't it? Definitely possible. Do you mind if I smoke?"

"Not at all, Mr Repton. Did you know about Mr Borthwick's friendship with Mr Geller prior to his death?"

"No. I only found out just now when you told me! It makes sense, of course. I remember reading about the murder in the newspaper, but I hadn't realised the poor chap was Borthwick's friend."

"What do you think Mr Borthwick meant in his letter when he said that he thought it best to die by his own hand rather than at the hands of theirs?" asked James.

"Oh, we're back to that again, are we?" Mr Repton looked at me and rolled his eyes. "Miss Green and I have already had this discussion. The answer is that I really don't know, Inspector. I would tell you if I knew, but that's the sort of thing that can only be found out through an investigation."

"I'd like to request permission to return here and read through any of Mr Borthwick's personal papers which are kept in this building," said James. "Would that be possible?"

"Absolutely. Help yourself to whatever you need, Inspector. Now that I've learned of the connection between the poor unfortunate hospital chap and Mr Borthwick I'm as keen as you to understand what happened on that strange day."

James and I left the works, passing the warehouses and timber yards of Upper Ground Street before walking across Blackfriars Bridge. It was only a short walk to Fleet Street from the other side and James could take an omnibus from there to Scotland Yard. I wiped the drizzle from my spectacle lenses.

"What do you think about our friends at the Southwark works?" asked James.

"I find Mr Repton rather amusing and charmingly eccentric," I replied, squinting through the smears I had added to my spectacles. "Copeland and Maynell seem rather guarded to me. I feel sorry for Lillian Maynell being married to that man. He's rather humourless, isn't he?"

"He is. I suppose he was angered by your meeting with his wife. But I feel there may be more to this than they're telling us. They didn't overstretch themselves when replying to our questions, did they?"

I stopped, struck by a sudden thought.

"I think Jeffrey Maynell could be the anonymous letter writer!" I exclaimed. "The malicious letters began shortly after I met with Lillian."

"There's a thought," said James. "I can imagine him doing such a thing, and perhaps he's adept at altering his handwriting."

"But how do we find out?"

"There must be a way." He smiled. "Leave it with me."

CHAPTER 33

The rain pummelled the windows of the reading room dome as I balanced on the ladder in the upper gallery, trying to find a book about Panama. I had no idea that someone else was in the gallery until I began descending the ladder and a woman in a grey dress and black hat pushed past me, almost knocking the heavy book from my hand.

"I do apologise," she whispered without turning to look at me. I found her manner rather brusque, but I thought little more of it as I returned to my desk.

As I leafed through the book I had the uncomfortable sensation that someone was watching me. I looked up and glanced around, but everyone seemed occupied with their work.

"Miss Green!" whispered Mr Edwards. "How are you this morning?"

"I'm well, thank you, Mr Edwards."

I hadn't seen him since he had made his comment about allowing me to continue with my work if I were to become his wife. I felt my cheeks redden slightly at the memory.

"You'll be relieved to hear that I haven't received any more unpleasant letters," he said.

"Good," I whispered in reply. "I don't know of anyone else who has received another, so hopefully the letter writer has stopped that nonsense. Actually, I'm wondering whether I met with him yesterday."

"Really?" Mr Edwards' left eyebrow lifted in surprise.

"Yes. I suspect the writer could be the engineer Jeffrey Maynell; one of Simon Borthwick's colleagues."

"Do you really think he could write such nasty letters about you?"

"He took exception to me meeting with his wife and discussing Simon Borthwick with her. And he warned me off again when I saw him yesterday. You found out some extremely useful information for me about Hugo Banister—"

"Would you like me to find out more about Mr Maynell?"

"If you could I should be extremely grateful. Thank you, Mr Edwards."

"My pleasure, Miss Green. I can't think why a scientist of his calibre should resort to writing unpleasant letters, but I'm quickly learning that one should never underestimate people."

"That's right, Mr Edwards. One shouldn't."

"I'm afraid my research into the various Bannisters hasn't come to much. I have spoken to a couple of people with the same surname. One chap took offence to the suggestion that he might have written such a letter."

"Don't worry about Hugo Bannister for the time being. Thank you very much for your help, though. I'll let you know if the matter needs to be investigated further."

He left my desk, but the sense that someone was watching me remained. I looked around and saw the young woman in grey again. The back of my neck prickled as she stared at me from a desk approximately ten yards away. Her face was angular and solemn, her hair dark and her black hat distinctly unseasonal.

I returned her stare and eventually she looked away.

❧

"If Father is still alive, I don't quite know what we're supposed to do about it," said Eliza as we sat in a box at the Theatre Royal in Drury Lane waiting for the performance of *As You Like It* to begin. We were located to the right of the stage in a position that afforded us a good view over the auditorium.

"How do we find him?" continued Eliza. "It would cost such a vast sum of money. We were so fortunate that Lizzie Dixie funded the first search. I cannot even begin to think where we might find the money a second time."

"Do you think Father is still alive?"

"I like to hope that he is, Penelope. Don't you?"

"I do and I don't."

"What's that supposed to mean? You can be so terribly confusing at times."

"If he is alive I can only guess that he has been unwell or in prison, and I don't like the sound of either possibility."

"Perhaps he simply doesn't care about us any more."

"Ellie!"

"But it could be true, couldn't it? Maybe he hasn't written because he doesn't consider us to be important any longer. Perhaps he's quite happy where he is and feels worried that if he contacts us we'll beg him to come home against his will."

"How could he be happy there? Surely he would rather be at home with his family."

"You'd like to think so, wouldn't you? I should also like to think that. But there is a possibility that he chose not to come back. We must be ready to cope with that eventuality, Penelope."

"Wouldn't it be wrong of us to go looking for him again if he has made that decision?"

"No, I don't think it would be wrong. After all, I think he owes us an explanation, doesn't he?"

"If he's alive, that is. I'm not sure he can be. It isn't the sort of thing Father would have done."

"Maybe he suffered a blow to the head and forgot all about us," suggested Eliza. "It happened once to my friend's spinster aunt. She was found wandering about in Elephant and Castle, which is no place for a lady from Belgravia."

"I'm not sure about this, Ellie. I don't like having to consider all these possibilities when there is nothing to suggest that Father might still be alive. If Fox-Stirling hadn't mentioned it we wouldn't have found ourselves in this turmoil again. And what does he know, anyway? It's just something he said in passing, and I wish he hadn't because it took so long for us to accept that Father might not be alive any more. I don't think it's fair of him to have mentioned anything of the sort!"

"I disagree. I think he was quite right to say something. If he has the slightest suspicion that Father might be alive he should say so while we still have the time to do something about it."

"But can we really find the funds to pay for someone else to travel to Colombia and find him? What if they couldn't find him? What if there are no further answers about what has happened to him? Then it will all have been for nothing."

"But we would feel better for having tried again, don't you think? Don't you agree that we should do everything we possibly can to find out what has happened to him?"

"I thought we had."

"As long as there is a possibility that he is still alive, I want to find him. I'm surprised to hear that you don't feel the same way, Penelope."

"I want to believe that he's still alive, Ellie, truly I do. But it's so hard having to adjust my feelings about him all over again. I don't want to raise my hopes for it all to be a complete waste again."

I pulled out my handkerchief and wiped my eyes.

"I understand."

A great fanfare rose up from the orchestra pit and startled us both.

"Time for curtain up," said Eliza with a sense of relief to her voice.

Just before the lights dimmed I looked down at the audience and saw a face upturned towards me. It was the face of a woman.

The woman in grey I had seen in the reading room.

CHAPTER 34

I searched for the woman again during the play's interval but was unable to see her. Either she had stopped staring at me or she had left the auditorium altogether.

"Are you all right, Penelope?" asked Eliza. "You seem rather distracted."

"I'm fine, thank you, Ellie. Just a little tired."

"Well you do work tremendously hard, it has to be said. Have you found out who sent me that odd letter yet?"

"I think I know who it is. His name is Jeffrey Maynell and he took offence after I spoke to his wife about the inventor who committed suicide."

"That Borthwick fellow?"

"Yes. Mr Maynell's wife once courted him and I had lunch with her to discuss his death. She swore me to secrecy about our meeting, as presumably she knew that her husband would be upset if he found out about it. Then for some odd reason she went and told him about our meeting."

"Oh dear. Let's hope he hasn't been cruel to her about it in that case," said Eliza.

"He doesn't seem to be a very pleasant man. I think she

would have been better off staying with Borthwick. Actually, on second thoughts I don't think she would have been."

"Why not?"

"I think she would have been wise to choose a different man entirely. Oh look, the curtain's about to go up again."

I felt relieved that this slightly evasive conversation had been brought to an end.

We left the theatre shortly after sunset and it was dark by the time I got out of my cab on Milton Street. As I climbed the steps up to Mrs Garnett's front door I caught sight of a figure standing under a gas lamp further along the street. As I stopped and stared I saw that it was a woman.

Was it the woman in grey again?

She stood facing me, as if she wanted me to see her there. *Did she want to talk to me?* I descended the steps and began walking up the street towards her. But as I did so she stepped out of the pool of light beneath the lamp and into the darkness.

"Wait!" I called out.

There was no reply.

I quickened my step, hoping to catch up with her. I caught a glimpse of her under the next gas lamp as she ran across the bridge that straddled the railway lines. I also began to run, crossing the bridge just as the train beneath it blew a great plume of smoke and steam into the night sky.

The brewery was ahead of us on the left of Milton Street, but I knew that there was a maze of narrow passageways on the right which someone could easily escape down. Predictably, the woman turned right into a covered walkway. It wasn't a place I wished to find myself in after dark, but I needed to find out what she was doing there.

I followed her into Hanover Court and slowed to a walk as I could barely see anything in the dark. The cobbles were uneven beneath my feet and only a dim light glowed from a curtained window. There was an unpleasant damp smell, which often seemed to lurk in narrow, hidden places such as this.

My heart thudded in my throat.

"Hello?" I called out.

I felt sure that I could hear footsteps up ahead.

I continued walking, holding my hands out in front of me in case I bumped into something. A passageway opened up to my right and I could see a faint light at the end of it.

I had lost her.

I turned into the passageway and stumbled towards the light. I discovered that it led to Moor Lane, a street which ran parallel to Milton Street. There were a few people standing around but none that I recognised as the woman in grey.

I turned right, and a swaying drunk lurched up to me.

"'Ow much?" he asked.

I pushed him away, then ran down the street and back over the railway lines again.

The woman had completely disappeared.

I walked past The Greyhound public house and its neighbouring police station. I paused outside the doors of the station, wondering whether to report the woman.

But was the woman who had been watching me actually committing a crime?

Deciding that a police officer probably wouldn't be interested in helping me, I walked home, turning right into Fore Street and right again into Milton Street. It had been a fruitless chase.

As I climbed the steps to Mrs Garnett's house for the second time that evening I noticed something had been written on the front door in white. It seemed to be chalk, and I could only just make it out in the gloom.

Stay away!

I shuddered and spun around, searching for the woman. But there was no sign of her or anyone else. I turned back to the door and rubbed at the writing with my hand. The chalk came away easily, but while I was still halfway through the task the door swung open.

"Oh, it's you, Miss Green!" said Mrs Garnett. "I've heard all sorts of strange noises out here this evening." She glanced at the powdery chalk on my hand and dress, then looked at the door. "Goodness gracious! What are you doing to my door?"

"Trying to clean it, Mrs Garnett."

Part of the writing remained.

"Oh no, it's begun again," sighed Mrs Garnett.

"Again? What do you mean?"

"This happened a long time ago when Hercules was still alive. People used to write all sorts of things on our door because we were negroes."

"No, it's not that this time. It was directed at me," I said. "I even saw the woman who did it!"

"Then why didn't you stop her?"

"I didn't catch her in the act of writing on the door. She was watching me over there under the lamp, so I gave chase but lost sight of her. While I was looking around for her she must have returned and written this."

"What's it supposed to say?"

"'Stay away.' It's to do with my work. Please don't worry; it's nothing."

Mrs Garnett sucked her lip. "It's not nothing. It may only be chalk, but she could have scratched the paintwork on my door. Stop rubbing it with your hand, Miss Green! I'll fetch some water and a cloth. Is it something to do with that letter I received?"

"It might be, I can't be sure, I'm afraid."

She tutted. "Get inside and go up to your room. You'll need to clean the chalk off your hands and dress."

"I'll stay and clean up the door first."

"No, I'll do that. I want it done properly."

CHAPTER 35

I received a telegram from James asking me to meet him at the Borthwick family's law firm in Berkeley Square.

I travelled by omnibus and found the premises on the west side of the square. The company name, Newbolt & Dimsdale, was etched onto a brass plaque beside a polished black door.

"Penny!" James greeted me inside a high-ceilinged room with two tall windows looking out over the square. Several piles of papers and a pot of coffee sat on a large table at the centre of the room.

"Hello, James. I can't stay long, I'm afraid," I sat down at the table. "I have to write an article about the death of Alexander, the Prince of Orange."

"That is sad news."

"He died from typhus fever. He was only thirty-two."

"Such a young age. I shan't detain you for long in that case."

"Are you wearing a new suit?"

My question appeared to startle James and he looked

down at his suit as if he had only just noticed that he was wearing it.

"As a matter of fact, it is, Penny." He smiled.

"You look very smart in it."

"Thank you. And you look very umm, fetching in your, umm blouse and—"

"There's no need to return the compliment James!" I laughed.

"No, I see. Very fetching, though." He cleared his throat. "Can I pour you some coffee?"

"Thank you."

"As you can see, I managed to obtain permission from Simon Borthwick's family to look at his papers," said James. "I've had a quick read through some of these. There is rather a lot of engineering speak in the letters, but the long and short of it is that there has been a dispute over a feature of the incandescent lamp which Borthwick patented. Maynell was demanding financial compensation for an idea which Borthwick supposedly stole and Borthwick was refusing to pay it."

He slid a cup of coffee across the table to me.

"Does Maynell use any threatening language?" I asked.

"Not particularly, no, but it's rather hostile, as you'll see. And I have found a few photos," said James, passing them to me. "I don't know what Borthwick looked like, but you met him, didn't you?"

I nodded and examined a photo of him standing next to a generator. He wore a frock coat with a wide velvet collar and the customary floral buttonhole.

"Yes, that's him all right," I replied. "And I'd say the photograph was taken fairly recently, too."

"There are a few more here," said James, passing them to me.

Borthwick was pictured on his own, then with some of his

colleagues – I recognised Jack Copeland – and there were four photographs in which he was pictured with a serious-looking young man with a heavy brow, spectacles and a slightly receding chin. I laid the photographs out on the table and placed the latter four in a separate pile.

"I don't recognise this man he's with," I said. "I don't suppose you know who he is?"

"I have no idea," replied James. "Perhaps it's Richard Geller? I think we need to go and ask Mr Kurtz to confirm it."

As I leafed through some of the papers on the table I told James about the woman in grey.

"You should have called in at Moor Lane police station as you passed by and reported it."

"But they couldn't have arrested her for standing under a lamp and watching me!"

"If you'd told them about her presence in the reading room and at the theatre they might have decided she was worth talking to. Mind you, they may not have been much help. Moor Lane is a City of London police station after all," he said with mock derision.

I laughed. "Well, whoever she is I have no doubt that Jeffrey Maynell is behind all of it. If he's writing unpleasant letters and telling people to follow me about, perhaps he did the same to Simon Borthwick."

"He may well have done. And perhaps he also murdered Richard Geller."

"Could Jeffrey Maynell be a murderer?"

"I don't know. He doesn't have a particularly pleasant manner, does he?"

"Perhaps you could question him again."

"I think I will need to."

"I've asked Mr Edwards to find out more information

about Jeffrey Maynell. I'll let you know as soon as he's finished doing so. He is usually quite thorough."

"I'm sure he will be. Is this a service reading room clerks routinely offer?"

"Not routinely, no."

"It's the sort of thing they do for their friends, I suppose."

"It is, yes. He has been quite helpful since he was sent one of those malicious letters."

"Mr Edwards is always helpful where you're concerned, Penny."

"To be honest with you, James, I'm surprised he is still helpful having read that letter. There were a few upsetting things in it."

"Such as?"

"I'd rather not say. It's embarrassing."

"You can tell me."

"I'd rather not."

"Why not?"

"Because it concerns you."

"Then I have a right to know!"

"Do you?"

"Yes! Come on, now. Tell me what it said."

"There is no truth in it, of course. And please don't pass it on to the future Mrs Blakely because people can be very sensitive about these matters."

"What did it say, Penny?" He took a sip of coffee.

I took a deep breath and raised my eyes to the ceiling. "It advised Mr Edwards to consider marrying me, but implied that my friendship with you might have raised questions in his mind."

I paused for a while before feeling brave enough to look James in the eye again.

He frowned. "I see. And why should that be embarrassing?"

"It suggests that there is something untoward about our friendship."

"But there isn't."

"No, I know that. It's a friendship between professional colleagues, nothing more. We don't meet socially because you are engaged to be married."

"And you're not far off it yourself from the sound of things."

"I am a long way off it! Mr Edwards is merely an acquaintance."

"Even though you're terrified that he might ask you to marry him?"

"Oh, that. I was mistaken on that front. The unpleasant letter he received suggested he marry me so that he could stop me from working as a news reporter."

"I can perfectly imagine how you'd feel about that!" He laughed.

"Mr Edwards has assured me that he would never ask me to stop pursuing my profession."

James stopped smiling. "Has he, indeed? That's reassurance for you, then."

"Not that I need any reassurance, because I would never consider marrying him."

"You wouldn't?"

"Of course not."

"You have often told me that one of the reasons you haven't married is that a husband would stop you from working. Now you have the prospect of a husband who would allow you to work."

"But I have no wish to marry Mr Edwards."

"So what is the nature of your relationship?"

"We are acquaintances."

"You're acquaintances with Mr Edwards and I'm your professional colleague."

"Yes, like Edgar Fish."

James almost spat out his mouthful of coffee.

"Are you comparing me to Fish now? Have I really dropped so low in your estimation?"

We both laughed, but my heart ached. I wished I could tell James how I really felt about him, but with his wedding only two months away I knew there was no use in broaching the subject.

CHAPTER 36

James and I sat at the table in the law offices and continued to read through Simon Borthwick's papers and correspondence.

"Now I can see what Jeffrey Maynell's handwriting is like," I said. "And it doesn't match the writing on any of the anonymous letters."

"Except one," said James.

"No. It doesn't match any of them."

James gave a slight cough. "There's another letter."

"Another one?" I felt puzzled. "One that I haven't yet seen"

"Yes."

"Addressed to whom?"

"It was sent to me, Penny." He turned to face me, his blue eyes apologetic.

I felt a burn of anger in my chest. "And you didn't tell me?"

"It is a horrible letter. You won't want to read it."

"Do you have it with you?"

"As a matter of fact, I do. I brought it here for the

purpose of comparing the handwriting, and it seems that I have found a match."

"I would like to see it."

"Penny, please. You mustn't."

"I've read all the others."

"It will upset you."

"It won't! I've coped with far worse in the past. Please show it to me, James."

"Penny..."

"What are you trying to protect me from?"

"Hurtful remarks which bear no element of truth."

"And you think I have never encountered such untruths before? I wish to see it."

James sighed and reached into his pocket.

"I can't believe you hid it from me! I trusted that you would tell me about a matter such as this."

He retrieved an envelope and slowly held it out.

"Penny, can I ask you one last time not to read it? It's hurtful and was written purely to upset you. There are some things it is better to remain ignorant of."

I thought of the letter which had been sent to Mr Edwards and how it had momentarily upset me as we stood in Russell Square. *Surely the letter James had been sent couldn't be any worse.*

I held out my hand and took it. "I don't need you deciding what will and won't upset me, James. I can look after myself. The letter was written about me and I have a right to read it."

He got up from his chair and walked over to the window while I read the note.

A detective of your calibre should know better than to associate with a woman like Miss Penelope Green. She is a nosey ink-slinger who insists on poking her proboscis into matters which don't concern her.

I'm unsure why the Morning Express *insists on employing her. Perhaps its editor keeps her as his concubine. That is certainly a profession to which she is more suited judging by the manner in which she conducts herself around a man who is engaged to be married.*

With little skill or talent to her name, Miss Green clearly relies on her feminine wiles to succeed. I'm surprised that you haven't realised this yet. Perhaps you should observe how she plays the reading room clerk off against yourself. The woman is only interested in furthering her own interests, and she will use whatever means she can to get there.

You should stay well away from her if you wish to have a happy marriage, Inspector Blakely.

I felt a heavy sensation in my chest as I finished reading. I laid the letter on the table and looked through the photographs of Simon Borthwick again, as if unaffected by what I had just read. I understood now why James had tried to keep the letter a secret from me.

He turned away from the window and regarded me.

"I hope you know that there isn't an ounce of truth in what you've just read," he said. "It seems Jeffrey Maynell is a bitter and vindictive man."

I realised that I would emit a loud sob if I tried to speak.

I nodded, cleared my throat and wished that my eyes didn't well up quite so easily.

"It's upset you, hasn't it, Penny?" said James. "I knew it would. No one could read something like that and not be upset. Curse that man!"

He strode over and snatched the letter away from me.

"Don't destroy it," I said in a cracked voice. "We need to keep it." A tear rolled down my cheek.

"Curse him!" James said again.

He scrunched the letter up into a ball and dropped to his

knees beside my chair. He put an arm around my shoulders and wiped the tear from my cheek with his thumb. His face was close to mine.

"It's not true, Penny, do you hear me? Nothing that he says is true. He simply wishes to hurt you."

"I know."

"You've rattled him, that's all. You're on to him and we need to do everything we can to pin something on him. He's a cruel man and I am going to make him pay. Trust me."

"I do."

I turned to look at him. Our faces were practically touching, and everything suddenly seemed very quiet.

His eyes moved over my face as if he were planning to kiss me. I held my breath, not daring to move and ruin the moment. Then he seemed to check himself. He released his arm from my shoulder and slowly stood to his feet.

Disappointment descended upon me and I felt an undeserved loathing for the woman who was keeping us apart.

"I will do everything I can to gather evidence of what Maynell's been doing," said James. "I already have this letter he's sent to me. The man was foolish to think that I would be unable to match his handwriting to the letters he sent Borthwick."

He picked up the ball of scrunched paper and opened it out again.

"He must have assumed that you had never seen these letters," I said.

"Well, he assumed wrong. We're one step ahead of him now."

"Perhaps Jack Copeland is also in on this," I suggested. "We need to see an example of his handwriting to know for sure."

"You think the two men could be co-ordinating this cowardly attack?"

"It's worth investigating. Let me give you the other letters I have," I said, delving into my carpet bag to find them. "And you can tell me if you find any handwriting which matches the writing on them."

I gave James the letters. His expression was grave, as if he were saddened that I had received any of them.

"Would you like to join me at the medical school museum at ten o'clock tomorrow?" he asked. "We need to ask Mr Kurtz if Richard Geller is the man in these photographs."

I smiled and nodded. "Of course, James. I'll see you then."

"And please don't worry about that letter, Penny. It's all nonsense."

"I have forgotten it already."

I stepped out into the bright sunshine of Berkeley Square and tried to push the words of Jeffrey Maynell's letter to James out of my mind. I longed to confront Maynell and find out why he had written it. But doing so at this stage would place the investigation at risk. For the time being we needed to gather as much evidence as possible so that he could be confronted properly at a later date.

You should stay away from her if you wish to have a happy marriage, Inspector Blakely.

I recalled the moment when I had thought James was about to kiss me. I had to reluctantly admit that there was an element of truth to this phrase. *Was there any truth to the rest of the letter?*

As I looked about me before crossing the road I caught a glimpse of a familiar figure. She stood watching me from further down the street. She wore a pale blue skirt and jacket with the same dark hat as before.

It was the woman from the reading room again.

I felt an uncomfortable flip in my chest. Then I gritted my teeth and strode towards her.

She turned and walked swiftly away down Charles Street. I began to run and she did the same, pushing past people on the pavement.

She was a good deal faster than me.

"Oi!" I called out, aware that my shout was unladylike and unexpected to the people around me. I attracted a few disapproving glares, and my boots pinched my toes as I ran.

The woman turned into Queen Street and I followed. She turned again into a narrow street, and I expected to see her ahead of me as I followed in her footsteps. Instead, the narrow road ahead of me was empty.

I walked slowly, checking doorways as I went. *Was she waiting for me? Would she ambush and attack me?*

I gripped the handle of my carpet bag, ready to swing it at her should I need to defend myself. But after a further search there was no sign of the woman. It was as though she had disappeared into thin air.

CHAPTER 37

"You've just missed the lovesick gentleman from the library," said Mrs Garnett as I returned home that evening. "He's been writing things for you again." She handed me a sheaf of papers.

"Thank you, Mrs Garnett." I glanced quickly at them and saw that they were the notes he had written about Jeffrey Maynell.

I spent some time at my writing desk reading through Mr Edwards' notes. Rain lashed against the window while Tiger slept on my lap. Jeffrey Maynell appeared to have enjoyed a good education, studying in the Department of Engineering at King's College. He had joined Repton, Borthwick and Company shortly after his graduation and didn't appear to have achieved much that was remarkable during his time there. *Was it possible that he had been envious of Simon Borthwick's success?*

It was about eight o'clock when I heard voices downstairs.

"Miss Green!" came a shrill summons from Mrs Garnett.

Sensing that something was wrong, I put down my papers and went to find out what was the matter. Mrs Garnett stood in the hallway with a young woman in a cloak, which was soaked through with rain.

"You shouldn't have come out in this weather!" Mrs Garnett scolded.

"I need to speak to Miss Green," said the woman, looking up the stairs at me.

"Lillian?" I asked in puzzlement. "What is it? Has something happened?"

"She needs to dry out beside a proper fire," said Mrs Garnett. "You can both come and sit in my parlour."

We followed my landlady past the staircase and into a small room at the back of the house.

"Let me take your wet things," said Mrs Garnett, holding out her hand for Lillian's bonnet and cloak. "Take a seat and I'll make you some tea."

"What an attentive landlady you have," said Lillian as Mrs Garnett went off into the kitchen.

We sat down at the small round table, which was covered with a lace tablecloth. Golden ringlets hung about Lillian's pretty, youthful face in wet coils.

"What brings you here, Lillian?" I asked." If your husband finds out you have spoken to me again he'll be extremely angry."

"I know," she replied, "but I'll make sure he doesn't find out this time. I've made a promise to myself not to tell him. I refuse to give in to his bullying."

"I don't want you to put yourself at risk."

"Let me take responsibility for it, Penny," she replied. "I chose to come here, didn't I? I've been thinking about Simon and there are a few things I wish to tell you. I met Jeffrey when I was courting Simon. We attended an event to celebrate Repton, Borthwick and Company installing its electric lights at the Law Courts. From the moment I met Jeffrey I could see that he had an interest in me. He kept glancing over throughout the evening, which I thought most rude because I was accompanied by Simon.

"After that evening he sent letters to my parents' home and paid them a number of visits. It wasn't long before he had convinced them that he was a worthier suitor than Simon. And then I was told Simon had unhealthy interests and that I shouldn't be consorting with a man of his ilk."

"What kind of unhealthy interests?"

"That was never elaborated upon."

"Were you aware that he had these so-called interests?"

"No. I didn't even know what they were. But before long everyone was telling me that he wouldn't be a suitable husband."

"Everyone?"

"My parents, my sister, Jeffrey."

"What about your friends?"

"They wanted me to choose the man I would be happiest with, but they were concerned by the reports they had heard about Simon and told me there had to be something behind them."

"What did Simon have to say on the matter?"

"He denied that he was involved in anything untoward, but I noticed a change in him after that. He withdrew and I wonder now if there was something he was keeping from me. I can't think what it might have been, as I have no doubt that he loved and cared for me. He wasn't as indifferent as I suggested at the restaurant. I only told you that because I had to provide a reason for leaving him. I found it difficult to tell you the truth when I had only just met you, and we were chatting in such a public place."

Lillian stopped talking as Mrs Garnett brought in the tea

tray and placed it on the table. My landlady stood with her hands on her hips and regarded us both.

"I'm judging by the silence in the room that you don't wish to speak with me present," she said.

Lillian pulled an awkward grimace.

"We only need a few minutes, Mrs Garnett," I said, feeling rather uncomfortable.

"Fine," she replied curtly. "You pour the tea, Miss Green, and I'll wait in the kitchen."

Once she felt sure that the kitchen door was shut, Lillian continued with her story. "It was extremely difficult for Simon and me to be as happy as we had been," she said. "Eventually he told me that perhaps it would be for the best if I married Jeffrey. I still don't understand why he said that. It was as if he was pushing me away, albeit reluctantly; as if he didn't want the relationship to end, but he had no choice. Does that make any sense to you?"

"Perhaps. Does Georgina know all this?"

"Some of it. She has been a good friend to me. I've spent a great deal of time at her home, as I can't bear to be around Jeffery at the moment. He's so terribly possessive of me. He doesn't like me talking to anyone; least of all someone who wishes to discuss Simon Borthwick."

"I realise that. He was quite angry with me when I spoke to him at the works down in Southwark."

"Oh dear. I do apologise.'

"No, you mustn't apologise for your husband's behaviour. I'm worried about you, Lillian. Who else do you have living with you?"

"We have a housekeeper and a maid. And Jeffrey has a valet."

"I think you need someone to protect you. Do the servants realise what he's like?"

"Oh yes. They often see his rages."

"Can they help in looking after you and protecting you from him?"

"I don't know. I think they're rather scared of him too, if truth be told."

"Lillian, I think you need to spend as much time as possible elsewhere. It sounds as though Georgina and Edgar are helpful. Some men can be unpredictable, and you shouldn't have to endure your husband's rages. I'm interested to know if there was anyone else at Repton, Borthwick and Company who pressured you to leave Simon and choose Jeffrey instead."

"I remember that on one occasion Jack Copeland told me I would be better off without Simon. It was an odd comment which he made during a dinner at Mr Repton's home. He didn't know me very well, but he was a friend of Jeffrey's, so I suppose that was the reason why he said it."

"Is your husband much of a letter writer, Lillian?"

"Not really. Why do you ask?"

"Some unpleasant letters have been sent to my family and friends, and as your husband was angered by our meeting I wondered if he might be behind them."

Her eyes widened. "What a mean thing to do! Are you all right, Penny? I didn't realise such a terrible thing had happened to you!"

"I'm fine, please don't worry. Could your husband be behind the letters, do you think?"

"I don't know. He does spend a lot of time in his study and I can't be certain what he's doing in there, but I don't like to think that he could be writing letters of that kind. What a horrible thing to do!"

"Have you ever met a young woman who wears grey and runs quite fast?"

"She *runs?*"

"She keeps following me, and whenever I try to confront her she runs away. I thought perhaps your husband had asked her to follow me, but... I feel terribly awkward levelling such accusations at him."

"Oh, please don't worry." She rested a hand against my arm. "He doesn't help himself with his bad moods and tempers. I'm quite sure he wouldn't write unpleasant letters or ask someone to follow you about, but I can quite understand why you might think him capable of it."

"Did Simon Borthwick ever mention a man named Richard Geller?"

"No, who's he?"

"A friend of Simon's who was unfortunately murdered."

"Oh goodness!" Lillian flung her hands up to her mouth, and I wondered if I had been foolish to mention Mr Geller.

"But that's dreadful!" she continued. "Richard Geller, you say? I really don't remember the name. Who murdered him?"

"The police don't know yet."

A line from Borthwick's letter came back into my mind: *Everything I care about has been taken away from me, piece by piece.*

"Lillian, is it your belief that your husband pursued you while you were courting Simon?"

"Yes, he did. It began with that event celebrating the electric lights at the Law Courts. It was particularly ill-mannered of him."

"Perhaps Simon viewed Jeffrey's actions as some sort of persecution."

Her eyebrows crumpled. "Why would he think of it in that way?"

"I'm not sure. I'm just trying to make sense of the words he used in his letter."

"He thought Jeffrey was persecuting him by stealing me

away?" She laughed derisively. "No, that would be ridiculous. I chose Jeffrey because Simon withdrew from me. I decided that Jeffrey was the better suitor." She laughed again. "And now I'm not sure either man was a good choice!"

"What makes you say that?"

She waved the comment away. "Please forget that I said it."

"If I understand you correctly, Lillian," I ventured. "You have visited me this evening to tell me that Jeffrey pursued you, even though you were courting Simon. And you were warned that Simon had unhealthy interests."

"Yes. Although, on reflection, I'm not sure how useful this information is to you. And I still don't understand what was meant by 'unhealthy interests'. Have you any inkling?"

"None, I'm afraid," I lied.

"I hope you don't mind me visiting you, Penny. I suppose I felt the need to explain how matters really stand. I didn't feel I could speak freely at the restaurant."

"You told your husband that we met there, didn't you?"

"I'm afraid I did." She bit her lip nervously. "Either he can read my mind or I'm a hopeless liar. But he knew that I had kept something from him and I felt it would be easier to tell him the truth. I'm sorry he was angry with you about it. He was angry with me, too."

"Well he shouldn't be angry. You've done nothing wrong."

"It's just the way Jeffrey is. He likes to know what I do each day and the people I meet with."

I felt momentarily pleased to be a spinster.

"To tell you the truth," Lillian lowered her voice and leaned in closer to me, "I feel quite afraid of him sometimes."

I felt a rising concern for her. "Where is he now?" I asked.

"At the Garrick. He doesn't go there very often, but when he does he stays out late, so I knew I would have time to come and see you this evening and return home before he did."

"But what happens when he either reads your mind or you find it impossible to lie about this evening?"

She sighed, and I noticed that her eyes were damp. "I don't know, Penny. Some days I wish I could leave him and return to my parents' home."

I understood her predicament but had no idea what the solution might be.

"It sounds like you've taken a significant risk in coming to see me this evening, Lillian. I don't want you to find yourself in trouble with him again. Perhaps in future you could write to me instead. I think it would be safer that way."

She looked at me sadly. "It would be, wouldn't it? I've been quite foolish this evening. I'm sorry. I felt the need to explain matters to you a little more clearly, and as soon as he left the house I dashed over here without giving the situation much thought."

"How did you find out my address?"

"Edgar gave it to me."

I watched her hands fidget nervously and I felt a deep hatred toward Jeffrey Maynell for the fear he had instilled in his wife. I was becoming increasingly convinced that he might be capable of murder.

"I shall come outside with you now and help you hail a cab," I said. "And if you end up having to explain to your husband that we met this evening, please tell him that I was responsible for asking you to come here."

"No, Penny! I couldn't do that!"

"Please do. It will be safer that way. I have people who can protect me, such as Inspector Blakely from Scotland Yard. When it's just you on your own in your home with him... I can't bear to think what he might do. Please blame me for this if he finds out the truth."

"I don't think there's any need —"

"*Promise* that you will," I urged.

"All right, Penny." She fixed me with her large blue eyes. "I promise."

CHAPTER 38

James was already talking to Mr Kurtz inside the medical school museum when I arrived there the following morning. I had kept my eyes open for the woman in grey during my walk to St Bartholomew's Hospital but had seen no sign of her.

"I've told you everything you need to know, Inspector," said Mr Kurtz. "What else can there be?" He paused to look me up and down. "Good morning, Miss Green. I didn't realise you'd be joining us." His bloodless lips formed a sinister smile.

"Mr Kurtz, I have a question about some photographs I have come across," said James. "Would you mind taking a look at them for me?"

He laid the four pictures we had found at the law firm out on the table.

"Goodness, what's that?" James asked, peering at the contents of a large jar to his right.

"A pair of lungs," replied Mr Kurtz.

"So that's what they look like, is it?"

"They do indeed. Would you like to see the cross-section

of a lung? We have a few samples here, and you'll find the bronchioli quite fascinating, I'm sure. The diseased samples are particularly intriguing."

"Perhaps another time, Mr Kurtz. I should like you to examine these photographs for now," said James. "We know that one of these chaps is the late inventor Simon Borthwick, but we were wondering about the other fellow. I suspect it may be Richard Geller. Am I right?"

Mr Kurtz glanced down at the photographs. "Yes, you're right," he confirmed.

"Did you know of the friendship between Mr Geller and Mr Borthwick?" asked James.

"Richard mentioned him to me once or twice, so I knew they were acquainted, if that's any help. Clearly they were close friends if they paid to be photographed together."

"You weren't aware that they were close friends?"

"No."

"What did Mr Geller tell you about Simon Borthwick?"

"Nothing specific. He occasionally mentioned him while discussing an evening he had spent with friends or something of that kind. Why do you ask?"

"You do realise that both men died on the same day, don't you?"

"Was it the same day?" asked Mr Kurtz in surprise. "I thought it was the same week, but the same day is quite extraordinary. Do you think there may be a connection between their deaths?"

"That's exactly what we're assuming, Mr Kurtz. Can you think of any?"

"No, none at all."

"You suggest that Mr Geller didn't mention Mr Borthwick often. However, were you aware of any change in their relationship before he died? A falling out over something, perhaps?"

"None whatsoever. He never discussed anything like that with me."

"Did Mr Borthwick ever visit Mr Geller here at the hospital?" I asked.

"No, Miss Green. I never saw him. I never saw the two together. I was under the impression that they socialised sporadically and that was all there was to it. I cannot understand why they should have died on the same day."

"One theory is that Mr Borthwick was so frightened by the murder of his friend that he took his own life, fearing that he would be next," said James.

"That is extremely tragic," replied Mr Kurtz, his face displaying little emotion.

"May I have a look inside the storeroom?" asked James, gesturing toward the door in the wall.

"Of course," said Mr Kurtz.

We followed him across the room and he opened the door. James and I stepped inside and saw that it was a gloomy, cluttered room. The wooden shelving that ran all the way around it was loaded with jars and cases. The only light came from a small window at the far end.

"This is where we keep the specimens we have no space for in the museum," explained Mr Kurtz. "We put them on display from time to time, and they're always here for medical students to look at should they request to do so."

James walked around the shelving, inspecting some of the items stored there. I peered at a number of jars containing various body parts, and a twisted spine mounted on a display stand.

"Do you mind if I open this window?" asked James.

"Not at all," replied Mr Kurtz.

James lifted the sash and peered outside.

"I see there is a roof below here," he said. "Do you ever keep this window open?"

"Only when the weather is particularly warm."

"How easy would it be to open the window from the outside?"

"For someone standing on the roof out there, you mean?"

"Yes."

"Why would somebody wish to do that?"

"Someone may have wanted to enter the storeroom surreptitiously and lurk in here until the opportunity came to murder Mr Geller in the museum."

Mr Kurtz's mouth hung open. "Do you think that's what happened?" he asked.

"It's a possibility. Now, could this window be opened by someone who was standing on the roof outside?"

"I don't know. I can't say I have ever tried it."

"Let's give it a try then, shall we?" said James as he pushed the sash up a little further. He handed me his bowler hat and began to climb out.

"Be careful, James!" I said, seeing that the roof was steeply sloped.

"Shut the window behind me, please, Penny."

I reluctantly pulled down the sash and watched him examine the window frame as he balanced precariously on the steep roof. My heart rose into my mouth as he spent some time pushing his fingers against the sash, trying to gain enough traction to lift the window. It took a fair bit of effort and he almost overbalanced, causing me to emit an involuntary shriek of alarm.

"That was close, wasn't it, Miss Green?" said Mr Kurtz. "Your inspector almost fell and dashed his brains out!"

Eventually, after a considerable struggle, James was able to slide up the sash and climb back in through the window.

"There we are," he said. "It's not impossible for a chap to open the window from the roof. Do you ever lock this window, Mr Kurtz?"

"No. I didn't think anyone would ever be foolish enough to climb onto the roof out there."

"And you leave it open in warmer weather, you say?"

"Yes."

"That could explain how the culprit got into the museum without Geller noticing him," James said, glancing around the storeroom. "There are plenty of hiding places in here for an intruder. Is the window ever left open overnight, Mr Kurtz?"

"I like to ensure that it's closed at night, but I cannot say, with certainty, that it has been closed every night. I may have overlooked doing so on occasion."

"And it certainly wasn't locked, seeing as you felt it unnecessary to do that," said James.

"You think, Inspector, that a man gained access to this room some time during the night of the sixteenth of June and lay in wait for an opportunity to murder Richard?"

"That's exactly what I think. Has this room been thoroughly searched for clues?" asked James.

"Inspector Stroud searched it."

"Let's look again, in that case," said James. "You two start at either end of the room and I'll begin in the centre here."

I moved to one side, staying as far away from Mr Kurtz as possible, and began searching among the shelves, unsure of what I was looking for. There were many empty jars and others with contents I had no wish to look at closely. To my left was a small skeleton in a case.

"I can't see anything out of place in here," said James after a while. "What about you, Penny? Have you found anything?"

"Nothing."

"Mr Kurtz?"

"No. As I said, Chief Inspector Stroud has already searched this room."

We looked around for a little while longer before reconvening in the centre of the room.

"Can you be sure that the murderer climbed in through the window and lay in wait here, Inspector?" asked Mr Kurtz.

"I cannot be entirely sure, but neither can I disprove the theory," replied James, still looking around in case there was something he had missed.

I left the confines of the small room and walked back into the museum. *Was there a hiding place in one of the galleries above?* I walked over to the spiral staircase and some jars on a low shelf caught my eye: they appeared to contain the cross-sections of lung which Kurtz had referred to earlier. I bent down to inspect them, wincing at the darkened, diseased tissue. Then something small and glittering behind one of the jars caught my eye.

I retrieved it and was surprised to discover that it was an earring. It was a drop pendant style and appeared to be made of diamond and pearl.

"What have you there, Penny?" asked James as he and Mr Kurtz stepped out of the storeroom.

I showed him what I had found.

"Interesting," he said. "Mr Kurtz, do you have any idea how an earring might have found its way into the museum?"

"An earring, you say?"

He stepped over to look at it as I held it out in my palm.

"No," he concluded.

"You don't recognise it?"

Mr Kurtz shook his head.

"Your nurse friend," ventured James. "Has she ever visited this room?"

Mr Kurtz's pale face flushed red. "No, never," he replied curtly. "Besides, nurses don't wear earrings like that one."

"Is there any other woman you're aware of who might have entered this room?"

"None that I'm aware of."

"Are there any female medical students at the current time?"

"No, not at the moment."

"So it would be quite unusual for a woman to visit this museum."

"It would be fairly unusual, yes, although they do visit now and again. As does the occasional nurse."

"But a nurse wouldn't wear jewellery like this as a rule."

"No."

"It is a very fine earring," said James, gently lifting it from my hand and holding it up to the light to examine it more closely. "I'm surprised Inspector Stroud didn't find it, perhaps it was dropped here after his search. I shall ask around the medical school to see if anyone has reported it missing. It would be extremely useful to identify its owner, don't you think, Mr Kurtz?"

"It would indeed, Inspector. I can't think how on earth it has found its way in here."

"There's another interesting discovery I need to tell you about," said James as we left St Bartholomew's Hospital. "I've been able to match the handwriting of another of the malicious letters."

"Whose is it?" I asked. "Tell me!"

"I'm about to, Penny! The handwriting on the letter sent to Mr Edwards matches the handwriting on a letter sent to Borthwick by Jack Copeland."

"Jack Copeland?" I stopped. "Why should Jack Copeland write a letter like that?" I paused for a moment to think it over. "So Jeffrey Maynell and Jack Copeland have both been writing unpleasant things about me."

"It appears that way. But please don't take it to heart."

"It's rather difficult not to, isn't it? Why would they write so maliciously and then speak to me as if they had never done such a thing? What have I done to upset them?"

"You are trying to investigate Borthwick's suicide. I suppose they object to it."

"Mr Maynell I can understand; he's such an unpleasant man. Oh, I meant to tell you that his wife paid me a visit yesterday evening."

"Did she?"

I told James about my conversation with Lillian.

"Poor woman," he said. "She seems rather frightened of him."

"She is. And Mr Maynell must have told Mr Copeland to write the letter to Mr Edwards," I said. "Perhaps Mr Copeland is frightened of Mr Maynell There's no doubt the man is a bully."

"Did Mr Edwards uncover anything interesting about him?"

"He didn't, I'm afraid."

"But we know from Borthwick's papers that Maynell was demanding financial compensation from Borthwick for an idea he supposedly stole. I shall have to return to Maynell and ask him about that."

"Please don't tell him that his wife visited me. She would be in terrible trouble again if he found out."

"I won't, don't worry. I'll have to watch my step with him. I don't think he's a man who should be crossed."

CHAPTER 39

"Tiger!" I called out of my window that evening.

The only reply was a train letting off steam as it pulled out of Moorgate station. I peered through the dusk at the chimneys and rooftops, but there was no sign of my cat.

"Tiger!" I called again, leaning out of the window and placing a bowl of sardines on the roof tiles. It was unlike her to ignore my calls. In fact, she was usually waiting for me when I returned home each evening.

A shaky panic began to rise in my chest. I tried to quell it by reassuring myself that she had been distracted by a pigeon or another cat.

I sat down at my writing desk and returned to my work on Father's book, but despite my attempts to concentrate my eyes kept wandering up from my papers to the window in front of me.

Had I heard a miaow? Perhaps Tiger was injured.

I tried to push these thoughts away and continue with my work. But just as I began to get some words down on the page I was disturbed by a knock at my door.

"Who is it?"

"It's your sister!"

I rose up and opened the door for Eliza, who stood on the landing in a shimmering blue dress.

"I hope I'm not disturbing you, Penelope, only George and I were passing on the way back from dinner at the Mansion House and I wanted to let you know about a wonderful idea we've just had." She paused to look at me, then added, "Are you all right?"

"Tiger hasn't come home."

"Oh, don't worry about her. She's a cat."

"But she's never disappeared before."

"There's a first time for everything, Penelope."

Eliza walked into my room with a swish of satin.

"I shan't stay long, as George is waiting outside in the cab. At dinner we discussed Father's disappearance and decided that we should ask Mr Fox-Stirling to go back to Colombia to look for him again."

"You and George have decided that?"

"Yes. It makes perfect sense, doesn't it? And we'll make sure he takes a Spanish speaker with him this time."

"But isn't he about to travel to the Himalayas?"

"He is, yes. But we will need some time to raise the money. We were hoping that Mr Fox-Stirling could go out next year to search for him."

I sank down onto my bed.

"I don't know about this, Ellie. It's an awful lot of money to spend. Besides, Mr Fox-Stirling didn't find him last time, so why would he find him at the second attempt?"

"Having a Spanish translator with him would be of enormous help. And Mr Fox-Stirling knows where he's going. He found Father's hut, didn't he?"

"But it's been nine years! If Mr Fox-Stirling goes there next year it will be ten years since Father disappeared! How can he hope to discover anything more about his whereabouts?"

"If Father is still alive he has every hope!"

"And if he isn't?"

"I think we must at least try to find out, Penelope. For as long as there's hope we need to keep trying."

"But if he were still alive he would have contacted us by now. It's been so long. And if he's alive yet hasn't contacted us... Well, I suppose he has a reason for that. Perhaps he wishes to be left alone."

"He has no right to be left alone!" Eliza barked. "He has a wife and two daughters. We are entitled to know what has happened to him!"

I shrank back from my sister's anger.

"I apologise for my outburst, but I have given this matter a great deal of thought. I realise there is a possibility that he may have started a new life out there and no longer wishes to have anything to do with us, but we're his daughters!"

"I know." I felt tears pricking my eyes. "But I don't think it's possible that he could still be alive, Ellie. Sending Mr Fox-Stirling out there again would be a waste of time. Besides, I don't even like the man. If we were to go to all the trouble of raising the money I should like to choose someone different."

"But he already knows the country. Who else is as well acquainted with Colombia as he?" She sighed. "Oh, I really thought you would be supportive of this plan. George and I have just had the most pleasant meal discussing it, and I felt certain you would agree that it was a good idea. It's rather disappointing that you don't. Would you prefer to believe that Father is dead? Does that make life easier for you in some way?"

Eliza's eyes were damp, and I felt a lump rise up into my throat.

"It was a fact to which I had grown accustomed," I replied quietly.

"And so had I! I appreciate that this feels like the opening of an old wound, but we have to try, don't we? He's our father!"

"I know!" I replied irritably.

I got up from the bed and walked over to the window, hoping my cat would appear at that very moment.

"I shall give you some time to ponder the idea," said Eliza. "Perhaps I caught you rather unawares."

"Yes, you did. I'm sorry, Ellie," I said, turning to face her. "I'm rather worried about Tiger at the moment, so I'm not in the most receptive mood. I'll have a think about it."

"But she's a cat! Cats always come back. If you had children to worry about you certainly wouldn't waste time worrying about an animal in this manner. In fact, you wouldn't even have noticed she was gone."

"You're not making me feel any better, Ellie."

My sister moved toward the door. "I can see that. I should leave. Perhaps you can get in touch with me when you've thought more about what we have discussed."

"I will."

My sister closed the door behind her, and as I looked out of the window my heart felt even heavier. It was close to nightfall and the sardines on the roof lay untouched. I was unable to concentrate on my work, so I decided to go out and look for Tiger.

She had to be in trouble.

I descended the steps outside Mrs Garnett's front door.

"Tiger!" I called, scouring the street around me for the slightest movement in the dark. I strained my ears to listen out for her miaow, but all I could hear were the trains and the distant clop of horses' hooves.

I walked up and down the street calling for her, but there was no sign. I peered into the shadows of the gutter, worried that she might have fallen prey to an unforgiving carriage wheel.

Then I caught sight of a figure further up the street. I stopped and stared, my heart pounding in my ears.

It was her. The woman in grey.

"Oi!" I shouted, throwing all thought of manners aside.

The figure moved slightly in response.

"Why are you watching me?" I shouted. "What do you want?"

There was no reply, and as I watched she began to walk away from me.

"Come back!" I called out, marching after her. Although I wanted to run I was wary that doing so would cause her to sprint off again. "Have you got something to tell me?"

"Stay away!" came the reply, echoing the words she had chalked on my door.

"Why?" I called back. "What will you do to me if I don't?"

The woman broke into a run and I knew there was little use in chasing after her again. Then a horrible sickening sensation lurched in my stomach.

Had she harmed Tiger?

"Have you taken my cat?" I shouted as loudly as I could. "Have you harmed her?"

But the woman was gone.

She had taken Tiger. She had done something cruel to her.

I tried to tell myself that I was imagining it. I could accept that the woman was willing to threaten me by writing messages on the door, but I couldn't believe that she would harm a poor little animal.

She had warned me to stay away and I had ignored her. Had I paid a heavy price for my disobedience?

“Miss Green, whatever is the matter?” asked my landlady as I stood in the hallway, my face wet with tears.

“She’s done something to Tiger!” I cried.

“Who has?”

“The woman who wrote on the door. I saw her out there just now and Tiger is missing. She *never* goes missing!”

“I’m sure she has done nothing of the sort.”

“She did! I know she did! Tiger hasn’t come home!”

Mrs Garnett took me by the arm and guided me into her parlour where I had sat with Lillian Maynell just a few days before.

“Sit yourself down there, Miss Green, and I’ll fetch you some of Dr Cobbold’s Remedy.”

I sat on the chair and wiped my face with my sleeve, but still the tears continued to flow. *What had happened to Tiger?* I thought of her alone and suffering without me there to help her.

Mrs Garnett returned and poured some amber-coloured syrup from a brown bottle onto a spoon.

“Here, this will see you right.”

I opened my mouth as she spooned in the remedy; a cloying mixture of sugar and tar. As I reluctantly swallowed a sharp tingling sensation ran up my nose and across my forehead.

“Now you must sleep,” said Mrs Garnett. “Take yourself up to bed, Miss Green. Your cat will be back by the morning, I’m sure of it.”

“But that woman has taken her!”

“No one has taken Tiger. She’s out enjoying the summer

night. Cats have no loyalty, you know, much as you like to think otherwise."

"Tiger does," I said sorrowfully.

Mrs Garnett shook her head and sucked her lip. "Only because you feed her. Now, no more arguments, Miss Green. Up to bed with you."

CHAPTER 40

I endured a sleepless night and felt bereft when there was no sign of Tiger the following morning. I called at our neighbours' homes to ask whether anyone had seen her, but no one had. Mrs Garnett assured me that she would keep a lookout while I was at work.

I arrived at the newsroom to find Frederick and Mr Sherman peering out of the narrow grimy window together.

"What is it?" I asked. "I've just been out in the street, but I saw nothing untoward."

"Ah, Miss Green," said Mr Sherman. "Good morning."

We exchanged a glance. I felt there was a new understanding between us following our secret meeting.

"Has something occurred out there?" I asked.

"Not out there, no. But in here, perhaps."

He stepped away from the window and I saw that the glass had been smashed.

"Oh dear! How did that happen?" I asked as Miss Welton entered the newsroom with a dustpan and brush.

"It seems that someone decided to hurl something at us," said Mr Sherman.

My boots crunched on broken glass as I walked closer to the window.

"What?" I asked.

"This," said Frederick, holding half a brick in his hand.

He was trying to pull away some string which was wrapped around it. Attached to the string was a piece of paper.

"What's that?" I asked.

"Nothing, just rubbish," replied Frederick, tugging even harder at the string. "Miss Welton, do you have a pair of scissors?"

"I do, but I'm busy brushing up the glass at the present time," replied the secretary, who was on her knees with the dustpan and brush.

My attention was still focused on the piece of paper attached to the brick. Someone had carried out a vindictive act, and had presumably attempted to justify it in the note.

"Can I see that piece of paper, please, Frederick?" I asked.

"There's no need, Miss Green." He pulled it off the string and crumpled it into a ball.

"Show me this instant!" I shouted.

Everyone in the room stopped and stared at me.

I had surprised even myself with my outburst, but my patience was in short supply. I was worried about Tiger, and Dr Cobbold's Remedy had left me with a thick head.

"I want to see what is written on that piece of paper," I said quietly but determinedly. "Especially if it concerns me. I have seen the letters which have been written about me, and now my cat has been taken."

"Taken?" repeated Miss Welton in horror.

"Yes, by a woman who has been following me these past few days. So I demand to see what is written on that piece of paper."

Frederick glanced at Mr Sherman, as if checking for his

approval. The editor gave a slight nod as Frederick slowly held out the ball of crumpled paper for me to examine.

"It doesn't say much at all," he said. "It's just a name."

I opened out the ball of paper, confident that the name written on it would be mine.

And sure enough it was. Written in blue ink were the words: 'Miss Penny Green'.

"As I thought," I said stiffly, staring at the handwriting. "It's probably that Maynell chap again."

"The man could have killed someone!" said Mr Sherman.

"When did this happen?" I asked.

"About five minutes before you arrived," said Frederick.

He went on to describe how the half-brick had come crashing through the window while he and Edgar were sitting at their desks. It had hit my desk and bounced off onto the floor.

"We need to summon the police," said Mr Sherman. "Someone has attempted murder here this morning!"

The culprit must have been on Fleet Street as I arrived for work that morning. I tried to recall whether I had seen anyone throwing something or running away.

"Someone in the street must have seen who did it," I said.

At that moment, the newsroom door opened and a red-faced Edgar strode in.

"No, nothing," he said breathlessly. "Good morning, Miss Green."

"Have you been out searching for the person who threw the brick through the window?" I asked.

"Yes. But he got away quickly, that's for sure. I found a few people who were able to describe him to me."

"What did he look like?"

"A chap in a cap. Brown jacket. Young fellow. Ran off in the direction of St Bride's."

"Maynell must have paid him to do it," I hissed.

"Do you really think so?" asked Edgar.

"I can't think who else it could have been. He has employed someone to follow me and now my cat is missing!"

"Your cat?" asked Edgar incredulously. "What's the cat got to do with anything?"

"I don't know." I felt fresh tears in my eyes. "But Jeffrey Maynell needs to be arrested and I'm going to see to it that he is!"

I had visited James' drab, smoky office in Scotland Yard a couple of times before. As I approached his desk, various police officers strode in and out of the room carrying piles of books and papers.

"Penny!" James rose to his feet as soon as he saw me. "Is everything all right?" He was in his shirtsleeves and wore a dark tweed waistcoat.

"No, it's not." I placed my heavy carpet bag on his desk, opened it and pulled out the brick which had been thrown through the window.

"My goodness," said James. "Have you just lugged that all the way from Fleet Street?"

"I took the omnibus."

"Where's it from? Why's there a string wrapped around it?"

I showed him the note. "It was hurled through the window of our offices this morning."

"Was anybody hurt?"

"No, but they easily could have been. I want you to arrest Jeffrey Maynell, James. He has to be behind this." I told him about the young man who had reportedly thrown the brick.

"That doesn't sound like an accurate description of Maynell," said James.

"He obviously paid someone to do it!"

"Hmm, it would be rather difficult to prove that Jeffrey Maynell is responsible for this attack," said James.

"But it has to be him! He wrote the letters."

"He wrote *one* malicious letter."

"He forced Copeland to write another. He's got that woman following me about and she's taken my cat!"

"Tiger?"

"Yes!"

"Are you sure about that?"

"Tiger has vanished, James. All of this is connected, and Jeffrey Maynell is behind the whole thing."

"Well, we can certainly link him to the letter he sent me, so I can question him about that. But as for the rest—"

"There's no one else it can be, James! And I should imagine that he murdered Richard Geller, too!"

James put on his jacket. He picked up a bundle of papers from his desk and folded them into his pocket. Then he fetched his bowler hat from the hat stand.

"I was planning to go down to Repton's works this afternoon, but there's no time like the present. We must be careful, Penny. I know you think Maynell is behind this, but we can't accuse him of everything just yet. I'll speak to him about the letter and about the disagreement between him and Borthwick. Let's see where that gets us."

"He could have killed someone this morning! We need to stop him, James. And I need to know where Tiger is!"

"I know, but we must remain calm. I can't take you with me to Southwark unless you promise to keep a cool head. Patience gains the day."

"But if you arrest Maynell today he can't do anything else, can he?"

"By the sound of things, Penny, he may have other people

doing his dirty work for him. Let's go and see what he has to say for himself."

"Shall I bring the brick?"

James laughed.

"What's so funny?" I asked. "It's evidence!"

"The brick can stay here, Penny."

CHAPTER 41

"We should speak to Donald Repton first," said James as we climbed out of the cab outside the Southwark works.

"Must we?" I said. "Surely he has no idea what Jeffrey Maynell has been up to. His mind is muddled by brandy half the time."

"It's important that he knows what's going on."

"Inspector Blakely! Miss Green! Do come and sit down. To what do I owe this pleasure?"

James and I declined Mr Repton's offer of a drink and took our seats opposite him. "How's the investigation going, Blakely?"

"Progressing, sir, but not as quickly as I'd like. I wish to speak to you about two members of your staff."

"Do you indeed?"

James pulled the bundle of papers from the pocket of his jacket.

"I received a rather unpleasant letter last week," he said,

unfolding the letter which Jeffrey Maynell had sent him. "It contains rather derogatory comments about my colleague, Miss Green."

"Oh dear. Really?"

"I have the evidence here in my hand, but I hope you won't mind if I don't show you what the letter says to save Miss Green's embarrassment."

"Goodness, is it that bad?" asked Mr Repton with concern.

"It's all nonsense, of course," said James. "However, it is also—"

"I think it would be better if Mr Repton read what his colleagues have written about me," I interrupted.

"Are you sure, Penny?" asked James.

"Yes, I don't mind. It's all nonsense, as you say."

"Of course."

James passed the papers to Mr Repton, who fitted a monocle into his right eye. I felt my teeth clench as he read it, acutely aware that he was reading comments of a most personal nature about me.

"Well, that won't do at all," said Donald Repton. "Who wrote this? There's no signature."

"The sender chose to remain anonymous," said James. "That's rather typical of a coward, I'm afraid. Fortunately, I was able to identify the sender when I came across this."

He handed Donald Repton another letter.

"This was sent to Borthwick!" exclaimed Donald Repton. "And it is signed, I see. Jeffrey Maynell. I'm sorry, but I don't see the connection. I thought this was to be another unpleasant letter, but it merely discusses the patent."

"Do you not notice the similarity in the handwriting?" asked James. "It confirms that Jeffrey Maynell sent both letters."

"What? Maynell sent you that nasty letter about Miss

Green?" Mr Repton raised his eyebrows and his monocle fell out.

"Yes."

"No, there must be some mistake!" He pushed the monocle back into its place. "He would never do such a thing!"

"He already bears Miss Green a grudge, sir. However, to be completely certain I need to discuss the matter with the man himself, and I wish to make you aware that I intend to do so."

"Yes, of course." Donald Repton sat back in his chair. "If he's written that letter he must be admonished for it!"

"I have another unpleasant pairing of letters here." James unfolded the bundle of papers again. "Here is a letter written to Mr Edwards, an acquaintance of Miss Green's. Do you mind if Mr Repton reads this one as well, Penny?"

"Not at all."

Once again, I felt embarrassed that Donald Repton was to read the disparaging remarks about me. I watched his face as he read it, his brow knitting together.

"And this is another letter sent to Simon Borthwick," said James, handing it to Mr Repton. "It's rather long and there's no need to read it. The important matter is the signature at the end."

"Jack Copeland," said Donald Repton. He pulled the monocle away from his eye and stared at James. "You're telling me that Jack Copeland said those dreadful things about this pleasant lady here?"

"It certainly seems that way when you compare the handwriting,' said James.

I shifted uncomfortably in my seat. Two men had attempted to sully my name. They had once been Borthwick's persecutors and now they had turned on me.

"I am struggling to believe it," replied Donald Repton.

"You're perfectly entitled to speak to both of them, of course, but I cannot believe that it's true. There must be a plausible explanation."

"What explanation can there be other than malice?" asked James.

"I agree with you," he replied. "Perhaps the two men can clear this all up. Let me know once you're finished with them, for I should like to speak to the pair of them myself."

He turned to face me. "Miss Green, I'm struggling to understand how something as dreadful as this could have happened to you. All I can do at the present time is apologise for the upset this has caused. I do hope you haven't taken it to heart."

"Thank you, Mr Repton, and no I haven't. It's something that sometimes has to be endured in my line of work."

I could see that Mr Repton wasn't entirely convinced by my reply. It was difficult to conceal the fact that the letters had upset me greatly. His kind smile made my eyes feel watery.

"Penny, I don't think it's a good idea for you to see Jeffrey Maynell with me," said James as we made our way to Mr Maynell's office.

"Why not?"

"You know the reason. You have seen the things he wrote about you. And after the brick was thrown through your office window this morning you're understandably upset at the present time."

"I can remain calm about such matters."

"Are you sure? It's important that we keep our interview with him controlled. We cannot accuse him of throwing bricks or stealing your cat or any of the other matters which have occurred, or he will become uncooperative. We don't want to upset him. If we can keep our interview conversational we might be able to coax him into incriminating himself."

"Can we ask about the woman in grey?"

"Let's see how the conversation progresses, Penny."

CHAPTER 42

Jeffrey Maynell kept us waiting as he finished some correspondence. James and I sat silently across the desk from him, the tick of his clock on the mantelpiece almost deafening amid the silence.

Had Mr Maynell found out about his wife's evening visit to my lodgings? I hoped Lillian had managed to remain silent on the matter.

He eventually laid his pen down and regarded us coolly.

"What can I help you with, Inspector? And what's this ink-slinger doing here again?"

"There is no need to be impolite to Miss Green," responded James. "We shan't detain you for long. The matter pertains to a letter you've written."

"Which one?"

"This one here," said James, passing the letter across the desk to him.

Mr Maynell unfolded it and I watched him scowl as he read it.

"What nonsense is this, Inspector?"

"Is that your handwriting, Mr Maynell?"

"It looks similar, but it's not mine. The letter isn't even signed. How can you possibly attribute it to me?"

"It bears a remarkable resemblance to this letter, which you sent to Simon Borthwick. Even the ink is the same."

Mr Maynell read the second letter. "Yes, I recall writing this. I can vouch that this one was written by me and I have signed it. I would never send an unsigned letter, Inspector. Why on earth would you think I had sent this anonymous letter?"

"Because you appear to bear some animosity towards Miss Green."

Mr Maynell laughed. "Why should I bear Miss Green any ill will?"

"When we visited this establishment the last time you had some rather strong words for her."

"I was angry because Miss Green had arranged a secret meeting with my wife to discuss a former suitor. Any other fellow would have been equally annoyed."

"So you deny that this anonymous letter was written by you, Mr Maynell," said James, "even though the handwriting matches that of another letter you wrote?"

"Absolutely, Inspector. It is mere coincidence. Have you had a graphologist analyse these letters?"

"Not yet," replied James with a hint of awkwardness to his voice.

"May I suggest that you do so? I'm certain that you're a good detective, Inspector Blakely; however, you are clearly no expert in handwriting. You need to have these letters analysed by someone who knows what they're talking about."

"If this letter was not written by you," said James, "how do you explain why someone has gone to the trouble of forging your handwriting?"

"I don't believe anyone has attempted to imitate it, Inspector. It's merely coincidence, as I have already said!

There is nothing to connect me with that letter other than a passing similarity in the handwriting. That is all, Inspector. I would thank you to trouble me with this no longer."

"Can you explain your request to Simon Borthwick for financial compensation in return for an idea that he supposedly stole?" asked James.

"Oh, that." Maynell sat back in his chair and interlocked his fingers. "It's rather long and complicated, and it has nothing to do with this letter you've shown me."

"The tone of your correspondence to Borthwick on the matter suggests that there was a significant disagreement between the two of you."

"Not significant, Inspector. He borrowed my idea to use a filament made of carbonised paper; an idea which he had begun to pass off as his own."

"But his patent used a carbonised cotton filament, didn't it?" I said. "I found a letter accusing him of stealing that idea from an inventor named Hugo Bannister."

"We are always attempting to find filaments which burn for longer," replied Maynell. "And as soon as someone else found a more suitable material Borthwick was quick to adopt it."

"Without giving credit where it was due?" asked James.

"Exactly," said Maynell. "I did not consider the disagreement between us significant, but I was rather tired of his behaviour and decided that demanding financial disbursement would dissuade the man from continuing in the same vein. The chap never had an original idea of his own."

"Do you think Borthwick might have interpreted your letters to him discussing this matter as persecution?" asked James.

Mr Maynell laughed coldly. "Probably! It wasn't persecution, though, was it? I find it impossible to believe that a few letters mentioning the idea he had stolen could have driven him to his death."

"You were first introduced and became attracted to your wife while she was courting Simon Borthwick, is that right?" I ventured.

Maynell's eyes flashed angrily. If James hadn't been sitting next to me I should have felt fearful of him.

"Is that what she told you?" he snapped.

"I deduced it," I replied as calmly as possible.

"There was nothing dishonourable about my behaviour, if that's what you think. I cannot deny that I was drawn to Lillian, and when I heard rumours about the man – rumours which I dare not repeat – I decided that she needed saving."

"I'm interested in the rumours you mention, as it happens," said James. "What were they?"

"You will hear nothing of them from me, Inspector! I suggest you continue with your own investigating if you truly wish to find out."

"Simon Borthwick may have felt that you were persecuting him because you had contested his ideas and then married Lillian," I suggested.

He shook his head, then fixed me with his pale gaze. "If that's what the man thought, then God help him. If Borthwick's mind was so disturbed as to view matters in that way it's no wonder he took his own life, is it? What could I have done otherwise? Left Lillian to her unhappy fate? Allowed him to continue stealing other people's work? What else could I have done with regard to this matter? The man was troubled. He wasn't anything like the genius everyone believed him to be. Can we leave this conversation alone now? I'm tired of it, I really am, and so is Lillian. It's beginning to affect her health. She is currently nursing a mild fever, and I can only hope that it doesn't progress into anything worse."

I remembered how soaked through she had been on the evening of her visit. I sincerely hoped that hadn't been the cause of her illness.

"Of course, Mr Maynell," said James. "Another quick question, though, if I may. A brick was thrown through a window at the *Morning Express* offices this morning. Do you know anything about that?"

Mr Maynell's expression turned to one of incredulity.

"A *brick*, Inspector? Do you honestly think I would throw a brick through a window?" He stood to his feet. "Do I look the brick-hurling type?"

"No," James quickly replied. "Finally, do you mind if I ask where you were on the morning of the seventeenth of June?"

I saw Mr Maynell's fist clench involuntarily. "That was the day Borthwick died, wasn't it? I was at the Crystal Palace, but then you already knew that."

"You were there all morning?"

"Yes. I got there at about ten o'clock," he replied curtly. "You can ask my wife if you have any doubt. I really don't understand your line of questioning, Inspector. You seem extremely muddled. First you accuse me of sending you a strange letter, and next you suggest that I was somehow persecuting Borthwick. Then there are questions about a brick and my whereabouts on the day Borthwick shot himself! Where is this all leading, Inspector? What's going on?"

"I wish I knew," replied James. "Thank you for your time, Mr Maynell."

"We didn't ask him about the woman who has been following me," I hissed to James once we had left Jeffrey Maynell's office. "Or about Tiger!"

"You saw how his patience had run out, Penny."

"But what if he asked that woman to follow me? And what about Tiger?"

James stopped. "You really think Maynell would steal a cat?"

He noticed my lower lip wobble slightly.

"I'm sorry," he added hurriedly. "I didn't intend to sound dismissive. I know how important Tiger is to you. A lot has happened over the past few weeks, and it wouldn't do us any good to level all of it at Maynell in one go. Perhaps he is responsible, perhaps he's not. There's a great deal more investigating to do."

"Do you believe him about the letter?" I asked. "Do you believe anything he said?"

"I'm not sure that I did," replied James. "Either the man is innocent, or he is well practised at shaking off accusations."

"Which leaves us no closer to the truth!" I hissed.

"Penny, I asked you to remain calm, didn't I?"

"It's rather difficult to do so!"

"I know, but you must. Will you be able to stay calm while we speak to Jack Copeland, or is it best that you occupy yourself with something else?"

"I *will* be calm!" I snarled.

James watched me for a moment, then his lips formed a smile. "I do find you comical at times, Penny."

"I fail to see what could be funny about all this!"

"You are when you're seething with anger but claiming to be calm. I asked you to keep a cool head, didn't I?"

"If you refer to a *cool head* again my temper will be lost for good!"

"Can I trust you to conduct yourself with decorum when we speak to Jack Copeland?"

"Of course you can trust me," I replied, marching off ahead of him. "Let's get it over with."

CHAPTER 43

Jack Copeland occupied himself with a tall piece of apparatus holding various vessels connected by several lengths of tubing.

"Oh, it's you again, Inspector," he said glumly. "I really don't have any time for you, I'm afraid."

"May I ask what you're doing, Mr Copeland?" asked James.

"Creating a vacuum with a Sprengel pump."

"How fascinating. May I ask what substance that is?" James pointed to a container filled with a thick, shiny liquid.

"Mercury. Each drop which travels down this tube here takes a pocket of air with it, gradually reducing the air pressure within the bulb I've attached. Eventually, a vacuum will be created in the bulb."

"Impressive," said James. "I think I should have quite liked to be a scientist."

"But instead you are a police officer," replied Copeland, his long moustache twitching. "What do you want? I'm rather busy."

"The vacuum takes a little while to develop, does it not?"

asked James. "That will allow you a short amount of time to examine a letter I have here."

"What letter?" asked Copeland, suddenly growing more interested.

James handed the paper to him and I looked away as he read it, trying not to think about the words it contained.

"Who the devil is Mr Edwards?" asked Copeland.

"An acquaintance of Miss Green's," said James.

"I see. The author of this letter doesn't think a great deal of Miss Green, does he?"

"He's trying to stir up trouble," said James. "Do you recognise the handwriting, Mr Copeland?"

"I'm afraid not. This letter isn't signed. Why are you showing it to me?"

"You say that you don't recognise the handwriting, but it bears a remarkable resemblance to your own, does it not?"

Jack Copeland peered at the letter more closely. "Now you come to mention it, I suppose it does. But it is not my handwriting, I can assure you of that."

James showed Jack Copeland the letter he had written to Borthwick. "When you compare these two letters you can see that there is barely anything to differentiate the handwriting on either of them," said James. "The person who wrote one must have written the other. Can you see that now?"

"When you put it like that, Inspector, yes, I can see it. But surely it's nothing more than chance. Why would I write an anonymous letter to a man I've never heard of about a woman with whom I have had only the briefest of acquaintances?"

"You tell me, Mr Copeland."

"Now hold on, Inspector!" His bulbous eyes glared at James. "You cannot possibly think that I wrote this!"

"The handwriting is identical to yours, Mr Copeland."

"It is similar, Inspector, not identical. You can't just march in here throwing wild accusations around without any evidence. There is no proof at all that I wrote this letter. And there's no motive, either. Why on earth would I do such a thing?"

"Because Miss Green has been trying to find out who Simon Borthwick's persecutors were, and in doing so she has angered people who must be worried that she is getting closer to the truth."

"You think that I persecuted Simon Borthwick?" He shoved the letter back into James' hands.

"My mind is not yet made up on the matter, Mr Copeland."

"But you're considering it? What nonsense! He was a colleague of mine, and I respected him. We were friends."

"Where were you early in the morning of the seventeenth of June?"

"What does that have to do with anything?"

"Please answer my question."

"Now hold on a moment. What are you trying to infer? I think I need to take the advice of a lawyer before answering any more of your questions."

"If you require a lawyer, Mr Copeland, that suggests to me that you may have something to hide."

"What on earth are you talking about? Every man has the right to seek a lawyer's advice whether he's guilty of something or not! Do you really take the suggestion of a lawyer to be an admission of guilt? How preposterous! And you call yourself a detective!"

"I only enquired as to your whereabouts on the morning of the seventeenth of June, Mr Copeland."

"Why that day?"

"It was the day on which Mr Borthwick took his own life."

"Why, I travelled to the Crystal Palace of course! Where else could I possibly have been, Inspector?"

"I don't know. Hence the question."

"Are you trying to be smart with me?"

"Not at all, Mr Copeland. I am simply looking for an explanation as to how and why a malicious letter was written in your handwriting."

"You're not the only one! I should also like to know the answer to that question. If someone is trying to frame me for something I wish to get to the bottom of it as soon as possible!"

"An acquaintance of Mr Borthwick's, Richard Geller, was murdered inside the museum at St Bartholomew's medical school on the morning of the seventeenth of June. Were you aware of that?"

"No, but I suppose I'm guilty of that too, am I? A letter which resembles my handwriting is sent to someone I have never met and that implicates me in the murder of Borthwick's friend?"

"Not at all, Mr Copeland. You're the one making assumptions now."

"So why all the questions, Inspector? Are you attempting to manipulate me into divulging something?"

"No, I have finished with my questions for now. Thank you for your time, Mr Copeland."

"You're finished, are you? So you walk into my laboratory and rile me as if I were a bear to be poked with a stick." Copeland jabbed his finger angrily at James as he spoke. I had never seen him so animated before. "Well, let me tell you something, Inspector. This bear can roar if he needs to. And he can do far worse than that if necessary!"

James glanced at me and I could tell he was suggesting that we quit the room.

We turned to walk towards the door.

"That's it is it, Inspector?" Copeland called after us. "When shall I look forward to your next visit?"

James escorted me out of the laboratory without giving a reply.

"Well, that's two men angered in one morning," commented James as we left the works and made our way towards Blackfriars Bridge. "Who shall we rile next?"

I laughed. "What do you think? Was Copeland telling the truth?"

"He seemed to be. But the letters do appear to be in his and Maynell's handwriting. Both men claim it's a matter of chance or coincidence, but I need to have the letters analysed by a graphologist as soon as possible. We need to be able to prove that they wrote them."

The wharves were busy with steamboats and barges as we began our walk across the bridge. Sails flapped in the wind and trains clattered over the railway bridge alongside us. Clouds raced across the sun, casting brief shadows over the city.

"I need to finish my article on the statue France is gifting America tomorrow," I said. "Shall we meet at the Museum Tavern this evening to discuss Maynell's prospective arrest? He cannot carry on like this and get away with it. And neither can Copeland."

"I should like to, Penny, but I'm afraid I can't this evening."

"Do you have other plans?"

"I'm afraid so." He avoided my gaze.

"What are they?"

"Only dull plans, I'm afraid."

"I'm still interested to hear about them."

"I'm sure you wouldn't be."

"You might be surprised."

James turned to look at me, his expression weary. "You wouldn't be interested, Penny."

"Now I am extremely interested. We've been discussing your dull plans long enough for me to wonder what they could possibly be."

"Just wedding discussions."

"Oh, I see."

"There you go. I knew you wouldn't be interested."

"Perhaps we could meet at the tavern tomorrow evening instead?"

"I'm afraid that won't be possible either."

I felt puzzled. James was usually keen to meet me at the Museum Tavern to discuss whichever case we were working on.

"You're discussing wedding plans again tomorrow evening?" I asked.

We stopped midway across the bridge. A warm breeze brought with it the dank smell of the Thames.

James' eyes were fixed on a steamboat, which made its way downriver towards us.

"Penny... I'm not sure it's proper that I meet you at the Museum Tavern at all."

"Not proper? But we meet there to discuss our work. You've never said anything about it being improper before. I don't understand. Why should you no longer wish to meet me there?"

"I do!" He turned to face me again. "I do wish to meet you there, Penny. But... something has been said."

"By whom? Who has said something?"

"It doesn't matter."

"Of course it matters! Who told you that you shouldn't meet me there?"

"The person in question hasn't told me, as such. It has merely been implied."

"The future Mrs Blakely?"

He said nothing, but instead held my gaze. I realised my suggestion had been correct and tried to remain impassive.

"I don't see why she should prevent you from meeting with a colleague to discuss work. You're not even married to her yet."

"She views it differently."

"How does she view it?"

"To be honest with you, Penny, I'm not entirely sure. But there is some discomfort around the fact that you and I occasionally meet at a public house."

"Does she think I'm about to steal you away?"

James laughed awkwardly. "Of course not!"

"Then I still don't understand."

The truth was that I did understand. The future Mrs Blakely was concerned about James' relationship with me and I knew that she had every right to be. Perhaps I wanted to hear him admit it.

"It's just a notion she has at the present time," said James. "I'm sure it will die away in due course, but for the time being I think it best if Charlotte feels satisfied that I am not meeting with you at a public house."

He didn't often refer to her by name. I stared back at him, trying to ignore the tightening sensation in my throat.

"Are you saying that we shouldn't meet at all?"

"No, I'm not saying that. We have to meet during the course of our work, don't we?"

"But no more meetings at the Museum Tavern?"

"Perhaps not until the notion—"

"Forget about the *notion*," I said impatiently. "She doesn't want us to meet one another, and in a few months' time she will be your wife. She's already beginning to tighten her grip on you. I suppose I should have expected that. She's perfectly entitled to, of course. I don't even know why I'm surprised." I sighed. "But for some strange reason I am."

"I don't like this either, Penny," he replied quietly.

"It's a choice you have made, James! No one is forcing you to marry her."

I turned away from him and continued my walk along the bridge. I half hoped that he would call out or catch up with me.

But he didn't.

CHAPTER 44

Tiger's tin bowl sat empty by the stove as I got dressed the following morning. I turned to look at my bed, hopeful that I would see her sleeping there, but her favourite place was vacant. A tear ran down my cheek, swiftly followed by another.

Footsteps on the staircase up to my room prompted me to remove my spectacles and quickly dry my tears with the sleeve of my blouse.

"Telegram for you, Miss Green!" called Mrs Garnett.

I hoped she would push the envelope under the door, but she appeared to be waiting for me to open it.

I rubbed at my eyes, hoping my landlady wouldn't notice that I had been crying, and forced a smile onto my face.

"Good grief. Are you all right?" she asked as I opened the door.

"Of course," I replied with as much cheer as I could muster. But my voice cracked and the look of concern on her face gave rise to an enormous sob.

"You're certainly not all right."

My landlady took my arm, led me over to my bed and made me sit down.

"You need some rest; you've exhausted yourself. I'll be back in a moment with Dr Cobbold's Remedy."

"There's no need, Mrs Garnett!" I called out after her, but she was gone.

I wiped my eyes again and turned my attention to the envelope my landlady had placed next to me on the bed. Opening it, I saw that the telegram was from Mr Sherman.

Another unpleasant incident at office. Best to stay away for few days.

Had another brick been thrown through the window? Or something worse? Why hadn't he given any further detail about the unpleasant incident?

"Oh no! You look even worse now, Miss Green," said Mrs Garnett as she returned to the room. "Did the telegram bring bad news?"

"I have been advised not to go to my office," I said weakly.

"That's a good thing. You need a few days of rest," replied Mrs Garnett as she poured out a spoonful of the thick brown syrup.

"I don't need any rest," I protested. "I need to find Tiger!"

"She'll come back. She's a cat."

"She won't. They've taken her!"

"Who's taken her?"

"The woman who wrote on the door."

"I find that hard to believe." The spoon of remedy was poised by my mouth. "Open wide."

"I don't like this medicine, Mrs Garnett, and I'm not convinced that it does anything of use."

"Open!"

I felt my face crumple as I swallowed the syrup.

"Now you must sleep."

"What will happen if they don't want me to go back at all?"

"Who?"

"The newspaper. What if Mr Sherman decides he doesn't want me to write for him any more? You saw what it was like when it happened before."

"I remember that all right. What does the telegram say?"

I showed it to her.

"This doesn't imply that you're to lose your job; it only asks you to stay away for a few days. What could the unpleasant incident have been?"

"I have no idea. I only wish that I knew."

"What was the previous one?"

"What previous one?"

"It says here *another* unpleasant incident. Which suggests to me that there was one before it."

"Someone threw a brick through the newsroom window."

"That is indeed unpleasant. But why does it mean that you must stay away?"

"Because the brick was intended for me. It had my name attached to it."

Mrs Garnett gasped. "Whatever have you landed yourself in this time, Miss Green?"

"I don't know, but all of this has happened since I started taking an interest in the cases of Simon Borthwick and Richard Geller."

"Who are they?"

"Two people who appear to have died unnecessarily. I shouldn't have become involved."

"It certainly sounds like you shouldn't have if people are

throwing bricks at you through the window. They'd better not throw bricks through *my* windows!"

"I hope they won't, Mrs Garnett."

"You *hope* they won't? Is that all the reassurance you can give me? That woman wrote on my door, didn't she?"

"I'm sorry, Mrs Garnett. Please don't ask me to stay away from my home as well!"

"I don't understand exactly what it is you do, Miss Green, but I can see that it has involved you in a whole host of troubles. I don't really know how you manage it. As the good book says: *He that passeth by, and meddleth with strife belonging not to him, is like one that taketh a dog by the ears.*"

"But I'm a news reporter, Mrs Garnett. It's my job to meddle with strife!"

"You'll meddle yourself into an early grave if you're not careful."

"If I don't find out who caused the deaths of Simon Borthwick and Richard Geller the people responsible will get away with it. And they could do the same to someone else."

"Perhaps they'll do the same to you!"

I stared at Mrs Garnett and a shiver ran down my back. "Please don't say that."

"Whoever is responsible must be an evil person. Did you ever find out who wrote that letter to me?"

"Not yet."

"And what is your police officer friend doing about all this?"

"He's a detective. And he's doing his best, but it's difficult to prove anything against these people."

"That's because they're clever. They know what they're doing. You, on the other hand, do not. You need to stop this investigative work. Look what happened to the two unfortunate chaps who crossed these people."

"I'm not going to die, Mrs Garnett."

"How do you know that?"

The truth was that I couldn't be certain. The sickening sensation returned as I realised that Simon Borthwick had taken his own life because doing so had been preferable to living in purgatory.

"I wonder..." I found myself murmuring.

"Wonder what?"

"Was Richard murdered to punish Simon?"

"How would I know?"

"It was a rhetorical question, Mrs Garnett, but it has certainly made me think."

"You need to stop thinking, go back to bed and get some sleep. You saw your editor's telegram, and it was clearly written on my door. *Stay away.* How long will it take for you to heed the advice you've been given?"

CHAPTER 45

Miss Green

I was both distressed and saddened to learn of the despicable letters penned by Mr Maynell and Mr Copeland. I am writing to inform you that I have dismissed both men from the employment of Repton, Borthwick and Company, and wish to offer my sincere apologies for the distress they have caused you.

Respectfully,
Mr Donald Repton

I smiled as I read the letter. Despite the men's denials it seemed Mr Repton was convinced of their guilt. It was an honourable move and rather a brave one. Surely Jack Copeland had an important job to do at the Kensington

Court development. *Could he be easily replaced?* I folded the letter and felt pleased to have gained Mr Repton's support.

This was the second day I had stayed at home, having received no further word from Mr Sherman about the latest incident at the office. For the remainder of the morning I sat at my writing desk and watched the sun's passage over the rooftops of London. I couldn't remember the last time I had spent such a long time doing so little. All the while I hoped that I would hear a miaow and see Tiger jump into view on the roof tiles in front of me. But she never came.

I spent some time writing about my father's travels in Colombia. The words were beginning to come a little more easily and I found myself warming to the idea that Mr Fox-Stirling might undertake another search for him. It seemed preferable to taking no action at all.

My conversation with James on Blackfriars Bridge kept returning to my mind. *What exactly had Charlotte said to him about me? How had she guessed that we harboured feelings for one another?*

I tried to imagine how James felt about the situation. *Was he saddened that his fiancée sought to put an end to our friendship? Or was he prepared to accept it?* Perhaps I would never understand how he felt about it. I had to tell myself that one thing was clear. James had been forced to choose between me and his fiancée.

My little room grew hotter as the heat of the day intensified. I became restless and felt the need to venture outside. I wanted to talk to someone. I couldn't bear to sit around waiting for Tiger when I felt sure she would not return.

Mr Sherman didn't want me to attend the office but there was another place I could visit.

"Miss Green!" whispered Mr Edwards with a grin. "It's been a little while since I last saw you. How are you? You look rather tired if you don't mind me saying so."

"I am. My cat is still missing."

"Still? I didn't realise she had been missing."

"Yes, it's been three days now. I don't think she'll ever come back now."

He held out his hand as if to pat me on the shoulder, but seemed to think better of it.

"I'm sure she will come back, Miss Green. Cats often do this sort of thing."

"That's what everyone has said, but she has never done anything of the kind before."

"Perhaps it's the weather. We've had an unusually long spell of high pressure. Animals can react in strange ways to the weather."

"Perhaps."

Having taken a seat in the reading room I realised how hot the air was inside. Once again, I felt the need to move about.

"It's no good. I can't concentrate in here," I said.

I suddenly felt tearful again. *Perhaps it would have been better to remain in my room.*

"Miss Green, you don't look very well. Perhaps a short walk would do you good."

"I think it would."

"If you can bear with me for a few moments I could accompany you."

Mr Edwards and I walked around Russell Square. Birdsong rang out from the trees and two young children played on the grass with their nanny.

There was something rather calming about Mr Edwards' company. He had a soft, pleasant voice and seemed relaxed in my company. I no longer spent all our time together worrying that he might propose marriage to me at any moment.

We passed the Duke of Bedford statue and continued on our way.

"Has there been any progress with regard to all this malicious letter business?" he asked.

I told him about James' conversations with Mr Maynell and Mr Copeland.

"They most certainly wrote the letters," I said. "And yet they deny everything!"

"Unpleasant men indeed," said Mr Edwards. "I should like to have a word with them myself. Fancy writing such unkind things about a lady!"

"I don't care about the letters," I replied. "I just want Tiger to come home."

"She will; I feel sure of it, Miss Green. She is probably engaged in asserting her territorial rights, as is common among the Felidae."

"Felidae?"

"The cat family. Subdivided into the Pantherinae and Felinae groups. Your Tiger is one of the latter, though her name is synonymous with the former!"

"Is that so?"

We walked around the perimeter of the square once and then began a second lap. A child's nurse passed us pushing a perambulator, and behind her walked a woman in a plain grey dress. A large black hat partly shielded her face.

I glanced at her as we walked past and thought it unusual that she was looking so directly at me. All the while Mr Edwards was talking about cats. It was only once we had passed her that I felt a sickening lurch in my stomach. I stopped.

"It's her!" I said.

"Who?" asked Mr Edwards.

I spun around to see the woman running away from us. She had removed her hat and was holding it in one hand as she sprinted off.

"The woman in grey! I think she took Tiger!"

"She took her? Are you sure?"

"She keeps following me!"

I began to run after her.

"Miss Green!" Mr Edwards cried out from behind me.

"I need to catch her this time!" I called back.

But as I ran after the retreating figure I knew that, as before, I had no hope of catching her. My legs felt heavy and my breathing was constricted by my corset. As I slowed to a walk a figure ran past me at a great pace.

"Hold this!" came the instruction as he flung a bowler hat over his shoulder for me to catch.

Mr Edwards' arms and legs moved like pistons as he sprinted along the path. People dodged and dived out of his way, appearing as surprised by his speed as I was.

The woman in grey was at the far end of the park. She must have heard the pounding of Mr Edwards' feet, for she turned and saw him closing in on her. Apparently unfazed, she darted toward the edge of the park and vaulted over the wrought iron fence in one swift move.

I blinked, not wholly convinced that I had just seen a woman perform such a manoeuvre while wearing skirts. But the vault did nothing to deter Mr Edwards. He performed the same action and the pair vanished from my view.

I ran to catch up, but there was no sign of them by the time I reached the fence. I dropped my carpet bag and Mr Edwards' hat onto the other side of the fence and managed to slowly clamber over it, feeling rather foolish and conspicuous as I did so.

I crossed the road and peered along the stretch of large

houses which lined Upper Bedford Place. There was no sign of Mr Edwards there.

I continued on to the next street, Woburn Place, which was busy with traffic. I felt sure that I saw a running figure up ahead. Then I saw the woman's black hat lying on the ground, so I picked it up. It was made from black silk and had a bow wrapped around it.

I ran as best as I could with my bag and two hats, but as I reached the junction with Great Coram Street I could see no one running on ahead of me. Unless Mr Edwards and the woman in grey had run exceptionally fast, they must have turned off somewhere. The only other turning I could see was a small lane between the large terraced homes which led to the mews.

I ran through the entrance to the mews and along the uneven cobbles.

"Help!" I heard a woman's voice call out.

I turned into the mews on my left, where horses were hanging their heads over stable doors and chickens pecked at the gaps between the cobblestones. At the far end of the mews I saw Mr Edwards clinging to the arm of the woman in grey. She was trying to pull herself away.

"Robbery!" she shouted.

A stable lad appeared, followed by another. They immediately set themselves upon Mr Edwards.

"No!" I called out, running up to them. "It's not a robbery! He is not harming her. Leave him alone!"

Mr Edwards tried to duck the stable boys' blows while still clinging steadfastly to the woman's arm.

"Stop hitting him!" I shouted. "Everybody stop!"

The stable lads paused to stare at me and I held out the woman's hat. She snatched it and glared at me with dark eyes. She looked twenty-five or so in my estimation.

"Get him off me," she ordered as if Mr Edwards were a dog and I were his owner.

"You'll run away again if he lets go," I replied. "Who are you?"

She ignored my question.

"What's goin' on 'ere?" asked one of the stable lads.

"Fetch a police officer," I replied.

"I ain't fetchin' no one till yer tell us what's goin' on," he said.

"Ow!" said the woman as Mr Edwards held tightly to her arm.

"Who are you?" he asked her.

"Let go. Yer hurtin' 'er!" said the stable lads, who looked as though they were about to start beating Mr Edwards again.

"Hold on, Mr Edwards!" I called to him. "I'll go and fetch a police officer to place her under arrest."

I turned to summon help but was confronted by a small crowd wearing quizzical expressions. As I did my best to run around them I stumbled upon a police constable.

CHAPTER 46

"She's been following me for several days!" I explained to the dour police constable in the small, airless room at the police station. "And I think she's stolen my cat."

"Do you know who she is?" he asked.

"No! That's why Mr Edwards chased after her, so we could find out! She runs too swiftly for me to catch her. Has she told you who she is?"

"Not me personally."

I sighed. "Can I ask you *again* to please send a telegram to Inspector James Blakely at Scotland Yard. He will be able to deal with this matter. He knows this woman has been following me."

"I'll have to let Inspector Rigby decide whether that's a good idea or not."

"Tell him to do it!" I demanded. "And then this whole mess will be sorted out for good!"

An hour later I was permitted to sit at a table with Mr Edwards. The dour police constable sat with us, as did

Inspector Rigby: a large man with heavy jowls, black whiskers and unblinking eyes. He scribbled copious notes onto several sheets of paper.

James had also joined us, though there wasn't a chair available for him to sit on. He paced the room and I tried to pretend that he didn't look handsome in his smart grey suit. Our conversation on Blackfriars Bridge weighed heavily on my mind. I knew I had to accept that he had chosen Charlotte instead of me, but I felt a twinge of sadness whenever I looked at him.

"I have never been arrested before," said Mr Edwards. "Do I need to find myself a lawyer?"

"There will be no need for that," said James. "We'll have the charges dropped and get you out of here as soon as possible."

"We'll see about that," retorted Inspector Rigby.

"Mr Edwards was merely helping Miss Green," said James. "That woman has been pestering her for a number of days now. When will you allow me to question her?"

"There is no need for you to do so."

"I'm afraid there is, Inspector Rigby. There is a connection here with the murder of Richard Geller at St Bartholomew's Hospital and I am currently investigating that case."

"Doesn't St Bartholomew's fall under the jurisdiction of the City of London police?"

"It does, but the commissioner was personally asked by the victim's father, an important Rabbi, to have the case investigated by the Yard."

"You mention a connection between that murder and Mr Edwards' attack on an innocent woman. What is the connection?"

"I shall be extremely happy to sit down with you later today to explain the situation to you, Inspector Rigby," replied James. "But in the meantime, I must ask that you allow my good friends here to leave and grant me fifteen minutes with the woman in question."

"I don't wish to discuss this in detail with you here, Inspector Blakely. Please come into my office so we can continue the debate."

The two inspectors left the room, leaving us alone with the dour police constable.

"How are you?" I asked Mr Edwards. "Did the stable lads hurt you?"

"Oh no," he replied gently touching a painful-looking bruise on his cheekbone. "Not much, anyway."

"I had no idea you could run so fast," I said. "It was quite astonishing to witness."

He blushed. "I was the hundred-yard flat race champion at university. I like to keep it up where possible, and I'm glad I did as it meant that we finally caught her."

"Yes, you did. Thank you, Mr Edwards. We'll be able to find out who she is now and put a stop to all this unpleasantness."

❧

"Her name is Miss Maria Forsyth and she denies ever having followed you," said James when he and Inspector Rigby returned to the room a short while later. "She says she has no idea who you are."

"What nonsense!" I leapt up from my seat. "You saw her following me, didn't you, Mr Edwards?"

"I saw her pass us in Russell Square," he replied.

"Exactly! She was following me!"

"Well, she was walking towards us if we're to be precise," corrected Mr Edwards.

"But she looked at me. You saw the look she gave me, didn't you?"

"Actually, the first thing that drew my attention was that you began chasing after her, Miss Green. Are you sure she's the woman who has been following you?"

"Of course she is!"

I felt my stomach flip with anger as I noticed a sceptical glance pass between Mr Edwards and James.

"If she's innocent, why did she run away?" I snapped. "You saw how quickly she scarpered and the way she vaulted over that fence! She was acting suspiciously and she didn't want to be caught!"

"That's a good point," said Mr Edwards. "She didn't half move. Have you encountered Miss Forsyth before, Inspector Blakely?"

"No, though Penny has mentioned her to me a few times."

"Can I speak with her?" I appealed to Inspector Rigby.

He sucked the air in through his teeth as he gave this some thought.

"Please?" I asked. "I only wish to know who she is."

"We know who she is," replied the Inspector. "She's Miss Maria Forsyth, and she appears to have done nothing wrong."

I snorted. "I disagree with that!"

"This gentleman, however," Inspector Rigby gestured toward Mr Edwards, "chased after the poor woman and manhandled her in Woburn Mews."

"Only because I asked him to, Inspector," I said. "I take full responsibility for his actions."

"It's a shame the chap can't take responsibility for himself," the inspector replied. "Do you do everything Miss Green asks of you Mr Edwards?"

"I think I probably do," he replied.

James rubbed his brow, seemingly bemused by this remark.

"However, Miss Green did not ask me to chase after Miss Forsyth," continued Mr Edwards. "I merely did so because I could see that Miss Green wished for her to be apprehended."

"If you let me speak to Miss Forsyth," I continued, "perhaps I can explain to her why Mr Edwards and I pursued her."

"Very well," replied Inspector Rigby. "But the woman is keen to leave the station and I have found no reason to hold her here any longer. You may have five minutes with her, and I shall be present throughout."

Inspector Rigby escorted me into the room where Miss Forsyth was waiting.

"When can I leave this place, Inspector?" she asked as we entered the room.

Then she saw me and curled her lip. There was no doubt in my mind that she was the woman in grey.

"Miss Green would like to speak to you for a few minutes, Miss Forsyth," said the inspector. "And then you can be on your way."

"What do you want?" she asked me coldly.

Her expression was haughty for someone so young. Her grey cotton dress, buttoned up to her throat, was trimmed with dark lace. Her black hat lay on the table in front of her and my eyes were drawn to the pair of earrings which glittered in her ears.

I immediately thought of the earring I had found inside the medical school museum.

"I want to know why you're following me," I said.

"Why would I follow you?" she replied with a seemingly confused expression.

"I saw you in the reading room and after that at the theatre. You were watching me on both occasions. And then you waited for me outside my home and chalked the words *Stay Away* on my landlady's front door. After that you followed me to Berkeley Square and I chased after you, but you escaped."

A smile slowly spread across Miss Forsyth's face as I spoke. "I have no idea what you're talking about. I don't even know who you are."

"You're lying!" I retorted.

"Now, now, Miss Green," said Inspector Rigby. "There is no need for anyone to lose their temper."

"Someone asked you to follow me," I said to Miss Forsyth, ignoring the inspector's admonition. "Who was it?"

The smile remained on her face. "It's clear to me and to the police that you have mistaken me for someone else."

"No, I haven't. I recognise you. And it is no coincidence that you were in Russell Square today."

"I was walking to my sister's house in Gordon Square when your uncouth friend decided to chase me."

"So why did you run away?"

"I was frightened! I didn't know what he was planning to do to me!"

Inspector Rigby glared at me as if to ascertain why I wasn't satisfied with this explanation.

"Where's my cat?" I asked.

"Your *cat*?" She laughed. "How would I know anything about a cat?"

"You took her!" I snarled.

Her laughter rang in my ears and I felt my fist clench as I fought the urge to strike her.

"Inspector, this woman is deluded!" chuckled Miss Forsyth. "I hope you intend to commit her to Bedlam."

I lunged towards her with no idea what I would do if I got

close enough. Inspector Rigby grabbed my arm and pushed me back.

"That's quite enough, ladies. Miss Green, leave this room immediately."

Anger boiled in my chest as he led me away.

"She's lying!" I said to him. "Everything she has said is a lie!"

"That may be so," he replied. "But we have no evidence to support your claims."

"So in the meantime you intend to arrest my friend, Mr Edwards, who has done nothing wrong!"

"No, he won't be arrested," replied Inspector Rigby as we walked back toward the others. "Miss Forsyth has graciously said that she does not wish to press charges."

"Miss Forsyth doesn't wish to press charges because she was up to no good in the first place!" I fumed as I walked back across Russell Square towards the British Museum with James and Mr Edwards. "Did you ask her about the earring we found at the museum, James?"

"Not on this occasion, but we have a record of her name and address now, so we can ask her about it later if necessary."

"If necessary? I think it rather essential."

"Penny, there's nothing to suggest that she has any connection at all to Richard Geller's murder."

"Not yet, but it's worth asking, don't you think?"

"I suppose it is."

I sighed. "I feel as though we have missed an opportunity to challenge her properly."

"Inspector Rigby was rather protective of her," said James.

"He seemed to view her as the victim of that whole business today."

"I shouldn't have grappled with her in that manner," added Mr Edwards with deep shame.

"What else could you have done?" I asked. "You did the right thing, Mr Edwards. Sadly, I cannot prove that she's the same woman who has been following me, and it seems that no one believes me, anyway."

"I believe you, Miss Green," said Mr Edwards.

"As do I, Penny," added James.

"Well it didn't seem that way at the police station!" I retorted. "I saw the look you gave each other."

"What look?" asked James.

"A look of exasperation."

"We did no such thing!" said Mr Edwards.

"You did so!" I replied. "You both say you believe me to keep me happy, but I don't think either of you actually does."

"That's not true," said James. "I understand you're upset about Tiger, but it's not fair to suggest that we don't believe you. We both wish to help as much as we possibly can."

"You cannot help me any further, James. The future Mrs Blakely has decreed it."

"Now come on, Penny. That's unfair." James stopped.

"Decreed what?" Mr Edwards asked, also drawing to a halt. "What's unfair? And what does it have to do with the future Mrs Blakely?"

"Ask James," I replied, walking on without them.

CHAPTER 47

"Miss Green! What brings you here at this hour?"

Mr Sherman's housekeeper had shown me into his study, which had crimson wallpaper and was as untidy as his office at the *Morning Express*. It was the first time I had visited my editor's home in Holborn and I could see that he was surprised and uneasy about my being there. A pipe was lodged in his mouth and he wore a velvet paisley smoking jacket.

"Is everything all right?" he asked, standing and gesturing for me to sit in an easy chair by the fireplace. Then he sat back at his desk.

"Not especially," I replied.

"Then you must have a sherry," he replied, picking up the decanter on his desk. "There is another glass somewhere about the place. It's East India sherry, Miss Green. Your favourite."

He found the spare glass, filled it and passed it to me. I took a sip and enjoyed the comforting warmth of it in my throat.

"What was the unpleasant incident?" I asked.

"Oh, you don't need to worry yourself about that."

"But I should like to know! Was it anything to do with Mr Maynell or Mr Copeland from Repton, Borthwick and Company?"

"I don't know who it was to do with, Miss Green, but there is no need to concern yourself about the incident."

"But how long do you wish me to stay away from the office?"

"For as long as it takes for matters to calm down. Sadly, I think you need to stop pursuing your current line of inquiry."

"But I can't stop!" I replied. "Jeffrey Maynell and Jack Copeland are writing poisonous letters about me, and a woman called Maria Forsyth has been following me. They all deny it, of course, but I have to continue with the investigation. I cannot allow them to get away with what they're doing. And there is also Richard Geller's murder to consider. Somehow these people are behind it, but we need to prove how exactly."

Mr Sherman blew out a puff of pipe smoke. "Leave it to the police, Miss Green. The very best course of action now is to distance yourself from it all."

"I can't leave it up to the police."

"Of course you can. It's their job to solve these crimes. Stop the work you're doing on this and I have every confidence that the malicious letters, the bricks through the windows and the other unfortunate incidents will come to an end."

"You still haven't told me what has happened at the office."

"Nor have I any need to, for the time being."

I felt sure that Edgar or Frederick would tell me if I were to ask them.

"If I were to stop my work on this case I would be giving up," I said.

"Is that such a bad thing?" he replied. "Sometimes perseverance tips over into sheer stubbornness. Now and again a little skilled judgement is required. You can't win every battle."

"Maybe I can't. But I know that I cannot leave this matter to the police."

"Why ever not?"

"Because you told me yourself that there are certain people who refuse to speak to the police."

"Well, that's the detectives' problem to manage, not yours."

"Do you think they might speak to me?"

"Miss Green, do not get involved! You will only make matters worse for yourself!"

"You didn't answer my question, sir. Would the men who refuse to speak to the police speak to me?"

"I don't know," he replied irritably. "But even if there's a chance they will, what of it? They can't help the case progress because there isn't the slightest chance they would agree to appear in court."

"I'm quite sure they wouldn't have to. Please will you help me try? Two men have lost their lives. Two innocent men. And I have been to the museum at the medical school and seen where it all happened." I shivered. "It was such a terrible thing to happen to Richard Geller."

"I heard that Rabbi Geller asked the Yard to investigate. They will get to the bottom of this very quickly now, you'll see."

"Not if people refuse to speak to them."

"I wouldn't be surprised if Inspector Blakely has been asked to work on it."

"As a matter of fact, he has."

"Well there you go then, Miss Green. You have every confidence in the man, don't you?"

"Yes, I do. But I'm not prepared to stop pleading with you, Mr Sherman. I need to speak to someone who knew Richard Geller well. And someone who knew Simon Borthwick. I would be discreet; you know that I would. I would never put anybody in danger and I won't tell the police who I've spoken to. Not even James.

"Please, Mr Sherman, will you ask the people you know and find out if there is someone who could speak to me about Mr Geller and Mr Borthwick? Even if they have nothing helpful to impart I shall at least know that I have tried. I cannot miss an opportunity to find out something more. I've tried speaking to the people who I feel sure are behind it, but I have made no progress. I need to understand more about Richard Geller and Simon Borthwick, and I feel sure that someone knows something which can be of some use to me."

"I must say that you're extremely persistent."

"That's why I'm a news reporter."

"I would much prefer you to devote your energies to the stories we print in the paper."

"I am more than happy to, but I need to see this one through as well. *Please*, Mr Sherman."

He stared into the middle distance and sucked on his pipe thoughtfully.

"I'm going to have to think about it, Miss Green," he replied after a long pause. "I can't promise you anything at all."

An envelope was waiting for me when I arrived home. Inside

it was an invitation to dine with Edgar and Georgina Fish. Initially, my heart sank at the thought of having to make polite conversation for a whole evening, but then I realised that Edgar could perhaps tell me what had been happening at the office in my absence.

CHAPTER 48

"I can't help thinking that my behaviour toward Inspector Blakely has been rather petulant," I said to Eliza as we had lunch together at The Holborn Restaurant. Another day away from work had provided me with a little extra time to meet with my sister.

"What have you done now, Penelope?" she asked as she dipped her spoon into her bowl of chicken consommé.

"I think I may have become rather sulky when he mentioned that his fiancée would prefer it if we no longer spent time together alone."

"Sulky? Oh dear, that's rather immature. It sounds as though his fiancée has finally realised that she has something to be concerned about."

"She has nothing to be concerned about!"

"Is that so?"

"Of course! However, I would probably say something similar if I were in her shoes."

"Why would you say something similar?"

"Because perhaps it isn't fitting for a betrothed man and a spinster to be meeting together unchaperoned."

"You have always told me that it was for professional reasons."

"That's right."

"In which case she has nothing to be concerned about."

"No, nothing at all. But it's not commonplace, is it?"

"No. But then you're not really a commonplace sort of woman, Penelope."

"It was unfair of me to be rude to Inspector Blakely about it. It's not his fault."

"If you say so."

"I think I shall need to apologise to him."

"If you've been petulant an apology sounds like the right course of action. Then you must learn to distance yourself from the man. He is to be married in September, after all."

"I know."

"It's been some time since I last saw the delightful Mr Edwards. How is he?"

"He's very well, thank you, Ellie. I must say that I was impressed by his running ability earlier this week."

"Mr Edwards is athletic?"

"Yes. He was the hundred-yard flat race champion during his university days."

I explained to Eliza what had occurred with Maria Forsyth in Russell Square.

Eliza stopped eating for a moment and shook her head in dismay. "Oh dear, Penelope. You had the poor man arrested!"

"He wasn't arrested, he was merely questioned. As was the woman who took Tiger."

"How do you know that she is the culprit?"

"I just know. She was hanging about nearby on the day Tiger went missing."

Eliza sighed. "Until quite recently I thought Mr Edwards was a suitable match for you."

"What's changed your mind?"

"I'm beginning to think that he could do with someone rather more sensible. You get yourself into such ridiculous scrapes, Penelope. And to think Mr Edwards ended up at the police station because you had a notion that some poor woman stole your cat."

"It's rather more than that, Ellie," I said, feeling exasperated.

"Yes, I suspected as much. It sounds to me as though you owe both Inspector Blakely *and* Mr Edwards an apology. Why they should choose to consort with you I'll never know."

"Perhaps they like a lady who gets herself into scrapes."

"I suppose they must do. But you can wipe that smile off your face. It's hardly something to be proud of!"

I occupied myself with my tomato soup and decided not to tell my sister that I had been instructed to stay away from the *Morning Express* offices for the time being.

"Have you considered the plan George and I suggested about asking Mr Fox-Stirling to look for Father in Colombia again?" asked Eliza.

"Must it be him? Can't we find someone else?"

"He knows the area better than anyone else."

"Yet failed to find any sign of Father's whereabouts the last time."

"But there's no better alternative, wouldn't you agree? We can insist that he takes a Spanish translator with him this time."

"It'll take us a long time to raise the funds."

"We'll manage it. In the meantime, shall I go ahead and ask Mr Fox-Stirling?"

I sighed. "Yes, I suppose so."

"Good. That settles matters, then. I shall invite him and his wife over for dinner and propose the idea."

After lunch I walked up to the post office on High Holborn and sent a contrite telegram to James.

I wish to apologise for my churlish conduct and have every respect for your fiancée's wishes.

Penny

I addressed it to his home rather than to Scotland Yard.

CHAPTER 49

A warm breeze whipped down the steps as I exited Westminster Bridge Station the following afternoon. Big Ben chimed three o'clock as I crossed the road and made my way toward Westminster Bridge.

I was on time.

I slowly walked to the centre of the bridge as a multitude of people bustled past me. I wasn't sure how I would identify the person I was supposed to meet there when I had no idea what he looked like.

I paused beside one of the large ornate lamps and gazed up the river, where the Houses of Parliament and St Thomas' hospital faced each other across the Thames.

There was no word yet with regard to when I could return to the *Morning Express* offices, but that morning I had received a telegram from Mr Sherman.

Mr Hamilton will meet you on Westminster Bridge at three o'clock today. Not his real name.

Was Mr Hamilton young or old? Short or tall? I wondered. I turned to watch the passers-by, wishing that Mr Sherman had given me a clue about the man's appearance in his telegram.

I had begun to doubt that Mr Hamilton would turn up when a tall man in a dark frock coat and top hat leant up against the wall next to me.

"Miss Green?" His voice had a slight Scottish lilt.

I looked up at him. "Mr Hamilton?"

He was about forty years of age and clean-shaven apart from a thin, dark moustache, which spread across his upper lip. He regarded me with cool green eyes.

"I'm only doing this because William is a good friend of mine and I owe him a favour."

"I appreciate you speaking to me. Thank you, Mr Hamilton. Did you know Mr Borthwick and Mr Geller?"

"I knew both of them," he replied, looking out over the river.

"Can you tell me anything further about their deaths?"

"I don't know. What have you already learned?"

I spent a few minutes explaining the work I had done. His face betrayed no emotion as I spoke.

"It sounds as though you've done quite a bit yourself," he replied. "I'm not sure how I can help you."

"Have you any idea who might have murdered Mr Geller?"

"I'm afraid not."

"Can you tell me anything more about him? Or about Mr Borthwick? How well did you know them?"

"I should think I usually saw them two or three times a month; sometimes at The Ha'penny and sometimes at other places. Friends' houses. I knew Geller much better than Borthwick, as I first met him about five or six years ago. He was outgoing with lots of friends. You know who his father is, I presume?"

I nodded. "A rabbi, I believe."

"He was concerned about his family finding out too much about him, so he was very careful. He had a passion for pathology, and once you had him on the subject he would continue talking about it until late into the night. He took a few of us to that museum where he worked one time." He gave a guarded smile. "There are some interesting things in there. He enjoyed his work very much."

"And Mr Borthwick?"

"He was quite different from Geller. He could be entertaining at times and tempestuous at others, but they got along extremely well. Borthwick had a great mind, but his work often consumed him. Sometimes he missed dinner parties because he was working late in his laboratory. That irritated Geller a great deal." Mr Hamilton gave a quiet laugh. "But on the whole they enjoyed each other's company and were very much looking forward to their move to America."

"They had planned to emigrate?

"Yes, didn't you know? Geller had secured a position with the Perelman School of Medicine at the University of Pennsylvania."

"And they were both going?"

"Yes. You seem surprised, Miss Green."

"I certainly am, as it's the first I have heard of it. But what about Borthwick's work? Everything appeared to be going so well for him here."

"I'm sure it would have gone just as well for him in America."

"Do you know what Borthwick planned to do when they reached America?"

"I believe he harboured hopes of working with Thomas Edison."

"That would have been a wonderful opportunity for him." I looked out over the river and felt a pang of sadness that the opportunity had never been realised. "When had they intended to travel?"

"I can't be certain. Within the next month or two, I suppose. I only heard of it shortly before Geller died."

"Have you ever come across a woman called Maria Forsyth?"

Mr Hamilton shook his head. "No."

"Are you acquainted with Jeffrey Maynell? Or Jack Copeland?"

"I'm afraid not."

"What do you know of Mrs Lillian Maynell?"

"Who's she?"

"She was briefly engaged to Simon Borthwick."

"Oh, of course. Lillian! I recall her now."

"Was Mr Borthwick fond of her?"

"He seemed to be. I suppose he would have married her if she hadn't left him for some other chap. I think Borthwick craved the respectability marriage would have afforded him."

"She married Jeffrey Maynell, his colleague."

"So that's who that Maynell chap he mentioned is. I understand now. I never met him, but I encountered Lillian once or twice."

"I don't think she knew anything of Mr Geller. She has never alluded to him."

"That doesn't surprise me." Mr Hamilton checked his pocket watch. "I'm afraid I must go, Miss Green."

"Thank you for agreeing to speak with me."

"William assured me that our conversation would not be repeated to anyone else." He took a pipe from his pocket and lit it.

"It won't be, Mr Hamilton. I can assure you of that."

"Thank you. In the meantime, we must hope that the police catch Geller's killer. They're taking their time, aren't they?"

"The case is not a straightforward one. In my mind there are a few obvious suspects, but it is proving impossible to gather enough evidence against them."

"Poor Borthwick," he said. "Geller's murder must have been devastating for him."

I nodded.

"I wonder if that was the intention of Geller's killer," he continued. "I can think of no reason why anyone should wish to harm Geller other than to make Borthwick suffer."

"You think that might have been the motive?" I asked.

"Does it make any sense to you?"

"It's a dreadful thought that someone would kill one man to wreak revenge upon another. But I must reluctantly admit that it does seem to make sense, Mr Hamilton."

❧

While I took the underground railway to Moorgate I wrote down what Mr Hamilton had told me. I had become accustomed to discussing the case with James, but now that he could no longer meet me at the Museum Tavern my work felt quite solitary. Everything seemed much easier when I had someone to discuss it with, but now I would have to work out the implications for myself.

It was busy on the platform when I disembarked from the train. As the crowd moved toward the stairs a man on my right suddenly lurched to one side, as if someone had pushed him. There was barely time for me to react before a shove into my back sent me flying to the floor. A woman cried out and I tried to get back onto my feet again, fearful of being trampled. A woman in a blue dress helped me stand up, her eyes wide with horror.

"Get a doctor!" she called out.

A man in a top hat suggested that I rest myself against the wall.

"I'm fine, thank you. I'm almost home," I said.

"She hasn't realised," the woman in the blue dress said to the man.

"Realised what?" I asked.

"Your shoulder."

As she said the words I noticed that my right shoulder felt cold and damp. I touched it with my left hand and realised it was wet.

"How did that happen?" I asked, looking at my left hand.

And that's when my head began to spin.

My hand was covered in blood.

CHAPTER 50

"Miss Green!" Edgar greeted me as I arrived at his home for the dinner party. "How are you? Have they found out who attacked you? Tell us what happened!"

"I'm fine thank you Edgar. The wound isn't deep, they didn't manage to cause me much harm."

"But who was it?" asked Georgina as she dashed over to me, her silk dress rustling.

"I didn't see, but I have an idea. A woman called Maria Forsyth has been following me and I recently confronted her, I think this attack must be an attempt at revenge. I've spent much of today at the police station in Westminster and I've told them to speak to Inspector Rigby in Bloomsbury who dealt with the previous incident. Between them I hope they find her."

"Well I think it's a dreadful business," said Georgina. "You don't deserve this at all, you're extremely brave Penny!"

Georgina introduced me to Frederick Potter's wife Clara. Mrs Potter was as portly as her husband and was laced extremely tightly into a dress of gold satin.

I wore one of the few evening dresses I owned. It was made of russet-coloured satin, with fringing around the hips, a small bustle and a buttoned bodice. A silk shawl covered my bandaged shoulder, and before leaving home I had hastily pinned some rather limp cotton flowers into my hair.

"How are you after the stabbing, Miss Green?" asked Frederick.

"Quite recovered, thank you," I replied. "What happened at the office? Mr Sherman told me to stay away, but I'm still not sure why."

"You don't know why?" said Frederick with surprise. Just as he was about to elaborate we were interrupted as a sixth guest was shown into the room.

Mr Edwards.

His hair was neatly parted and he was dressed in a smart evening suit I hadn't seen him wear before. I almost found him handsome, and I smiled warmly.

"I hope you don't mind us inviting Mr Edwards," Georgina whispered into my ear. "We couldn't think who else to invite to balance the numbers, and then Edgar remembered that you and Mr Edwards were acquaintances."

"Thank you, Georgina. I don't mind at all."

A large white cat curled around my skirts. I bent down to stroke it and felt a lump in my throat as Tiger came back to my mind.

"Are you all right, Miss Green?" asked Mr Edwards with a look of concern.

"Yes, it's only a superficial wound," I replied.

"It may be superficial, but the person who did it surely intended you serious harm!"

"They may have done, but fortunately it was easily treated."

"Have the police caught the culprit?" he asked.

"No. It was impossible to see who did it. The station was

busy, and it happened so quickly. It wouldn't surprise me if it was our friend Maria Forsyth."

"She wouldn't go to such extreme lengths, would she?"

"I don't know, Mr Edwards, but that foolish inspector let her go, and I have no doubt that she still poses a threat. The situation is extremely frustrating."

"Perhaps a glass of champagne will make you feel better, Penny," said Georgina.

"It's worth a try, isn't it? Thank you."

We dined on pigeon compote in a pleasantly furnished dining room with large windows overlooking the garden. I impatiently speared at my food with my fork, waiting for an opportunity to find out what had happened at the office.

"I can't help but admire your carriage clock, Georgina," said Clara.

"Thank you. We received it as a gift at our wedding, didn't we, Edgar?"

"We did indeed," replied Edgar. "I must say I was listening to the thing ticking the other evening and it got me thinking about where on earth seconds and minutes come from. And hours and days. How did that whole business come about?"

"It's the time it takes for the earth to rotate," said Frederick. "And for the earth to travel around the sun."

"I know that, Potter. What I mean is that some chap somewhere decided to count it all up into seconds and minutes, and so on. Who on earth did that?"

"We have the invention of the mechanical clock to thank for that," said Mr Edwards. "Until time was represented on a clock face nobody concerned themselves too much with minutes and seconds."

"How the dickens were they on time for anything?" asked Edgar.

Mr Edwards shrugged. "I don't suppose time mattered so much back then. Summer hours were longer and winter hours were shorter."

"Hours were longer and shorter?" asked Edgar. "What are you talking about, Edwards?"

Mr Edwards laughed. "It does seem rather confusing, doesn't it? To summarise, the measurement of time uses the sexagesimal system, which we can credit as an invention to the Babylonians. Coincidentally, it fits well with the duodecimal system, which the ancient Egyptians used to divide the day into smaller segments. They began this with the use of sundials, which were simple at first but became surprisingly sophisticated."

I sipped my wine as Mr Edwards spoke and recalled how quickly he had sprinted across Russell Square. There was no doubt that he was talented, both physically and intellectually.

"I'm sorry, but I found myself lost at sexa... What was it you said?" asked Edgar.

"The sexagesimal system," replied Mr Edwards. "It uses sixty as a base. There is also duodecimal, which uses twelve."

"I see," said Edgar.

"Twelve fits into sixty neatly five times over, which is rather convenient, wouldn't you say?" said Mr Edwards.

"And there are twenty-four hours in a day, which is twice twelve!" said Frederick. "It's all quite simple, Fish. I don't know why you're looking so baffled."

"Greek astronomers refined the system of timekeeping, of course," continued Mr Edwards. "And it would be remiss of me not to mention the Persians with their water clocks and the Chinese with their candle clocks."

"Important not to forget them," added Frederick.

"It may surprise you to learn that European monks were proficient manufacturers of clocks during the Dark Ages, and

I believe that Wells Cathedral housed one of the first ever mechanical clocks."

"You have an impressive capability for recalling facts, Mr Edwards!" enthused Georgina.

"It's because the chap works in a library," said Edgar. "I would know all this if I worked in a library."

"No, Edgar, you wouldn't," retorted his wife, removing a ginger cat from the table.

"Rather amusingly, the French attempted to implement a decimal time system about ninety years ago," continued Mr Edwards. "They had one hundred seconds in a minute, one hundred minutes in an hour and ten hours in a day."

Frederick snorted. "That's the French for you."

"I could listen to you all day, Mr Edwards," said Clara, her chin resting on her hands. "You're such a clever man."

Mr Edwards coloured slightly, and Frederick scowled.

"You must adore your job at the library, Mr Edwards," said Georgina. "It's clear that you have a passion for knowledge."

"Oh, I don't know about that," he replied, his face still slightly red. "My job can become rather boring at times, so that's when I turn to reading books. I can't say I relish the thought of working in a library for the rest of my days. There are far more interesting pursuits in life. Such as being a news reporter!" He looked at me and smiled.

"Oh no," said Edgar. "You wouldn't want to do that. Potter and Miss Green would agree with me, I'm sure."

"There are good days and bad days," I said. "But I must say I'm rather tired of trying to find out what incident has occurred at the *Morning Express* offices." I had been waiting impatiently to ask the question ever since we had sat down for dinner.

"They still haven't caught the chap who threw the brick," said Edgar.

"I'm not talking about the brick. I was present for the

brick incident," I replied. "I'm referring to the more recent incident, which Mr Sherman refuses to tell me about."

"It was nothing," said Edgar.

"Nothing at all," added Frederick.

"But it had to be something. Otherwise, why would he ask me to stay away?" I asked.

"Veal pie!" shrilled Georgina, clapping her hands together with glee as her staff served up the next course. "We've had some wonderful veal recently, haven't we, Edgar?"

"It really is delightful veal," said Edgar.

"I had some spectacular veal in Marseille once," added Frederick.

"I cannot help but notice that you've changed the topic of conversation," I said. "But I really must know what happened at the office."

"I'm sure it will only be a day or two before you can return," said Edgar. "They have almost finished the repainting now."

"Why did the office require repainting?"

"To cover up the smoke damage," said Frederick.

"Shush!" said Edgar.

"*Smoke?*" I exclaimed. "From what?"

"My pipe," chuckled Edgar.

"Please be honest with me," I said. "Was there a fire?"

"Only a small one," said Frederick.

"Shush!" said Edgar again. "We're not supposed to say!"

"Why aren't you supposed to say?" I asked.

"Mr Sherman doesn't wish you to feel worried."

"Someone set fire to the office?" I probed.

"They tried to," replied Edgar with a sigh.

"But that's dreadful! Was anyone hurt?"

"Thankfully, no. It was late in the evening and a chap from the *Holborn Gazette* spotted it before it really took hold."

"And scored himself a story at the same time," said Frederick.

"We didn't publish anything," added Edgar. "Mr Sherman felt those responsible should not be given any publicity."

"Have they been caught?"

"Afraid not," said Edgar.

"But there's no suggestion that this has anything to do with the brick which was thrown through the window, is there? It could have been entirely unrelated."

"Two attacks on our office within the same week?" said Edgar. "The same culprit must be behind both incidents."

"Oh, don't say that," I said. "I feel terrible knowing that I'm responsible for all this."

"Please don't feel terrible about it, Miss Green," said Edgar. "You weren't even supposed to know about the fire."

"Well I'm pleased that I know about it because I don't want anything to be hidden from me. I must find a way to make recompense for what has happened."

"I wouldn't worry about that," said Edgar.

"No, you shouldn't worry about that, Penny," said Georgina. "You're such a darling, delightful person that you mustn't concern yourself over these unpleasant matters. In fact, you mustn't think about them at all. How are you finding the pie?"

"It's lovely. Thank you, Georgina."

"I must say, Miss Green, that you have some wonderfully supportive friends and colleagues," Mr Edwards chimed in, holding up his glass. "I propose a toast to no longer worrying about such matters."

Everyone raised their glasses and joined in with the toast. I smiled, but inside I felt that they were all missing the point somewhat. The people behind Richard Geller and Simon Borthwick's deaths were still at large.

"How is Lillian faring?" I asked Georgina.

"She's well, thank you. She had a slight fever, which she's recovering from. However, there's been a slight hiccup as her poor husband has lost his job."

I felt my stomach flip. This was something else I felt partly responsible for. I decided to pretend that I had heard nothing of it.

"It's not too concerning for the Maynells," interjected Edgar, "seeing as Lillian comes from an extremely wealthy family."

"But it's still sad news for her husband," I said, aware of the insincerity in my voice. "Is Mr Repton laying off many of his workers?"

"Another of Jeffrey's colleagues also lost his job," continued Georgina. "But only the two of them, and Lillian was extremely surprised because she believes they were two of Repton's best men. Along with Borthwick, of course. Mr Repton has lost all three of them now."

"The company must be in rather a precarious position," said Mr Edwards. "It's committed to completing that large project in Kensington; one of the first of its kind in the world! How will Mr Repton achieve such a feat if he is losing all his staff?"

CHAPTER 51

"Good afternoon, Miss Green. Are you working?" Mr Edwards whispered as I sat at my desk in the reading room.

I quickly folded away the notes I had made from my conversation with Mr Hamilton.

"Yes, Mr Edwards."

"You shouldn't be, not with your injury. And are you sure that it's safe for you to be out and about? What if that woman tries to attack you again?"

"I'm keeping an eye out for her, Mr Edwards. I can't allow her to stop me from living my life. And the police should have her under arrest very soon."

I smiled in an attempt hide my anxiety. The truth was I felt quite nervous going about my daily business, finding myself checking my surroundings whenever possible. But to hide away would have been to admit defeat.

"If you're sure, Miss Green." Mr Edwards sighed. "Did you enjoy the dinner party?"

"I did, thank you."

"It was extremely pleasant to acquaint myself better with

your colleagues. The Fishes are wonderfully hospitable people."

"I must say that Edgar is more tolerable when accompanied by his wife."

Mr Edwards laughed, and I recalled how impressed Georgina and Clara had been with him. Perhaps I had failed to recognise his true eligibility.

"I hope you don't mind me asking, Miss Green, but would you? Oh—"

The smile disappeared from his face as he noticed someone walking towards us. "Inspector Blakely," he said. "You're here to see Miss Green, I take it."

"Absolutely." James grinned, and my heart skipped a beat. "I have an update for you, Penny," said James. "Do you have a brief moment?"

"I do indeed." I gathered up my papers and put them into my carpet bag under the watchful and disappointed gaze of Mr Edwards.

"I thought Charlotte had prohibited you from visiting the Museum Tavern," I said as we sat down at a table with our drinks.

James rolled his eyes. "I might have known you would refer to that again. She hasn't prohibited me from visiting this public house and neither has she prohibited us from speaking. It's just that... Actually, I don't wish to dwell on the matter any longer. How are you? I heard about the attack at Moorgate Station. Dreadful news. How's your shoulder?"

"It's fine, thank you, James. It hurts a little when I move my arm, but no real harm was done."

He shook his head. "It shouldn't have happened," he said. "And you should be at home recuperating."

"I've been sitting around at home for a few days and it's been thoroughly tedious."

"Have the City of London police arrested anyone yet?"

I laughed. "What do you think, James?"

"You didn't have to speak to Chief Inspector Stroud about it, did you?"

"No, it was one of his colleagues. I've told him I suspect that it was Maria Forsyth and that all he needs to do is contact Inspector Rigby to find out where she lives. I shall visit them again tomorrow to ensure that it happens."

"If only it were that easy."

"It must be, mustn't it?"

"Let me explain something else first, then I'll tell you where we've got to with Maria Forsyth."

He removed some folded papers from the inside pocket of his jacket. I could see they were the malicious letters which had been written about me.

"Thank you for your telegram and apology," he said as he unfolded them. "Although it wasn't necessary. There was no need to apologise."

"I felt I owed it to you."

We held each other's gaze and then James cleared his throat.

"I've had a graphologist look at these and the findings are, frankly, quite surprising. These letters are forgeries."

"Really?"

"Apparently so."

"But how can the graphologist tell?"

"I have no idea, but I trust the professional's opinion. I gave him the unpleasant letters which had been sent to your friends and family, and then the letters Maynell and Copeland had written to Borthwick. By comparing the handwriting in the letters he was able to deduce that the handwriting in the anonymous letters was copied."

"But how? They look identical to me."

"And to me. That's probably why we're not graphologists, Penny. He did try explaining it to me. Something about the upper and lower extensions not flowing as naturally as they should. He assured me that they were exceptionally good forgeries, however."

"So Maynell and Copeland weren't lying. They were telling us the truth! And someone framed them. You do realise that Repton has dismissed both men?"

"Yes, I did hear that." James rubbed his chin. "Perhaps I should have asked the graphologist to look at the letters before we spoke to Repton."

"With hindsight, yes."

"Repton didn't realise the letters had been forged, did he?" said James. "He was equally convinced by them."

"We all were. And as for the remaining letters, they were presumably written in the handwriting of other individuals the forger wished to frame. I wonder who they might be."

"Well, we could try to find out, but we don't want it to detract from the main course of the investigation. We need to find out who forged these letters. We must also rule Maynell and Copeland out and inform Mr Repton as soon as possible that he needs to reinstate them."

"Maria Forsyth," I said. "It has to be her! You need to speak to her again."

"I've tried," James said with a sigh, "but I don't think Maria Forsyth is her real name."

"What?"

"I asked Inspector Rigby for her address because I wished to discuss the earring with her. But the family at the address she gave him had never come across a woman matching her description."

"She gave a false name and address?"

"She certainly did."

"Inspector Rigby should have arrested her while he had the chance!" I fumed. "And to think that Mr Edwards caught her and then found himself in trouble for doing so! I *knew* she was a criminal, but no one would listen to me."

"With the greatest respect to Inspector Rigby, he had no evidence to suggest that she was a criminal."

"I told him what she was up to. It couldn't have been more obvious that she was trouble."

I gulped down the rest of my sherry and slumped back against the seat.

"Now what do we do, James? She stuck a knife in my shoulder and next time the outcome could be far worse! I am trying not to be fearful, James, but I can't help worrying now. We must find her, and fast!"

"We don't know for sure that it was her who attacked you, but I agree that it's a possibility. And I think you'd be far safer remaining at home until we've tracked her down. However, as you've already told me how boring that is I doubt I'll be able to persuade you to, will I?"

I shook my head in reply.

"I've had a jeweller look at the earring we found in the medical school museum," continued James. "It appears to be quite a costly item and was sold by Villier & Powell's in Burlington Arcade."

"So we must take it to the jewellers and find out who purchased it!"

"I have already done so, Penny."

"Then who bought the earrings?"

"The young gentleman at the jewellers didn't know."

"Oh."

"He found a record of the sale and was able to tell me that the purchase was made approximately three months ago for one hundred pounds."

"But he couldn't recall who had come into the shop that day and paid such a significant sum for a pair of earrings?"

"Sadly, he couldn't."

"It's her, isn't it, James? Everything now points to the woman who calls herself Maria Forsyth. We must make every effort to find her again. Where *is* she?"

CHAPTER 52

Donald Repton presented a lonely figure as he stood within the subterranean engine house at the Kensington Court development. Several paraffin lamps had been positioned on the floor.

"Hello, Inspector! Miss Green!" He smoothed down his shock of white hair. "What brings you down here again?"

"We wish to offer an apology," said James.

"Oh no, I'm quite sure there is no need for you to apologise for anything." He took a hip flask from his pocket and offered it to James.

"No thank you, Mr Repton. How is your work progressing?"

Two engines had now been installed, but I knew that another five were needed. And the space where the generators should have stood remained empty.

"I cannot deny that we're a little behind schedule," replied Repton, taking a swig from his flask.

"I'm sure you'll catch up before long," said James with a lack of conviction to his voice. "I must reiterate my apology,

Mr Repton. I've had the letters we believed Mr Maynell and Mr Copeland to have written examined, and it transpires that the letters are forgeries."

"Someone else wrote them?"

"That's what a graphologist has said."

"Oh, I see." Mr Repton's mouth hung open as he considered the implications of this.

"I'm aware that Mr Maynell and Mr Copeland were summarily dismissed," continued James. "May I suggest that you reinstate them as soon as possible? I regret the error I have made with my accusation and feel terribly conscience-stricken that two men have been dismissed from their profession as a result."

"Oh, don't worry about that," replied Repton. "I had planned to dismiss them anyway."

"Had you?" I asked. "Why?"

"The truth of the matter is I have found a buyer for the company."

"You're selling Repton, Borthwick and Company?" James asked.

"Yes, to a company in Doncaster. They have been manufacturing generators for longer than I have, and I've come to realise that the work required here in Kensington is more than I can manage."

"But surely Mr Maynell and Mr Copeland could be invited back to work for the new employer," I suggested.

"I don't have time for all that before I depart."

"Depart?" I queried. "Where are you going?"

"To America!" he replied. "I'm heading across the pond." He took another gulp from his flask.

"Why?" asked James.

"For the opportunities which that great nation presents, electricity is a burgeoning industry there. I could make three times the amount of money in America, it's an idea which I've been considering for a while."

"Wasn't Simon Borthwick also planning to move to America?" I asked.

"Was he?" asked James. "How do you know this?"

"His friend Richard Geller had been offered a position within the medical school at the University of Pennsylvania," I explained. "Apparently, Mr Geller had asked Mr Borthwick to accompany him."

"Were you aware of Borthwick's plans to travel to America, Mr Repton?" asked James.

"The matter was discussed between us," he replied with a hardened glance. His manner was notably less affable than it had been up to this point.

"And what was your reaction upon hearing that your most successful engineer and inventor was preparing to move overseas?"

"I assumed that he would soon change his mind."

"Did he mention to you what he planned to do in America?" asked James.

"He harboured a notion that he would perhaps be lucky enough to find work with Thomas Edison in New York."

"Did you do or say anything in a bid to convince him to continue working for you?"

"What company owner wouldn't? I had no wish for him to emigrate."

"How did you try to persuade him to stay?" asked James.

"I thought a few strong words would do the trick, but sadly his mind seemed to be made up. Anyway, this is all of no consequence now, Inspector. I cannot understand why someone would wish to write such unpleasant things about Miss Green here and then pretend someone else had written the letters. It makes no sense to me."

"What sort of strong words did you use when you spoke with Mr Borthwick?" asked James.

"The sort of words a chap uses when he is about to lose his best employee! That's all there was to it."

"Was there anything else?"

"What do you mean, *anything else*?" He scowled.

"What else did you do to persuade Mr Borthwick to stay?"

"That was all, Inspector! Strong words; nothing more."

"Do you know a woman who calls herself Maria Forsyth?"

"No. Why should I?"

"Can you think of anyone who dislikes Mr Maynell and Mr Copeland enough to forge malicious letters imitating their handwriting?"

"No, but I must say that I'm rather pleased now that I've sold the company and have the chance leave this whole sorry business behind me."

"When do you leave these shores, Mr Repton?"

"Next Monday. I'm to travel on the Britannia from Liverpool."

"We shall be very sorry to see you leave," said James.

"We need to think of a reason to detain Repton," James said as we walked toward Kensington High Street Station. "Once he's on that ship bound for America we will have lost him from the investigation. We only have five days. It's rather a sudden departure, isn't it? Suspiciously sudden, I should say."

"It's tempting to speculate as to whether he's running away from something," I added.

"I'd say he was, wouldn't you? How exactly did you find out that Borthwick and Geller were planning to move to

America? It's the first I've heard of it. You say Geller had secured a job there."

"Yes."

"Who told you such a thing?"

"I'm not at liberty to say. I made a promise to keep the person's identity a secret."

"But I'm investigating the case, Penny! You cannot withhold that information."

"I can, James, and I have to. I have made a promise."

"What else did this mysterious person tell you?"

"A little more about Geller and Borthwick."

"Such as what? You need to share this information with me right away!"

"I've written it all down and can show you my notes. There was little else that seemed to be of any use, although the person did suggest that Geller's murder may have been carried out in order to hurt Borthwick."

"Meaning what?"

"Meaning that no one bore Geller any ill-will. It was his association with Borthwick which caused him to become the victim of such a terrible crime. By harming Geller the culprit intended to injure Borthwick."

James nodded. "I see. And does your anonymous source know this for certain, or was it merely a supposition?"

"A supposition, I'd say."

"I should very much like to talk to this person, whoever it is."

"I don't believe the person in question would be willing to speak to the police. In fact, I feel sure of it."

"That's a great shame."

"He didn't even tell me his real name."

"So we have established that it's a man. That narrows it down a little, I suppose."

"Let's not become distracted by my source, James. Do you

really think Mr Repton's sudden departure for America is suspicious?"

"I think it could be. We need to ask ourselves what he stood to lose if Borthwick had left his company. He told us that he tried to persuade Borthwick to stay. Did he use more than strong words, I wonder?"

CHAPTER 53

"And do you really believe that a simple apology is sufficient recompense for causing me to lose my employment, Inspector?"

Jeffrey Maynell jutted out his jaw as he awaited James' reply. He had received us in the drawing room of his large home in Mayfair's Dover Street.

"I hadn't expected that Mr Repton would make such a rash move," explained James. "I thought he would await further evidence. I told him I planned to have the letters examined by a graphologist."

"You should have awaited further evidence before accusing us in the first place!" retorted Maynell.

"Are you aware that Mr Repton is to sell his company and move to America?" I asked.

"Yes, I've heard about that. The man's mind seems to have become rather muddled of late."

"So perhaps he was planning to dismiss his staff anyway." As soon as the words left my mouth I regretted them.

Maynell's face reddened with rage. "So I've been treated fairly after all! Is that what you're suggesting, Miss Green? It has nothing to do with the careless work of your inspector friend? The fact that Repton intended to sell his company absolves this detective of his responsibility, does it? The fact that his investigation has been clumsy and amateurish has nothing to do with it?"

"I take it you feel no loyalty toward your former employer now," said James.

"None at all! And I shall complain to the Commissioner of Scotland Yard with regard to your foolhardy conduct, Inspector."

"As you wish, Mr Maynell. You're perfectly entitled to do so."

"Indeed I am."

"Were you aware that Simon Borthwick was also planning to move to America, Mr Maynell?" asked James.

"Yes, I was. And it would have been good riddance to him. I was tired of playing second fiddle."

"So you wanted him to move there?"

"Of course! He was to emigrate with a friend, and don't ask me to elaborate on what sort of friend, Inspector. I have no wish to discuss such matters under my own roof!"

"How did Mr Repton feel about Mr Borthwick's proposed emigration?" asked James.

"He would have been nothing without Borthwick. That partly explains his decision to sell the company, I suppose."

"Mr Borthwick was that invaluable, was he? Even though he reportedly stole other people's ideas?" ventured James.

"He stole ideas but somehow improved upon them as well. He was impressive, though I'm reluctant to admit it even now," he said with a sneer. "And I cannot pretend, either, that a lot of our success wasn't down to him."

"Mr Repton told me that he tried to make Mr Borthwick stay. Do you know how he went about it?"

"He had words with him, no doubt."

"Might Mr Repton have threatened him?"

"He may have done."

"How threatening might he have been?"

"It depends on how much he'd had to drink."

"Mr Borthwick intended to move to America because his friend Richard Geller was emigrating there," said James. "The removal of this friend from the equation would presumably have changed Mr Borthwick's mind."

"*Removal?* What do you mean?"

"Murder, Mr Maynell."

"Ah, right. Borthwick's friend Geller was murdered in the hospital, wasn't he?"

"Yes. And perhaps that's why Mr Borthwick took his own life," James suggested. "An incident which Mr Repton could not have anticipated."

A sinister smile spread across Maynell's face. "I see now, Inspector. I know what you're suggesting. Mr Repton *removed* this friend so that Borthwick no longer had any reason to travel to America. But the plan backfired rather badly when Borthwick murdered himself!"

He gave a cackle before continuing. "And when Miss Green, the ink-scribbler, developed an unexpected interest in Borthwick's demise, Repton tried to warn her off with the unpleasant letters. But the letters would have incriminated him had they been in his own hand, wouldn't they? Better to have them written by two men he no longer had any use for. He tried to frame us! And now he's to sell the company and escape to America. I can only presume that you intend to arrest him before he quits these shores, Inspector."

"I shall do my best, Mr Maynell."

We were interrupted by Lillian, whose yellow satin dress brightened the room.

"Penny!" She smiled broadly at me, then glanced warily at her husband.

"Don't worry," he said impatiently, "I have no objection to you two ladies speaking. No further damage can be done now, and I think I've just solved the inspector's case for him."

"Have you, darling?"

"I believe so. You have an arrest to make now, don't you, Inspector?" said Maynell with a smug smile.

"I have indeed," replied James.

"That's wonderful news!" said Lillian. "Who do you intend to arrest?"

"Repton," replied her husband. "He's behind all this nonsense. You wouldn't think him capable of murder, would you?"

"No!" said Lillian with a look of shock on her face. "Mr Repton? Could he really have done such a thing? It was cruel of him to dismiss you, but surely he wouldn't carry out a murder. I once thought him such a kindly man."

Mr Maynell gave a contemptible laugh. "It was all an act!"

"Whom did he murder?" asked Lillian.

"Borthwick's friend," replied Maynell. "I'll explain it to you later, dear."

"I see." Lillian turned to me. "Georgina told me all about her dinner party, and what delightful company you and your friend were. He works at the British Library, is that right? She was very impressed by his extensive knowledge!"

From the corner of my eye I noticed that James had turned to gauge my response. I chose not to meet his gaze.

"It was a pleasant evening," I replied.

"Perhaps now that this sorry business is concluded we could host a similar dinner here. That would be pleasant, wouldn't it?" said Lillian. "We need a distraction at the present time. It's been so terribly difficult with Jeffrey losing his job. Georgina and Edgar are great fun, aren't they, Jeffrey?"

"You could say that."

"Oh, come now. A little socialising is just what you need. It does you no good to sit about brooding."

I didn't like the dark expression on her husband's face.

❧

James and I stepped out of the house.

"I need to go back to Kensington and catch up with Repton again," said James.

"Do you think he's the person Mr Borthwick believed to be persecuting him?"

"He must be."

"In that case, why didn't Mr Borthwick name him in his letter?"

"That's a good point."

"And how does Maria Forsyth fit in with all this?"

"There are still a few questions to be answered, Penny."

"Perhaps Maynell didn't quite solve it after all," I suggested.

James laughed. "We had to allow the man to think he had, though, didn't we? I had no wish to see him become any angrier than he already was."

"He might have exploded like one of Repton's light bulbs."

"That would have made rather a mess of the drawing room." He laughed. "Right, I must go. I don't want to let Repton slip through our fingers."

CHAPTER 54

Once James and I had parted company I walked along Piccadilly with its expensive shops and restaurants. Fashionable ladies with small, pampered dogs shielded themselves from the afternoon sun with their parasols. There was a dull ache in my wounded shoulder, but I tried my best to ignore it.

As I passed the Burlington Arcade I recalled James telling me that the earring we had found at the medical school museum had been bought at a jewellers' shop there. I turned into the covered row of little shops and searched for the sign bearing the name Villier & Powell. I walked past a milliner, tailor and stationer, each with their luxury wares displayed neatly in small-paned windows. I eventually found the jeweller about halfway along the row.

A young man with neat red whiskers stood inside the shop and the scent of expensive perfume lingered in the air.

"Good afternoon," I said with a smile. "I would like to enquire about a pair of earrings which were bought from this shop about three months ago. They were drop earrings made of diamond and pearl, I believe, and they cost about one hundred pounds. Do you recall them?"

"We've sold a few like that, madam."

"Would you be able to look over your records and find out who this particular pair of earrings was sold to?"

The man gave me a suspicious look.

"I'm unable to furnish you with that information, madam. Is there anything you wish to purchase from us?"

I glanced around at the shelves of glittering jewellery, acutely aware that there was nothing in the shop which I could afford to purchase. I tried to think of a reason to persist.

"If there is nothing else you require, madam, I don't believe I can be of any further assistance." He glanced toward the door.

"Did you sell the pair of earrings yourself, sir?"

"I am not obliged to share any more information with you."

The expression on his face was stony, and I felt the sensation of a door closing on me. *This was the only lead we had for the woman who called herself Maria Forsyth. It was the only possible hope we had of finding out her true identity. The woman who had taken Tiger and attacked me. The woman who might remain forever hidden if I failed to extract the information I needed from the jeweller.*

As I thought of Tiger and how long she had been missing, my eyes welled up. I saw a flicker of discomfort pass across the man's features.

"Please, madam." He gestured toward the door.

"It's just that..." I trailed off and rummaged around in my bag for a clean handkerchief.

"It's just what, madam?"

"It's rather important to me that I find out who purchased those earrings. This is a matter that is very close to my heart. It's my sister... the earrings were given to her shortly before she died."

"I'm sorry to hear that. Please accept my condolences."

"Thank you. She was too ill to ever tell me who gave her such a beautiful pair of earrings. I know they were quite costly and I wanted to inform the benefactor of my sister's passing. Oh dear, I'm sorry..." I feigned a slight swoon, as if overcome by emotion.

"Madam!"

The man dashed out from behind the counter and guided me into a plush velvet chair.

"Thank you. I do apologise for causing you such trouble," I said weakly. "You say that you don't recall selling those earrings, but perhaps one of your colleagues might."

I looked up at him with wet, sorrowful eyes.

He pursed his lips, realising that helping me was the only way he could hope to stop my tears.

"I suppose I could ask Mr Villier himself."

"Would you? That would be so kind of you. I do apologise for taking up your time in this manner, but it's rather important to me."

"I can see that."

A few moments later we were joined by Mr Villier, a round-faced man wearing a bright, patterned waistcoat. I tearfully explained my predicament to him.

"Drop earrings, you say, in diamond and pearl?"

I nodded.

"We have a few which match that description. Would you recognise the exact pair if I showed them to you?"

I nodded again.

Mr Villier unlocked several little drawers behind the

counter and proceeded to open a series of small, silk-lined boxes to show me the earrings inside.

"Those!" I said as he opened the fifth box. I recognised the style of the earrings immediately.

"A most excellent choice. Your sister's benefactor had good taste," he replied, closing the box and placing it back in its drawer.

He lifted a heavy ledger onto the counter and began to leaf through it. "We don't usually record the name of the person who buys a piece of jewellery; however, many of our customers are regular visitors and buy from us several times over. We pride ourselves on the quality of our jewellery and the excellence of our service, don't we, Wilson?"

The young man forced a smile.

A clock ticked as I patiently watched Mr Villier leaf through the sales ledger. He picked up a pencil and paper and made some notes on it before closing the book.

"My apologies, madam. I didn't ask your name."

"Miss Milligan."

"Very good, Miss Milligan. From our ledger I can see that we have sold five pairs of those particular earrings within the past three months. A beautiful pair they are, too, and certainly not cheap. Your sister must have been a popular lady."

"She was." I sniffed.

"I recall selling three pairs myself. Wilson, you must have sold one or two, I gather?"

"Yes, one or two I should think. Perhaps Mr Powell also sold a pair."

"He may have done," added Mr Villier as he examined the notes he had made. "Lady Hathaway bought a pair on the third of May. I distinctly remember her purchasing those earrings and my handwriting on the ledger records the sale. Is Lady Hathaway a familiar name to you, Miss Milligan?"

Could this be another pseudonym used by Maria Forsyth?

"It is not immediately familiar, Mr Villier."

"Very good. I shall continue."

Mr Villier and Mr Wilson discussed some of the other sales, suggesting the names of others that meant nothing to me. *What name had I hoped to hear? Perhaps Maria Forsyth was Lady Hathaway after all? Should I ask if Mr Villier knew where she lived?* I decided to wait until the two men had finished making their suggestions.

"This sale from the fifth of June is one I don't recall," said Mr Villier, "although it's in my handwriting. Do you have any memory of it, Wilson?"

Mr Wilson reopened the ledger and examined it closely.

"I'm afraid I don't," he said after a long silence.

My heart began to sink. This task was beginning to feel rather hopeless.

"And finally, we have a pair of these earrings bought by one of our regular customers. This sale was recorded by you, Wilson. However, I remember it as the chap bought a number of other items at the same time. There was a necklace in a similar style that he purchased. A Mr Maynell."

I blinked.

"Does that name mean anything to you, Miss Milligan?"

"I'm not sure. The fifth of June, you say?"

"Yes. Jeffrey Maynell is a good customer of ours."

My heart thudded heavily in my chest. I tried my best to appear calm and pretend that the name meant nothing to me.

"Perhaps the person who bought the earrings is the one you don't recall," I said. "It's a shame, as I did so wish to offer my thanks for the kindness." I rose out of my chair, attempting to look disappointed. "Thank you for your help, gentlemen."

"It's interesting that you should enquire about these earrings, as a detective visited us a few days ago to ask about a very similar pair," said Mr Wilson. "In fact, I think it may even have been the same pair."

"A detective?" said Mr Villier. "What did he want?"

"I'm not sure why he was asking. You were out of the shop at the time, and I'm afraid I wasn't much help to him."

"Never mind," replied Mr Villier. "Is there anything else you need help with, Miss Milligan?"

"No, thank you!" I replied over my shoulder as I swiftly left the shop.

CHAPTER 55

I marched along Piccadilly and hailed a cab to take me to Kensington. I predicted that James would have escorted Mr Repton to Kensington's Church Court police station for questioning. The distance wasn't great, but the journey seemed to take an inordinate length of time.

"Can't you ask the horse to trot?" I called to the cabman through the hatch in the roof. "I'm in a hurry!"

He paid me no heed. As I watched the horse lumber along Knightsbridge Road I tried to understand how Mr Maynell had manipulated us. He had claimed that Mr Repton was framing him, yet it now seemed to be the other way around.

As the traffic slowed along Kensington High Street I paid my fare and ran the rest of the way to the police station.

The constable behind the desk refused to allow me to interrupt James and Mr Repton, despite my earnest protestations. I sat on a wooden bench in the waiting room and agitatedly scribbled in my notebook, trying to piece together the information. *How did Mr Maynell know Maria Forsyth? Why should he have wished to kill Richard Geller? And what was Maria Forsyth's true identity?*

By the time James finally appeared it was almost six o'clock.

"Penny?"

I hurriedly told him what had happened at the jewellers' shop. He listened with interest.

"We must get back to Maynell," I said. "He's hiding something! Do you have the earring with you?"

"As a matter of fact, I do," said James, feeling around for it in his jacket pocket. "Are you sure about this, Penny? I've already upset the man by wrongly accusing him of writing that letter. Are you certain that the jeweller gave you the name Jeffrey Maynell?"

"Yes, I'm sure! He said Mr Maynell. It has to be him doesn't it? And anyway, we needn't accuse him of anything. All you need do is ask if he recognises that earring."

"And if he denies that it has anything to do with him?"

"I'm sure you'll think of something, James. Come on! We must find him without further delay."

"How did you find Donald Repton?" I asked as we sat together in the cab on our way to Dover Street.

"Rude and uncooperative," replied James, "which is hardly surprising. Guilty or not, the man had no wish to be questioned at a police station."

"Is he to be kept there?"

"Yes, they're detaining him overnight. But they cannot detain him forever and the chap has conveniently bought himself a ticket for the SS Britannia, so time is running out. I'm not sure about this Maynell business at all. I hope it is a worthwhile diversion, as I could do without any more of my time being wasted."

"Have you ever known me to waste your time?" I asked with a smile.

"No, but there's always a first time. I hope something will come of this conversation with Maynell."

"What is it *this time*, Inspector?" asked Jeffrey Maynell with an angry scowl.

I glared at him, unable to hide my dislike for the man. Not only was he dishonest; he was also a bully. It was highly likely now that he was a murderer to boot.

We stood in the hallway of his home. Maynell had been interrupted while eating supper in his study and still held his serviette in one hand.

"Just one question, Mr Maynell. That is all we're here to bother you with," replied James.

"Have you spoken to Repton?"

"Yes, we have, and he is currently detained at Church Court police station in Kensington."

"Arrested?"

"Not yet, but I'm working on it."

"That's a shame," replied Maynell. "This had better be quick, Inspector. My supper's getting cold."

"It will be. Do please apologise to your wife for the interruption."

"There's no need for that. She's dining out this evening."

James reached into the pocket of his jacket and brought out a folded handkerchief. He unfolded it to reveal the earring.

"Can I ask whether you recognise this piece of jewellery, Mr Maynell?"

He took a step closer and squinted at it.

"Yes, it does look familiar. I bought quite a similar pair just recently."

"May I ask where you purchased the earrings from, Mr Maynell?"

"I could tell you, Inspector, but what does this have to do with anything?"

"I would greatly appreciate it if you could answer my question, Mr Maynell. Where did you buy the earrings?"

"At my favourite jewellers' shop in Burlington Arcade. Villier & Powell."

I was taken aback by Mr Maynell's honesty. *Why had he made no attempt to cover his tracks?*

"Do you know a woman who calls herself Maria Forsyth, Mr Maynell?"

"No, I don't. Who is she?"

"We're not entirely sure yet. That is not her real name."

Mr Maynell laughed. "Inspector, I really have no idea what this conversation is about."

"For whom did you buy the earrings, Mr Maynell?"

"Well, I should think that would be quite obvious, Inspector. Why do you even need to ask? I bought them for my wife."

CHAPTER 56

"Are you sure you bought them for your wife?" asked James. "I have reason to believe that this missing earring may belong to another woman."

"I'm sure there are plenty of ladies who own the same style of earring," replied Maynell.

"Does your wife happen to be missing one of these earrings?" I asked.

"No."

"Can you be sure of that?" asked James.

"I think so. Although now I come to think of it I don't remember seeing her wear that particular pair for a little while. Is that the missing earring in your handkerchief? Where was it found?"

"Mr Maynell, allow me to reassure you that our utmost discretion is guaranteed before I ask you this next question," said James. "Did you gift a pair of these earrings to any woman other than your wife?"

"Certainly not!" Mr Maynell jutted out his jaw. "What an impertinent question!"

"My intention is not to offend," said James. "I only ask

such a thing to ensure that all possibilities have been explored."

"I bought the earrings for Lillian," said Mr Maynell. "Along with a matching necklace, which she adores."

"In which case, perhaps she has lost an earring," said James. "Are you able to look through her jewellery, sir?"

"I can't say that I have ever looked through my wife's jewellery box, but seeing as I'm rather baffled as to what all this is about I shall go and see now."

"Please could you bring us the other earring when you find it," James suggested. "Or both if the full pair is there."

We waited in the hallway while Mr Maynell went upstairs.

"It's not possible," I whispered to James. "Lillian cannot be involved in this, can she?"

"Anything's possible, Penny. You know that."

Maynell descended the stairs a short while later.

"How did you get on?" asked James.

"My wife has a lot of jewellery," said Mr Maynell.

"Have you found the earrings?"

"I found one of them," he said, holding it out. It matched the earring James held exactly. "Lillian has a great deal of jewellery, as I say. The other must be there somewhere. Are you going to tell me what this is about? Where did you find the earring you are holding in your hand?"

"I shall explain all in good time," replied James. "Can you tell me where your wife is dining this evening?"

"No," replied Mr Maynell. "I don't want you involving her in this nonsense. I want to know what's going on here, Inspector. What has happened with Repton? When are you planning to arrest him?"

"As I have just said, I shall explain everything to you when we have more time. Where is your wife this evening, Mr Maynell?"

"If you're not prepared to explain it to me now I shall

refuse to tell you."

James sighed. "That's a shame, as it would grieve me to arrest you for wilfully obstructing a police officer in the execution of his duty."

"You would arrest me for not telling you where my wife is?" His mouth hung open. "But Lillian hasn't done anything wrong!"

"Perhaps you can ask her yourself, sir," James replied. "Now where can I find her?"

"I used to think Lillian Maynell was perfectly nice," I murmured to James as we approached the restaurant, Les Jardins d'Harmonie, in Old Burlington Street. It was a small yet elegant establishment with a red and gold awning.

"Used to?"

"Until her earring was found inside the medical school museum."

"Let's not jump to any conclusions, Penny. We cannot be sure that it is hers as yet."

Mr Maynell had marched on ahead of us and was already deep in conversation with his wife when we entered the restaurant.

"I wonder what he knows," mused James.

Several diners turned to look at us as we approached them. Attired in my everyday blouse and skirt, I was not dressed suitably to dine in such an establishment. I smiled apologetically and wished the place wasn't so quiet.

Lillian had changed out of her yellow dress into a dark red one. Her brow crumpled, and she bit her lip as her husband spoke to her. Then she turned to face us, and her glance was not one I recognised at all. Her blue eyes were ice cold.

I noticed that her companion looked familiar.

It was the woman in grey.

"My goodness," whispered James. "I believe we have found Miss Forsyth."

He darted off and spoke quietly with a slick-haired man who looked to be the maître d'hôtel. I remained standing where I was in the centre of the restaurant with a number of people staring at me.

After his quick conversation with the maître d', James approached Maynell, Lillian and Maria, and asked them to accompany him to a room above the restaurant. There were some whispered words between the three, and Lillian seemed reluctant to move until she noticed that she and her friend were attracting inquisitive stares.

Mr Maynell looked on, rubbing his brow.

I had expected Lillian to be angry or upset once we reached the restaurant manager's office, but she was either an accomplished actress or completely innocent of any wrongdoing. She sat herself down behind the manager's desk beneath a painting of the picturesque French countryside, her golden ringlets framing her face.

"I must say that this is quite a surprise, Inspector," she said with a sweet smile. "And Miss Green! How lovely to see you again."

Maria Forsyth said nothing. Instead, she stood in the corner of the room and examined her fingernails.

"Will this take long, Inspector?" asked Mr Maynell. "My wife and I are well known in this establishment and it's rather embarrassing to be escorted off to a private room in this manner. What are your plans, exactly?"

James stepped toward the desk, took the item of jewellery from his pocket once again and showed it to Lillian in his outstretched palm.

"Do you recognise this earring, Mrs Maynell?"

CHAPTER 57

"Why yes, it's mine!" Lillian confirmed with a smile. "So that's what all this is about. Thank you for going to such great lengths to return my earring to me. I was wondering where it had got to. Where did you find it?"

"On the floor of the museum inside St Bartholomew's medical school," replied James. "Do you know how it came to be there?"

"In the what? The medical school? What a strange place for it to be found! How on earth did it get there?"

"I was hoping you might be able to tell me," replied James.

"I wish I could, but I'm afraid I have no idea. I'm very sorry, Inspector, though I'm extremely grateful to the person who found it. Did you make a note of his name? I should like to thank him personally for the return of my pretty earring."

She extended her hand to take the piece of jewellery, but James held on to it.

"Have you ever set foot in the museum inside St Bartholomew's medical school?" asked James.

"Never."

"You heard my wife, Inspector," said Mr Maynell with a sneer. "It doesn't matter how the earring got there. Please return it and allow Mrs Maynell and Miss Preston to continue with their meal."

"Miss Preston?" I said. "So you are not Miss Forsyth."

The woman glared at me.

"As we suspected, she goes by another name," said James. "We'll get to the bottom of that in a moment."

"Hang on a moment," said Mr Maynell, his face suddenly full of concern. "This medical school you mention. Wasn't Richard Geller murdered at that location?"

"He was indeed, Mr Maynell." James turned to face Lillian. "Did you ever know a Richard Geller, Mrs Maynell?"

"No, I can't say that I did. Who is he?" she asked.

"*Was*, Mrs Maynell," corrected James. "Richard Geller was found strangled inside the museum of St Bartholomew's medical school."

"Oh dear. How horrible!"

"I see now why you're so interested in this earring," said Mr Maynell, his voice quavering. "It was found at the murder scene."

"*Murder?!*" exclaimed Lillian, her lower lip trembling. "Oh goodness!" She clasped her hand to her chest. "I feel quite... Oh my."

"You are aware, I believe, that Richard Geller was a friend of Simon Borthwick's?" James asked her.

"Don't mention that name to my wife!" warned Maynell.

"I'm afraid it's unavoidable," replied James. "Can you explain how your earring came to be found at the scene of Mr Geller's death, Mrs Maynell?"

"No, I can't," she replied tersely.

"Did you know about Simon Borthwick's friendship with Richard Geller?"

"No, I didn't."

"You have never heard the name before?"

"No."

She stared down at the desk in front of her and I began to suspect that she was lying.

"You've heard what she has to say for herself, Inspector. Now leave!" said Maynell.

"I'm afraid I can't do that," replied James. "Not while I suspect that your wife had something to do with Mr Geller's death."

"But that's ridiculous! My wife had nothing to do with it. Look at the size of her! Do you think for one moment that she possesses the strength to overpower a man?"

I had to agree with Mr Maynell. As I watched his petite wife dab at her eyes with a lace handkerchief, it was impossible to imagine how she could cause anyone any harm.

"There's no doubt that she had some help," said James. "Presumably from her friend over there." He pointed at Miss Preston, who glared at him in response.

"Catherine Preston," I said, recalling Lillian and Georgina's reminisces from their school days. "You've known each other for a long time, haven't you?" Both women looked at me and said nothing. "Did you ask Catherine to follow me, Lillian?" I continued. "Was it Catherine who stabbed my shoulder with a knife?"

"I have no idea what you're talking about," replied Lillian haughtily.

I struggled to believe that she was the same fragile woman who had visited me in my lodgings.

Miss Preston curled her lip at me. "You interfere too much, Miss Green."

"So you admit to following me now?" I asked.

"There is no need for me to admit any such thing. I've done nothing wrong."

"Yes, you have! You wrote those letters and threw a brick through the window of my offices. And you tried to set fire to the place!"

Miss Preston laughed. "I did no such thing!"

"It's a shame we don't have Mr Kurtz here with us," said James. "As I feel sure that Miss Preston here would be familiar to him."

She gave him a quizzical look.

"I suspect she has been a regular visitor to the medical school at St Bartholomew's Hospital," continued James. "I'm not sure which pretext she would have used. Perhaps she pretended to be a prospective medical student. I'm sure she will have found some excuse to patrol the corridors of the medical school and establish the routine of the two men who worked at the museum."

"What are you talking about?" asked Lillian.

"And there's no doubt that Miss Preston possesses a physical ability which is slightly unusual for her sex," said James. "You've witnessed how fast she can run, haven't you, Miss Green? And I hear that she vaults a fence with great agility. Perhaps a woman of her abilities would be capable of climbing onto a roof and in through the window of the storeroom attached to the medical museum."

"What is this, Inspector?" scoffed Maynell. "My wife has already asked you what you're talking about, and I would ask the same question. Do you expect us to stand here and listen to this nonsense?"

Catherine Preston hadn't shifted her gaze from James since he had begun explaining his theory. She didn't even appear to blink. Her face was as still as a mask, and it made me shiver.

"Miss Preston," said James. "Did you hide yourself in the storeroom until Mr Kurtz left Mr Geller alone in the museum? And Mrs Maynell, did you wait for Mr Kurtz to leave the room that morning before you walked in there and confronted Richard Geller about his friendship with Simon Borthwick?"

Lillian shook her head. "Of course not!"

Catherine remained silent and Jeffrey Maynell's face was ashen.

"It is my belief that while Mr Geller was distracted by your conversation your friend Miss Preston crept out of the storeroom and looped the twine around his neck."

"No!" shouted Lillian.

"The man stood no chance," said James. "He would have struggled, of course, and that is how you lost your earring, Mrs Maynell. But there were two of you and one of him, and I have no doubt that he would have succumbed within minutes."

"It's not true!" said Lillian. "And you have no proof!"

"There are witnesses and alibis to call upon, of course," said James. "The usual procedures. The question is, can you disprove it?"

"Of course she can!" retorted Maynell. "She can and she will! She's my wife! She knew nothing about this Geller chap, and she couldn't have cared less for Borthwick. She ended their courtship herself! The man didn't care for her either. Their love affair was one monstrous mistake."

"It wasn't!" snapped Lillian.

Maynell turned to stare at his wife. His lips moved but no sound came out.

"He loved me," she said quietly. "He even apologised to me in his letter." A strange grimace broke across her face and I struggled to ascertain whether she was laughing or crying.

"He didn't love you," scorned her husband. "He loved that... I can't bring myself to even say it!"

"Mr Geller was in the way," said James. "Am I correct, Mrs Maynell? If it hadn't been for him Simon Borthwick would have given you his full attention. If it hadn't been for Mr Geller Simon Borthwick wouldn't have even considered moving away to America. Away from you. Am I right?"

Tears flowed down Lillian's face unchecked.

"No!" shouted Maynell. "No, I refuse to believe it! The man was a degenerate. Both of them were! But this has nothing to do with my wife; nothing at all. This is all wrong, Inspector! You've concocted this strange, twisted tale out of nothing. Nothing, I tell you!"

"And what do you say, Miss Preston?" asked James. "You've been rather quiet."

She took a few steps towards him, her eyes fixed on his.

"Miss Preston?" said James.

Without saying a word, she lunged forward and struck him in the stomach. James fell back, colliding heavily with a chair, and that's when I saw the flash of metal in her hand.

"She's got a knife!" I screamed. "Use your revolver, James!"

CHAPTER 58

James lay on his side on the floor, his face creased with pain and his hands clutched to his stomach. I bent down to retrieve the gun he kept in a holster beneath his jacket.

As I did so, Catherine lunged toward me. I sheltered myself with my arms, knowing that if I rolled away she was likely to stab James a second time.

I heard a shout and Catherine fell backwards. She had been hauled to the ground by Jeffrey Maynell.

"James!" I cried.

"I'm all right, Penny," he whispered. "Call for help, will you?"

"Someone fetch a doctor!" I shouted.

But Jeffrey Maynell was still grappling with Catherine and Lillian stood behind the desk, unsure what to do next. Blood began to seep through James' fingers and across his waistcoat.

I lifted his jacket to locate his revolver. Lillian walked over to her husband and her friend, and I wondered who she intended to help. I felt my fingers close around the cold metal of the gun.

"Stop!" I ordered, standing to my feet and pointing the gun at Catherine. "Stop now!"

Jeffrey Maynell had hold of Catherine's wrist as the pair scrambled around on the floor. They instantly froze, and the gas light flickered on the blade in Catherine's hand.

"Drop the knife!" I shouted, the barrel of the gun trembled so much in my hands that I could barely keep it pointed at her.

She kept her eyes on me as she allowed the knife to slide from her hand. It fell to the floor with a clatter.

"Mr Maynell, call for help!" I said. "James is injured!"

"Of course."

He began to get to his feet, while I kept the gun pointed at Catherine. I glanced briefly down at James, who had managed to push himself up into a sitting position.

"I'm all right, Penny." He forced a smile. "It's only a flesh wound."

Neither of us saw Lillian throw herself at me until it was too late. She grappled with me and extracted the revolver from my shaky hand.

"Stay where you are!" she shouted at her husband, who stood poised with his hand on the door.

"Lily..." he said, his eyes fearful. "Don't do this."

"Get your knife, Catherine," she said to her friend. "Between us we can finish them off. Jeffrey, get on the floor next to the inspector."

Maynell cautiously did as he was told, while his wife kept the revolver trained on him. Catherine grabbed the knife and moved toward the door as if planning to prevent our escape.

"James needs help," I pleaded. "He's injured."

"You think I want to help a police inspector who's about to arrest me?" Lillian asked. She shifted the barrel of the gun away from her husband and pointed it at me.

"Lillian, please don't make this any worse than it already

is," I said quietly, my eyes trained on the revolver. "You'll never get away with it. Just stop now for everyone's sake. Please."

"Simon apologised to me," she said with a cackle. "Isn't that the strangest part of it all?"

The door swung open, making Catherine startle and the slick-haired maître d'hôtel appeared in the doorway.

"Is everything all right? I..."

Lillian swung her arm around to point the gun at him.

"Duck!" shouted Mr Maynell.

James lurched at Lillian's legs and a gunshot rang out. Lillian was knocked to the floor and the revolver fell from her hand.

"Grab the gun!" shouted James, still holding on to her.

The stunned maître d'hôtel remained standing where he was, the gunshot having missed him by some stroke of good fortune.

Maynell and I both scrambled for the revolver, but he got to it first.

"Catherine!" Lillian cried out. "Help me, Catherine!"

Maynell got to his feet, clasping the gun firmly in both hands.

"She can't hear you, Lily," he said to his wife. "I'm afraid you've shot her."

CHAPTER 59

"How I've missed you, Tiger!" Tears dripped onto her fur as I hugged her thin, bony body. Her purr reverberated loudly in my ear.

"She's already eaten two tins of sardines," said Mrs Garnett. "And a slice of cake."

"Cake?"

My landlady shrugged. "She needed fattening up after ten days shut away in Mr Rumbelow's stable. The rats may have sustained her for a while, but after that she must have been rather hungry. Mr Rumbelow told me she's welcome to return any time for a spot of rat-catching."

"I shan't be allowing her back there in a hurry," I said. "She belongs here."

"Fancy getting stuck in a stable like that. Cats do such foolish things. I told you she hadn't been stolen, didn't I?"

"I didn't think Tiger would ever stray as far as Monkwell Street."

"I've always said that cats have a secret life we know nothing about. Who knows where she goes and what she does? You're lucky Mr Rumbelow happened to mention her to Mrs Hooper next door, otherwise I don't know how you'd ever have got her back."

I hugged Tiger even tighter.

"I am lucky, indeed."

"So, what of the woman you believed to have taken her?" asked Mrs Garnett. "What's happened to her?"

"She's dead."

"What?! How?"

"Do you remember that rain-soaked woman, Mrs Maynell, who visited me one evening? She accidentally shot her."

Mrs Garnett's mouth hung open.

"Mrs Maynell was arrested in Mayfair this evening. That's where I have just come from. Inspector Blakely has taken her to Vine Street police station."

"The people you associate with, Miss Green... That little fair-haired woman the size of a girl shot her friend? Did she do it because she thought the woman had taken your cat?"

"No. I shall have to explain it all to you in due course, Mrs Garnett. For the time being I'd rather make a fuss of Tiger now that she's returned."

"Yes, you do that. Just cuddle the cat and forget about all that horrible shooting business. The things women do these days." She sucked her lip disapprovingly. "And let's get some kerosene combed through Tiger's fur. She's covered in fleas from Mr Rumbelow's stable."

CHAPTER 60

"We passed a sleepless night at Puerto Cabello in Venezuela as our ship was moored beneath the prison there," said Mr Fox-Stirling with a glass of red wine in his hand. "Every half-hour the sentries called out from one man to the next. *Centinela alerta!* And no sooner had they finished one round when they struck it up all over again! Every half-hour. Day and night. *Centinela alerta!*"

"Presumably to ensure that no chap was asleep on the job," said Eliza's husband George.

"Exactly so," replied Mr Fox-Stirling. "And there was no chap asleep on our ship, either! There were magnificent palm trees in Puerto Cabello, however. I'd wager that some were one hundred feet high. And all the stems pierced with bullet holes!" He slapped the table as he laughed and gulped back a large mouthful of wine.

"Penelope and I are delighted that you are willing to return to those shores again and search for our father," said Eliza.

We were dining at my sister's home on a course of spiced beef with marrow au gratin. Mr Edwards sat opposite me, listening intently to Mr Fox-Stirling's tales of derring-do. The conversation had lost my interest some time earlier and I had spent much of the evening wondering how James was progressing with his questioning of the Maynells.

"I must say that I am very much looking forward to my return to Colombia," boomed Mr Fox-Stirling. "I've missed the fine cigars there."

"Don't forget that you have the Himalayas to see to first," said his wife.

"Forget the Himalayas? How could I forget them, Margaret?" Mr Fox-Stirling laughed again as Eliza's butler refilled his glass.

"That's the life of an adventurer!" said Mr Edwards admiringly.

"We're quite happy for you to proceed with your Himalayas expedition first, Mr Fox-Stirling," said Eliza. "It'll take us a while to raise the funds for your trip."

"On that note," said Mr Edwards, clearing his throat. "I should like to make a donation if I may."

"Really, Mr Edwards?" said Eliza. "That's terribly kind of you."

"My parents left me with a not-insubstantial inheritance," continued Mr Edwards. "It does nothing for me other than accrue a little interest in the bank."

"No, you must keep your inheritance," I said. "You may need it for something important."

"There is more than enough to meet my needs," he replied. "I should like to do what I can to help you discover what happened to your father."

"Thank you, Mr Edwards."

"Please call me Francis, Miss Green." He held my gaze and I smiled. "The same applies to everyone here," he said, turning to the other guests. "None of this Mr Edwards nonsense, please. Call me Francis."

"Of course, Francis," said Eliza. "And a handsome name it is, too. Thank you for your kind offer of help with our search for Father. It's much appreciated, isn't it, Penelope?"

"It is," I added. "Thank you, Francis."

He grinned, as if pleased to have entered this new state of familiarity.

The housekeeper entered the room and whispered something into Eliza's ear.

"Penelope," Eliza announced. "I'm informed that there is a caller for you."

CHAPTER 61

James stood in Eliza's hallway, his bowler hat clasped in one hand.

"How are you?" I asked. "How serious is your injury? You should be resting!"

"The injury's fine, it's healing quickly. Thank you, Penny." He glanced down at his stomach. "It's well bandaged and there's no chance of me resting at the moment. I've been busy interviewing the Maynells."

"You should come and join us in the dining room," I said. "There's far too much food and drink for our small party to get through. Eliza could have invited another four people!"

"That's a nice thought. I haven't eaten anything since breakfast. It's been rather a busy day down at the station in Kensington. Do you think your sister would mind?"

"Of course she wouldn't!"

James took a step forward and then hesitated. "Mr Edwards isn't with you by any chance, is he?"

"He is," I replied, "but that doesn't matter a bit. He'll be pleased to see you."

"On second thoughts, perhaps it's not a good idea after

all," James said, frowning slightly. "No, I'll journey home as I intended. The cab brought me through Bayswater and I remembered you telling me you would be dining here with Mr Fox-Stirling this evening. I only stopped by to tell you what has happened with the Maynells."

"Please, James."

"Please what?"

"Please stay."

"It's not appropriate, Penny."

"Tell me how you got on, then."

"Jeffrey Maynell knew nothing of what his wife had been up to. That much is clear."

"And Lillian?"

"She has confessed."

My heart skipped excitedly. "Well done, James!"

"It will make the trial easier to manage and by confessing Lillian's hoping the sentence will be more lenient."

"She doesn't deserve a lenient sentence," I scorned. "I don't suppose Simon Borthwick ever knew that Lillian was his persecutor."

"No, I don't think he did. He even apologised to her in his letter, didn't he? It seems he blamed himself for the termination of their engagement. And perhaps he suspected that Mr Geller had been murdered due to the nature of their friendship."

"Which is why he feared that he would be next."

"I think so. And Lillian was your persecutor, too. She sent many unpleasant letters about Borthwick, including the one you found in his book."

"She forged all the different styles of handwriting?"

"No, she paid a forger to do that. She had no qualms about implicating her husband and his colleagues in this tragic affair."

"Jeffrey was cruel toward her."

"It seems that he was; however, I don't think it ever truly broke her heart. Every move she has made since her relationship with Borthwick ended was part of a calculated scheme of revenge."

"And to think that she came dashing over to my home one rainy evening desperate to confide how beastly Jeffrey was!"

"That was all part of her clever manipulation. She was hoping to frame her husband."

"But the earring let her down."

"Indeed."

"She made the mistake of admitting that it was hers."

"Yes. I wondered why she didn't deny it. She may not have realised where she had lost it. And perhaps she was certain that Repton was about to be charged with Geller's murder. She'd evaded suspicion for so long that maybe she had become a little overconfident. Repton appears to be completely blameless. He has been released from custody, so he won't miss his ship after all."

"And I don't suppose we'll ever hear Catherine Preston's side of the story."

"No. Lillian's confession confirmed that Catherine strangled Richard Geller, but I would have liked to speak to the woman myself. Lillian put paid to that."

"I recall now something Lillian and Georgina told me about Catherine Preston," I said. "Georgina commented that Catherine had always done what Lillian had asked her to when they were at school. Lillian's explanation was that Catherine had a motherless upbringing. But that doesn't fully explain why Catherine was so willing to do Lillian's bidding. Did Lillian explain it any better to you?"

"I don't think Lillian really understands it herself. From what she told me she has always had an unusual hold over Catherine. Perhaps money played a part. Lillian's family was wealthy and Catherine's far less so, and it sounds as though she grew up without her mother, which must have affected her in some respects. Lillian is mortified that she has accidentally killed her friend, but she chose her path and now we must leave the rest to the judge and jury. I wanted to thank you, Penny, for persevering at that jewellery shop in Burlington Arcade. You put my work to shame!"

"Not at all."

"Well, you did, because I was unable to get Maynell's name from them."

"It was all down to a tall tale and a few tears. That combination is easier to conjure when you're a woman."

"Indeed it is, Penny. I couldn't have employed that same trick!"

We both laughed.

"I'll let you return to your meal. Apologies for the interruption." He placed his bowler hat back on his head.

"I wish you would join us, James."

"You know that it would make matters rather awkward."

I sighed.

"You were right, you know," said James, lowering his voice.

"About what?"

"What you said on Blackfriars Bridge. No one is forcing me to marry Charlotte."

"You made a choice."

"I did. But I made that choice before I met you. Had we met sooner, I believe things might be rather different now."

His words saddened me, and I couldn't miss the opportunity to respond. "But we didn't meet sooner, and nothing will ever change that. You can still make a choice, though. You know that, don't you?"

"I can, but the repercussions of such a choice would be..." He trailed off and stared down at the tiled floor. "I don't know. It would be quite dreadful. The wedding has already been postponed once before."

"And?"

James looked at me, his eyes searching my face.

"Can you imagine if I called it off?"

"There would be some fuss for a while," I said, "but it would eventually calm down and be forgotten about."

"An uncle of mine was once sued for breach of promise."

"Charlotte wouldn't do that, would she?"

"She would! And her mother would weigh in, no doubt. It would be awful."

"What else can I say, James? Yes, it would be awful, but only for a while. And then you would be free to pursue happiness with someone else."

"With you?"

"Yes."

No sooner had I said it than his warm lips were on mine. He rested his hand gently on my shoulder, which tingled beneath his touch.

But as quickly as he had kissed me, he drew away again.

"Miss Green?" came a voice from behind me.

I spun around to see Mr Edwards standing beside the door to the drawing room. He stared first at me and then at James.

A rush of heat flooded my face. I opened my mouth to speak but had no idea what to say.

How long had Mr Edwards been standing there?

"Your sister asked me to inform you that pudding is served." His voice betrayed no emotion.

He adjusted his tie and walked back into the drawing room.

THE END

THANK YOU

Thank you for reading *The Inventor*, I really hope you enjoyed it!

Would you like to know when I release new books? Here are some ways to stay updated:

- Join my mailing list and receive a free short mystery: *Westminster Bridge* emilyorgan.co.uk/short-mystery
- Like my Facebook page: facebook.com/emilyorganwriter
- View my other books here: emilyorgan.co.uk/books

And if you have a moment, I would be very grateful if you would leave a quick review of *The Inventor* online. Honest reviews of my books help other readers discover them too!

HISTORICAL NOTE

"And this invisible though mighty energy is day by day becoming more the obedient servant of mankind, whom once it only terrified in the lightning flash, or amused by the crackle of the philosopher's electrical machine." - *'Electric Lighting in America, An Interview with Dr J A Fleming'. Pall Mall Gazette, Thursday 18th December 1884. Retrieved courtesy of the British Newspaper Archive.*

Simon Borthwick is fictional, I borrowed his achievements from the British chemist and inventor Sir Joseph Swan. Swan obtained the British patent for the light bulb in 1880 and then began installing electric lighting in various buildings including the Savoy Theatre. It was Swan who lit the dancing fairies in the performance of Gilbert and Sullivan's *Iolanthe* in 1882.

Illumination displays were a popular form of entertainment in the early days of electricity. In the *Sporting News* of 9th June 1888 an advert reads:-

"Garden Fete - Crystal Palace - Today. Flowers, fountains, music, natural beauties of park, shrubberies and plantations revealed by electric light. Lakes, lawns, rosary and kiosks superbly illuminated by 50,000 fairy lights."

Donald Repton is also fictional, I borrowed his achievements from the pioneering British electrical engineer Rookes Evelyn Bell Crompton. Crompton established an engineering company and manufactured Swan's light bulb under licence. In the 1880s the company dominated the British lighting market and worked on projects such as Windsor Castle, King's Cross Station, The Mansion House and even Vienna Opera House. The Kensington Court project was built in 1888 (a few years later than 1884 when *The Inventor* is set). Crompton lived at the development for a time and it still stands today, Crompton's Electric Lighting Station where the generators were housed is used as offices.

So who actually invented the light bulb? The American inventor Thomas Edison is often given the credit but that's partly due to the success of his company General Electric (initially named the Edison Electric Light Company). Edison obtained the US patent for the light bulb in 1880. Despite my research I can't determine whether Edison sued Swan for infringement or whether it was vice versa (or both!), but the end result was the establishment of the joint company Ediswan which manufactured the light bulb in Britain.

Inventors worldwide worked on the light bulb throughout the nineteenth century, as well as Swan and Edison they include: Humphry Davy, Pavel Yablochkov, Frederick de Moleyns, Hermann Sprengel, Henry Woodward, Matthew Evans, William E Sawyer and Albon Man. With so many inventors working on the same idea in the latter part of the nineteenth century, litigation between them was to be expected.

The police raid on the fancy dress ball at The Ha'penny is inspired by a real-life event in 1880 in Manchester. On 25th September of that year police raided a private party at the Temperance Hall in Hulme where 47 men were guests: around half of them wore women's clothing. All the men were arrested and charged with 'soliciting and inciting each other to commit an unnameable offence'. In court they were fined on the surety of 'good behaviour' for the following twelve months, if they defaulted then the punishment was imprisonment for three months. The incident was widely reported in the press with *The Illustrated Police News* headline being: 'Disgraceful Proceedings in Manchester - Men dressed as Women.'

William Sherman is right to be cautious about his private life, the most extreme punishment at the time was imprisonment from ten years to life. In 1885 in Britain the Criminal Law Amendment Act recriminalized male homosexuality, one of the most famous cases tried under this act was the trial of playwright Oscar Wilde in 1895 for 'gross indecency'. He was sentenced to two years' hard labour which led to poor health and undoubtedly his untimely death at the age of 46.

The Crystal Palace was built for Britain's Great Exhibition in 1851, the first international exhibition of manufactured products. The enormous glasshouse was constructed in Hyde Park and 14,000 exhibitors were contained within its 990,000 square feet of space. The building was three times the size of St Paul's Cathedral.

After the Great Exhibition, the Crystal Palace was painstakingly dismantled and reassembled eight miles away at a park in Sydenham, south London. It reopened in 1854 and was used for various events, festivals and exhibitions over the years. The park was attractively landscaped and its lake was home to the famous concrete Crystal Palace dinosaurs.

Crystal Palace was destroyed by fire in 1936, an event witnessed by my Grandfather from five miles away on Clapham Common. Even at that distance he said the light from the fire was bright enough to read a newspaper by.

Some of the landscaped grounds of Crystal Palace remain: including the grassed-over Italian-style terraces, steps and a few statues. These days the park is famously home to the Crystal Palace football team's ground and the area itself is now called Crystal Palace. The 160 year old concrete dinosaurs are still there and the *Friends of Crystal Palace Dinosaurs* charity lovingly keeps an eye on them. Talk rumbles on of plans to rebuild the Crystal Palace but nothing has been confirmed.

St Bartholomew's Hospital remains on the site it was founded in the twelfth century. Some of its buildings date back to the eighteenth century and the hospital has a long-held reputation for teaching and research. Buildings for the medical school were constructed in the nineteenth century and among these was the pathology museum. I worked at the hospital in the mid-1990s and at that time the pathology museum was one of its best-kept secrets: a fascinating place to visit in my lunch break and I'm not sure I was actually allowed to be in there. I don't recall there being an attached store room - it was something I created for the story.

These days the pathology museum at Barts is now professionally curated and open to the public. Worth a visit if you're ever in the area.

The police station at Old Jewry was used as the headquarters of the City of London Police from 1863 until 2001. The building is now used for office space but it's popular with Jack the Ripper tours because officers in this building investigated the murder of Jack the Ripper's fourth victim, Catherine Eddowes, in 1888.

The upmarket Burlington Arcade on Piccadilly opened in 1819 and was a precursor to modern day shopping malls. It was given its own private police force which still looks after the arcade today: the Burlington Beadles. Singing and whistling is banned in the arcade: rules which were established when pickpockets frequented the place and brothels were to be found in its upper chambers.

Apparently in the mid-nineteenth century Madam Parsons ran a bonnet shop in the arcade, her shop was actually a front for a brothel in nearby Regent Street. Madam Parsons facilitated liaisons between gentlemen and ladies and it was only after her death that Madam Parsons was discovered to have been a man.

If *The Inventor* is the first Penny Green book you've read, then you may find the following historical background interesting. It's compiled from the historical notes published in the previous books in the series:

Women journalists in the nineteenth century were not as scarce as people may think. In fact they were numerous enough by 1898 for Arnold Bennett to write *Journalism for Women: A Practical Guide* in which he was keen to raise the standard of women's journalism:-

"The women-journalists as a body have faults... They seem to me to be traceable either to an imperfect development of the sense of order, or to a certain lack of self-control."

Eliza Linton became the first salaried female journalist in Britain when she began writing for *the Morning Chronicle* in 1851. She was a prolific writer and contributor to periodicals for many years including Charles Dickens' magazine *Household Words*. George Eliot – her real name was Mary Anne Evans - is most famous for novels such as *Middlemarch*, however she also became assistant editor of *The Westminster Review* in 1852.

In the United States Margaret Fuller became the *New York Tribune*'s first female editor in 1846. Intrepid journalist Nellie Bly worked in Mexico as a foreign correspondent for the *Pittsburgh Despatch* in the 1880s before writing for *New York World* and feigning insanity to go undercover and investigate reports of brutality at a New York asylum. Later, in 1889-90, she became a household name by setting a world record for travelling around the globe in seventy two days.

The iconic circular Reading Room at the British Museum was in use from 1857 until 1997. During that time it was also used as a filming location and has been referenced in many works of fiction. The Reading Room has been closed since 2014 but it's recently been announced that it will reopen and display some of the museum's permanent collections. It could be a while yet until we're able to step inside it but I'm looking forward to it!

The Museum Tavern, where Penny and James enjoy a drink, is a well-preserved Victorian pub opposite the British Museum. Although a pub was first built here in the eighteenth century much of the current pub (including its name) dates back to 1855. Celebrity drinkers here are said to have included Arthur Conan Doyle and Karl Marx.

Publishing began in Fleet Street in the 1500s and by the twentieth century the street was the hub of the British press. However newspapers began moving away in the 1980s to bigger premises. Nowadays just a few publishers remain in Fleet Street but the many pubs and bars once frequented by journalists – including the pub Ye Olde Cheshire Cheese - are still popular with city workers.

Penny Green lives in Milton Street in Cripplegate which was one of the areas worst hit by bombing during the Blitz in the Second World War and few original streets remain. Milton Street was known as Grub Street in the eighteenth century and was famous as a home to impoverished writers at the time. The street had a long association with writers and was home to Anthony Trollope among many others. A small stretch of Milton Street remains but the 1960s Barbican development has been built over the bombed remains.

Plant hunting became an increasingly commercial enterprise as the nineteenth century progressed. Victorians were fascinated by exotic plants and, if they were wealthy enough, they had their own glasshouses built to show them off. Plant hunters were employed by Kew Gardens, companies such as Veitch Nurseries or wealthy individuals to seek out exotic specimens in places such as South America and the Himalayas. These plant hunters took great personal risks to collect their plants and some perished on their travels. The *Travels and Adventures of an Orchid Hunter* by Albert Millican is worth a read. Written in 1891 it documents his journeys in Colombia and demonstrates how plant hunting became little short of pillaging. Some areas he travelled to had already lost their orchids to plant hunters and Millican himself spent several months felling 4,000 trees to collect 10,000 plants. Even after all this plundering many of the orchids didn't survive the trip across the Atlantic to Britain. Plant hunters were not always welcome: Millican had arrows fired at him as he navigated rivers, had his camp attacked one night and was eventually killed during a fight in a Colombian tavern.

My research for The Penny Green series has come from sources too numerous to list in detail, but the following books have been very useful: *A Brief History of Life in Victorian Britain* by Michael Patterson, *London in the Nineteenth Century* by Jerry White, *London in 1880* by Herbert Fry, *London a Travel Guide through Time* by Dr Matthew Green, *Women of the Press in Nineteenth-Century Britain* by Barbara Onslow, *A Very British Murder* by Lucy Worsley, *The Suspicions of Mr Whicher* by Kate Summerscale, *Journalism for Women: A Practical Guide* by Arnold Bennett and *Seventy Years a Showman* by Lord George Sanger, *Dottings of a Dosser* by Howard Goldsmid, *Travels and Adventures of an Orchid Hunter* by Albert Millican, *The Bitter Cry of Outcast London* by Andrew Mearns, *The Complete History of Jack the Ripper* by Philip Sugden, *The Necropolis Railway* by Andrew Martin, *The Diaries of Hannah Cullwick, Victorian Maidservant* edited by Liz Stanley, *Mrs Woolf & the Servants* by Alison Light, *Revelations of a Lady Detective* by William Stephens Hayward and *A is for Arsenic* by Kathryn Harkup. The *British Newspaper Archive* is also an invaluable resource. For more about Edison and the beginning of the electricity age you might like *The Last Days of Night* by Graham Moore.

GET A FREE SHORT MYSTERY

Want more of Penny Green? Sign up to my mailing list and I'll send you my short mystery *Westminster Bridge* - a free thirty minute read!

News reporter Penny Green is committed to her job. But should she impose on a grieving widow?

The brutal murder of a doctor has shocked 1880s London and Fleet Street is clamouring for news. Penny has orders from her editor to get the story all the papers want.

She must decide what comes first. Compassion or duty?

The murder case is not as simple as it seems. And whichever decision Penny makes, it's unlikely to be the right one.

Visit my website for more details:

emilyorgan.co.uk/short-mystery

THE RUNAWAY GIRL SERIES

Also by Emily Organ. A series of three historical thrillers set in Medieval London.

Book 1: Runaway Girl

A missing girl. The treacherous streets of Medieval London. Only one woman is brave enough to try and bring her home.

Book 2: Forgotten Child

Her husband took a fatal secret to the grave. Two friends are murdered. She has only one chance to stop the killing.

Book 3: Sins of the Father

An enemy returns. And this time he has her fooled. If he gets his own way then a little girl will never be seen again.

Available as separate books or a three book box set. Find out more at emilyorgan.co.uk/books

30133035R00222

Printed in Great
Britain
by Amazon